Cheating on
Myself

ERIN DOWNING

CHEATING ON MYSELF

Cover Design and Interior by The Killion Group

DEDICATION

For my amazing husband, who always makes me laugh.

BOOKS BY ERIN DOWNING

For Adults:

Cheating on Myself

For Young Adults:

None of the Regular Rules
Kiss It
A Funny Thing About Love (Three Book Collection)
Drive Me Crazy
Prom Crashers
Dancing Queen

For Tweens:

Best Friends (Until Someone Better Comes Along)
Juicy Gossip

PROLOGUE

When I was fifteen, the year my mom died, I made a checklist of my life's goals.

Kissing Trent Sloan was at the top of that list. The list wasn't meant to be in order of importance. But even if it had been, there's a decent chance Trent would still have been in that top slot. He played center on the hockey team and had a perfect, un-ironic mullet that just *worked*. After Trent came the usual things: stellar high school GPA, get the hell out of Nowhere, Iowa, college plans, a reliable job, travel to interesting-but-safe places, a good husband, and a wedding dress so classic I could never regret it.

(Give me a break. I was fifteen. These things mattered then. Some still do.)

It was a long, ambitious novel of a list. I really dug in to some categories, expanding my goals to cover critical items like dorm room color palettes and what style of bed I would buy for my first apartment. I made things intentionally difficult for myself in some cases, mapping out the preferred location to experience my first college campus kiss and the song that would be playing when I finally had sex.

Call me anal, but I had a plan. And that plan helped me get through the grief of losing my mother. It was a plan I felt good about, and it represented a life I knew would make my mom proud. (Except maybe Trent. Mom always thought he was a little greasy, and there were allegations that he'd once kissed my friend Carrie's mom. I don't believe everything, but that wasn't such a stretch. Carrie's mom got around.)

When I'd finished the list, I was confident I had plotted out a perfectly achievable and idealistic life, complete with adventure, romance, and true love. I'd sighed happily, tucked the list inside my freshman yearbook, and called Trent Sloan.

When I kissed Mr. Mullet a few weeks later, I found out his mouth tasted like school cafeteria tacos (and I later learned he had slept with Genelle Henderson right before she found out she had genital warts). It didn't matter, because the kiss was all I needed to check off the first box on my list.

In the twenty years since, I'd escaped the confines of my small-town upbringing and proudly marched my way through the rest of the boxes. Until I'd checked all but one.

Unfortunately, the last thing on my list wasn't falling out of love.

But I guess it should have been.

CHAPTER ONE: AUGUST

"Do my boobs look uneven in this shirt?" Lily Sparrow studied her reflection in the dirty glass of our office microwave. Her dark chocolate-colored hair fell in perfectly cascading waves around her slim shoulders. She turned, fixing her emerald green eyes on me. I swallowed, despite the fact that Lily shouldn't and couldn't intimidate me. Nearly everyone else at Centrex Corporation feared her, but I was immune to her intensity. Even still, the expression on her drop-dead gorgeous face was somewhat terrifying.

"Can you stop looking at me like that? Hardcore Lily freaks me out." She grinned at me, displaying a mouthful of mostly-perfect teeth. Lily's only imperfection was the tiny chip in her left front tooth—a permanent reminder to always check to make sure they used pitted olives in every martini before taking a bite. "And what do you mean by uneven?" I asked.

In the ten years I'd known Lily, I'd learned to expect random questions like this to pop up out of the blue. We'd been talking about spreadsheets mere moments before, but the topic-shift didn't faze me. I sipped from my latte and stood sentinel in the door of our office's twelfth-floor coffee pantry. This was our regular midday routine, and I'd come to look forward to some sort of random Lily conversation right around two every afternoon.

"Balanced. You know, does one look bigger than the other? Are they wonky?" She unbuttoned her conservative gray suit jacket, but stopped before taking it off all the way. "Anyone coming?"

I peeked my head out and looked both ways down the hall of cubicle walls. "Coast clear." Lily slipped her jacket off and I shook my head when I saw she was wearing a two-sizes-too-tight jeweled tank top. Most people at the office knew Lily as a conservative Marketing Director with a zero-tolerance-for-stupidity policy. But I knew Lily's carefully groomed image was just her way of managing office politics, since the Lily I was familiar with conjured up images of tight, tiny tank tops and cocktails. But I'd known her for more than ten years, and she'd spent a lot of time grooming her work image since our entry-level days. I guess there was a reason everyone was afraid of her—she just kept that side of herself away from me. She knew I wasn't going to fall for her shit.

"Hmm. They appear to be straight. Very sparkly and perfectly symmetrical."

"Do you think they *feel* even?" Lily pulled her Lean Cuisine meal out of the microwave with one hand, while threading the other arm back into her suit coat.

"You want me to touch your tits?" I tucked my latte-free hand into my dress pocket, just in case that's what she was getting at. If James Davis—VP of Marketing and the Captain of Inappropriate Comments—were to walk by while I fondled Lily's chest in the pantry, I was pretty sure all hell would break loose at the marketing summit later that week. "Why the breast obsession today?"

"Interns. They make me feel insecure. And the one with the red hair—Charlie, Chirpie, or something?—she has a chest I'd pay money for. I'm seriously considering it." Lily murmured. Then she pulled her Blackberry out of her suit coat to check for emails while forking up a steaming bite of pasta and something that looked like broccoli. The bite made it to her mouth without her ever looking at the food. It was obvious she didn't bother to taste it before swallowing, either. Lily's eyes were fixed on her tiny Blackberry screen, her face a mix of emotions as she scrolled through the dozens of emails that had probably come in while she heated her food and obsessed over her chest. She shook her head as she thumbed through an email.

"Fucking James. He's making me prep the interns for this week's marketing summit. Stella, I hate interns. They come floating in here every semester with their tight little business school bodies and their smug attitudes, and I'm supposed to pretend I love teaching them everything I know." She stopped to blow on her next bite, finally looking up when she dropped her Blackberry back in her pocket.

I swallowed the last of my latte and smiled as Corinne Andrews and Greg Kling from HR walked by. Corinne trilled out, "Hello, Stella. See you next week at the on-site off-site?" A blast of cigarette stench wafted through the hall as they breezed past.

"You bet!" I chirped. I noticed Corinne and Greg's fingers brush together as they turned the corner at the end of the cubicle hall, and realized there was a little something more than smoking motivating them to take their breaks outside. Fascinating. Who would date a coworker?

"Lil, interns are a fact of corporate life." That was true, but the other truth was, I disliked interns just as much as Lily. Anyone in their late-twenties (or, um, mid-thirties) who pretended to enjoy an onslaught of young, up-and-comers was a big, fat liar. I mean, let's face it: women like me have finally gotten to a place in our careers where we're not faking every decision, and suddenly, *kaboom!*, some twenty-four-year-old with long, shiny hair and fresh "Managing Change" expertise pops up and "makes suggestions." Who likes "suggestions" in the workplace? No one. "Suggestions" just lead to "rethinking" which leads to "explorations" which lead to a whole lot of busy work. I can finally do my job (very well, I might add) in just over forty hours a week, but when interns pop up and start trying to meddle in a perfectly mediocre organization, middle-management marketers like me take the brunt.

Oh, and more to the point, my boyfriend thinks all interns are "adorable." That worked out in my favor when *I* was an intern and he first asked me out, but I can't help but wonder if interns are part of the reason Erik refuses to grow up and commit already. It's like he thinks we're still the know-it-alls we once were, and if we just freeze time and commitment where we were when we were twenty-three and twenty-four, we'll never get old. Well guess what, Erik? Your hair *is* going to fall out, you've *already* up-sized the waist-size of your jeans, and you aren't even very good at texting. You're getting older, buddy, like it or not.

"Lily, we were both interns once. So they can't all be bad."

"Exactly. *We* were interns. That's how I know just how smart they all think they are. And how stupid they think *we* are. Well, they're probably not begrudging you, but they're surely eyeing my job."

Lily was a VIM—James' acronym for Very Important Marketer. That meant Lil sat on Centrex's marketing council, made important decisions, and got to sit in an office (Centrex was opposed to doors on offices, but still—she had real walls). I, on the other hand, was one of James' "Bears." Technically, my title was Senior Marketing Analyst, but the other people in my pod were told to call me "Share Bear." I earned that adorably moronic name when I was honored with a spot on the task force responsible for morale and team spirit at Centrex. "The Bears" don't make any important decisions. Instead, we sit in nubby cloth cubes, and are required to smile a lot. There's no room at the Inn for a bad attitude, even when everyone around you is acting like an idiot. Marketing is *such* bullshit.

Lily jabbed another mouthful of pasta between her lips. This time, she took a moment to chew. "This is disgusting, you know. I blame the interns for making me eat this crap." She tossed the rest of her microwave meal in the trash and dug through the reusable lunch bags in the fridge that were carefully labeled with other peoples' names. I guess she thought Eve Overstreet wouldn't miss her Strawberry Yoplait, since Lily seemed perfectly comfortable stealing it.

"I don't see any interns holding an Econ textbook to your head and insisting you have to eat cardboard to stay slim. You're a big girl. An important girl. Need I remind you that you have the intelligence and cash to buy whatever you want to eat for lunch?" I raised my eyebrows.

Lily knew I wasn't going to get into a ridiculous discussion about whether or not she was fat—and we both knew that was where this was headed. Of all the reasons to hate interns, their looks and slim hips were at the bottom of the list. But even worse, there was nothing I enjoyed less than talking to Lily Sparrow about cellulite, chubby thighs, or love handles. Like I said, Lily was perfect. She just didn't realize it. The good thing about Lily's lack of self-awareness was her blindness to her friends' shortcomings. I think she truly believed my size twelve thighs looked just like her size four thighs, the only reason for the difference in pant size being that my legs were longer.

Lily polished off the yogurt in six or seven very large and messy bites, stuffing the container in the trash when she was done. "I gotta go. Why aren't you eating?"

We lowered our voices for the walk down the hall of cubicles. "Erik is taking me out to the new place on Washington tonight. He booked us in at the kitchen table."

"Ooh, I heard about that place," Lily said, obviously both hungry and jealous. "I read somewhere that the chef brings you little portions of every single dish that gets ordered. I don't know how you stay so skinny."

See what I mean? Even though she should be easy to hate, there was something about Lily Sparrow that made her very lovable. "What are you doing tonight?"

"Sitting on my ass, alone and miserable, as always."

I rolled my eyes and said nothing. I wasn't being cruel by ignoring this comment. I heard some version of the same thing most days, even when we had plans to go out. Her boyfriend, Chad, was a management consultant, and traveled to his clients' offices every week. Many times, instead of flying home for the weekend, Chad would get his company to fly him to Connecticut to visit his parents or his college buddies instead. I was convinced their relationship only worked because of how infrequently they actually saw each other.

Lily sighed hugely. "I might have to make myself an alcoholic milkshake. Guilt bingeing." We'd reached her office, but since there was no door she went inside and brought her voice down to a whisper. "Did I tell you I have to fire two of the marketing assistants today?"

"Why?" I honestly didn't care *who*. There were so many marketing assistants that they all blended into one perky, post-internship blur. Yes, even the guys. Again, this was marketing. According to "The Bears" code of rules, we were all required to be perky and optimistic. James' motto is, "Culture, kindness, and sharing foster innovation." Interestingly, James was sharing a bed with his boss, Terese Fitzgerald, despite the fact that he was a newly married man. I guess he believed this was his contribution to the Centrex culture: kindness through orgasm and sharing spit with a superior.

"Why are they getting fired?"

Lily shrugged. "Performance issues, maybe? Excessive sick days? Bad attitude? The usual crap, but we're calling it a layoff for legal reasons. 'Downsizing.'" She made air-quotes and rolled her eyes. "I get to do the honors, as usual. Everyone thinks that just because I'm a bitch, I'm heartless."

I laughed. "Well, you're welcome to join me and Erik. At least then you won't be drinking alone."

"As if," she murmured. "There's nothing more attractive on a date than a drunk third wheel. And you never know... tonight might be the night, Stella Dahl." She rolled my first name and last name together, Stella-doll, like I was a sad sub-brand in the Barbie franchise. Then she moved toward her desk and logged in, glancing at her email as she lifted her eyebrows at me. "Maybe?"

"Hardly," I said, but the thought *had* crossed my mind. It was ever-present, actually. After twelve years together, I wasn't foolish enough to think a surprise proposal was likely (especially since Erik and I didn't exactly *do* surprises), but Erik knew I was waiting and wouldn't wait forever, so it wasn't totally out of the question. "Of course, you'll be my first call if it does happen tonight."

"I should hope so," she said. "Now get the hell out of here so people don't think I've gone soft. I don't want anyone to see me smiling. I have a reputation to uphold."

"Yes, ma'am!" I announced loudly, as I left her office. "So sorry to bother you, VIM!"

"Stella?" Lily shouted this, drawing attention from the collection of interns who were gathered around a computer monitor at the cube directly outside her office. "One more thing..." I peeked in and saw that Lily was holding up a piece of paper with "Will You Marry Me?" scrawled across it in black Sharpie. She tipped her head back, propped her feet up on her desk, and laughed. At least someone was asking me.

"If I get a glass of the Malbec, will you get the Cab so I can try it?" I gazed at my boyfriend, Erik, across an expansive wood table in the bright and bustling kitchen of *Molto* later that night. He was studying the wine list carefully, looking hopefully for one of his favorites, I was sure. I'd already scanned the list of reds and saw none of the wines we were familiar with were featured on the list. We'd have to take a chance and try something new. Admittedly, this wasn't something either of us did very well.

Both Erik and I were creatures of habit. Planners by nature. That's part of the reason we worked so well together. We had both been the type of kids who knew exactly what we wanted out of life, and had taken all necessary steps to get there. I'd gotten near-perfect grades through high school, had piled on extracurricular activities to get myself into a great college, and landed the perfect internship at Centrex right out of undergrad. I never really had any clear vision of life after that, but that's where Erik came in. He gave me a new goal for my adult life. I'd immediately fallen head over heels for him, and focused everything I had on our relationship and the new goals we'd made together. Before we met, Erik had followed almost exactly the same path as me. He'd been working at Centrex as a Marketing Assistant when I started as an intern, his sister introduced us, and the rest is history.

We'd spent our twenties focusing on careers and our relationship, and the problems only started to creep in a few years ago when I started asking about marriage. We'd always talked about commitment and staying together and making a life as Erik and Stella, but it was only then that he made it clear that he felt traditional marriage was an unnecessary formality. "Things are perfect the way they are," he'd said that first time I brought it up with any real pressure. "Neither of us wants kids, so why do we need to spend twenty thousand to throw a party to get a form that tells us what we already know? I consider you my life partner—do you need a certificate to remind you not to leave me?" He'd smiled and kissed me and we'd made love on the couch, and I'd felt happy again.

I sometimes lost touch with what I wanted, but Erik was always there to remind me what I was looking for. It just seemed like fewer and fewer of our goals were mine, and more and more of them were his. They just suddenly *felt* like mine.

After the first conversation about marriage, I eased off for a while, but the truth was, I wanted to get married. It was part of my plan, the last thing on my list, and I was going to get it. So I started bringing it up more frequently. I know, I know... the women's magazines would have had a field day with me. Whether I wanted kids or not (they weren't a goal that was included in my list, and Erik and I had decided together that we did not), there was something romantic and powerful about commitment and compromise and the permanence of marriage, and I believed in it. But I was starting to wonder if I had to give that up if I wanted to stay with Erik.

At that point, I hadn't even considered how much I was giving up by staying with him.

"You know I like Malbec." Erik announced at *Molto* that night, finally looking up from the wine list. "I'm going to get that."

"But that's what I want." I sounded like a whiny kid. "I just thought it would be fun to try two wines we've never had before. But if we both get the Malbec, then we only get to try *one* wine."

Erik grinned. "If we both get Malbec, we can get a bottle. Isn't that a better deal anyway?" He reached for my hands across the table. He lifted my left one off the table and held it up to his lips. His mouth grazed across my knuckles, dusting little kisses from pointer finger to pinky. I watched him as he ordered the wine, and thought about how well we fit together. He was right—if we picked the same wine, we could get a bottle. And then I'd get two-and-a-half modest glasses, the perfect amount. It was the smarter strategy, and this was usually what we did. When the waiter left, Erik continued to gently stroke my fingers. His focus on my left hand made me think about a ring again, and the thought made me wonder.

Each of his kisses sent the tiniest shock up my arm, reminding me of the time when his touch always made me feel like that. I still remembered that new love feeling, the sense of excitement and uncertainty and self-consciousness and curiosity. I missed the way he'd held me and wrapped his arms around me, even when people were watching.

That night, the kisses on my fingers and the anticipation and wonder about whether maybe tonight was the night, the night he'd see it my way, gave me delicious, tingly shivers. I pulled my foot out of my black slide beneath the table and reached it up, up, up Erik's leg.

The bottle of wine arrived just as my toes found their way to his inner thigh, and he reached under the table to push my foot away. Erik wasn't big on PDAs. Not that I was going after true affection... I just wanted to be sexy. After he tasted the wine and approved, Erik furrowed his dark eyebrows at me across the table. He needed a haircut, I noticed. His sideburns were too long, and his blackish hair was extra-puffy.

"What's going on?" he asked, as my foot continued its path up his thigh.

"What's going on with you?" I purred back, lifting my foot into his lap again. I wiggled my eyebrows at him and twirled a short curl around my finger. "Hi there." I wasn't much of a seductress (it happens when you ditch the dating scene at twenty-two), but I had a few decent moves. I licked my lips.

"Aren't you going to try the wine?" Erik asked, widening his dark brown eyes at me and shifting in his seat. "Can you please stop?"

"Stop what?" I asked, using something that might pass as a sultry voice.

"That." He blushed and pushed my foot away again, dropping my other hand in the process. "Seriously, Stella. That's really embarrassing. What if someone saw you? This place is crawling with Centrex people. You should be more careful if you want to be taken seriously there."

I bit my lower lip and looked down at the menu. He was right. Who did I think I was—Angelina Jolie? I was a decent-looking, overly conservative, mid-level marketer with shortish dull-brown curls (flecked with sixteen rogue grays that I routinely plucked), size twelve jeans, and a bad case of PMS-bloat. I didn't need to do stuff like play footsie with my boyfriend—we were beyond that. I mean, we lived together and he peed with the door open and watched me pluck my grays. We weren't the kind of couple to do spontaneous, faux-sexy stuff.

"What do you think they'll bring us first?" I asked, perking up at the thought of food. "I skipped lunch today so I can eat a ton."

"Did I tell you I gave the intern learning lunch presentation today?" Erik asked, easily shifting into a new conversation topic along with me. "One of the interns asked me to be her mentor. I guess it must have been a decent talk, if someone wants a longer lesson from me on online community activation." Erik had transferred from his first job at Centrex into a Marketing Director position at a consumer products company called *Zoom!* several years ago. His job was to convince people to buy soap. Eventually, Erik's goal was to start up his own company manufacturing organic baby products, but he hadn't yet taken the leap. I guess his fear of commitment extended beyond just me.

The chef came over to our table carrying three tasting plates.

"Good evening." He grinned sheepishly, as though he was embarrassed to have discovered someone sitting in his personal kitchen. He was obviously young—perhaps not even thirty—and looked like a little kid in a big kitchen. His white chef coat was too big, and something about his awkwardness made me laugh. Erik looked at me like I'd gone crazy, and the chef stammered on, talking about the dishes he'd brought over to our table. "This first plate features a sampling of our mini tacos—carnitas, beet and goat cheese, and sliced prime rib with raddichio."

"You can put the beet and goat cheese taco on my side of the table," Erik said. He knew I've never liked goat cheese. This was the good thing about life partners—they knew your dining preferences, and no one had to waste their time trying something they were sure not to like. We made a good team.

The chef cleared his throat and set a second plate on our table. "This is a tasting of our famous tater tot casserole. House-made tater tots broiled over a stew of lamb, locally-farmed carrots, and mini-potatoes from my own garden." I lifted my eyebrows. The chef grew his own potatoes? And how was this dish famous? The restaurant had been open less than two weeks. Still, tater tots were hard to beat.

"The third dish marries grass-fed beef and onion slivers in a perfect union inside a puff-pastry shell. I think you'll find it light, yet surprisingly filling." He bowed, then swished back to the kitchen in his big boy coat.

I reached for my fork to start with the tater tots. "Is it just me, or did that waiter look like a little kid dressing up as a chef for Halloween?" I popped a hot tot in my mouth and let the soft, potato goodness melt in my mouth. "Yum."

Erik shook his head. "He's twenty-six. He was just featured in Midwest Magazine's ten under thirty this year."

I'd refused to read that feature ever since I lost eligibility. So sue me: I was thirty-four and petty. I didn't need to read about people younger and more successful than me. "How can you be a professional chef with your own restaurant at twenty-six?"

"One of our interns sold her management consulting business while she was still in business school—she's on her second career."

I snorted through a mouthful of light-yet-filling beef. "And she's an intern? She started a business, sold a business, and has decided an internship selling cucumber-melon *soap* would be fulfilling?"

The look on Erik's face reminded me how sensitive he is about his products. Unlike me, he was a true marketer. He really believed in his product, and thought about the merits and advantages of *Zoom!* hand-soap often. He loved his job, and didn't like people—me, for example—poking fun. It was a sensitive subject, and I'd crossed the line.

"It's a great internship," he said through thin lips. Erik's lips stretched tight whenever he was frustrated. "It's not Centrex, but still. And our interns are bright self-starters with a lot of great ideas."

"Oh, come on! What is with the intern obsession today?" I reached for one of the tacos and inadvertently grabbed the beet and goat cheese one by mistake. Erik pulled it out of my hand before I could take a bite and replaced it with the carnitas taco.

"What if I wanted to try the goat cheese one? Maybe I want to try something new. Is that a crime?"

"God, Stella, you're in a foul mood tonight." He refilled my wine glass, which had somehow emptied itself while I was on my little tirade. "What's going on?"

I wasn't sure what was going on. I was obviously feeling feisty, and Erik was there to take the brunt of it. I'd noticed this had been happening a lot lately—I'd get frustrated, start picking on Erik, he'd put his guard up, and all hell would break loose. We weren't fighters, but the cold, irritable squabbling felt a whole lot worse.

"Are we ever going to get married, Erik?" It slipped out of my mouth before I could stop it, and as I said it, I could feel the tears prickling behind my eyelids. I squeezed my eyes shut and took a long, deep swallow of wine.

Erik took the wine glass out of my clenched fist and held my hands in his. This time, I felt no shivers, didn't fool myself into hopeful anticipation, and I certainly wasn't tempted to rub my foot up his thigh. I still had my eyes closed, but I knew exactly what expression was on his face when I heard him sigh. We were seated at the bustling kitchen table on a loud Friday night, and *still* I could hear his sigh, loud and clear.

Somehow, we got through the rest of our dinner that night. We made it home, we tucked into bed, we wished each other good night, and I read a single chapter in my book while Erik caught up on articles on his iPad. Business as usual. We predictably followed the routine of our life partnership and the monotony of each day-to-day. Unfulfilling, yet comfortable. Perfectly-matched, but taking each other for granted. We went on that way for another seven weeks.

Until I'd had enough.

CHAPTER TWO: SIX WEEKS LATER

Looking back, I guess I first let myself imagine what life might be like without Erik late in the night after our dinner at *Molto*. The sheer logistics were overwhelming at the time, so I'd considered it only briefly at first. There were the trivial things, such as the fact that I couldn't make coffee myself. Thirty-four years old and unable to correctly figure out the right ratio of water to beans. Somehow, every time I ground coffee, I would end up with little chunks of coffee bean in the filter or a pile of ground coffee on the floor. I could learn to do it, sure, but the thing that immediately jumped into my head was the fact that the easier option—purchasing coffee for myself at the office—would add nearly five percent to my monthly budget.

Erik was also always willing to let me put my frozen feet between his thighs at night when I first climbed into bed, even if he'd already been asleep for an hour. I hated sleeping in socks, and my boyfriend was always there with a warm and toasty spot for them. He made really good chicken wild rice soup, and only fake-complained when I put "sappy" movies— anything with Sandra Bullock or Reese Witherspoon or Colin Firth—in our Netflix queue.

The little things like hot coffee and cold feet added up, but on top of that were the big things... our life together, the carefully-negotiated morning bathroom ritual, his house that we'd made "ours," his family coupled with my lack of family. There were enough things tying us together that it seemed impossible I could ever consider a life without him.

And more than anything, I loved him. I didn't know an adult life without Erik, and I'd never let myself think one existed.

That, ultimately, was the problem. I'd had goals for myself—a list that told me who I wanted to become—when I'd been younger, and they were goals that had failed to evolve after I'd found Erik. At twenty-three, I'd achieved almost everything I'd ever thought I could want: I lived in Minneapolis-not-Farmville, had an enviable job, hilarious and reliable friends, and a seemingly perfect boyfriend. I'd checked off most of the things on my list that seemed to matter, but lost any desire for fun and spontaneity in the process. My life's ambitions started to merge with Erik's, and I found myself forgetting to think about me.

Initially, it was little stuff. I gave up pizza when Erik decided to do the South Beach diet, even though a carb-free day made me miserable. Then, Erik was always there to remind me how lucky I was to have my Centrex job, even though it was so unfulfilling I had lost my ability to be creative. I had always wanted to go to Italy, but since Erik had already been there on an art history trip during undergrad, we went to London and Brussels the only time we'd gone abroad. I'd never really thought about how much of myself and my own opinions I'd lost during our time together.

But new thoughts had crept in the night after *Molto*, and little incidents kicked me closer to the night I eventually left. I guess I started paying closer attention to what I wanted out of life, and other things began to bug me. A new list started to take shape in my mind, though this time I didn't write it down. I just started paying attention to the little things, and when there were enough things on the naughty list, I knew it was time to go.

First, there was the baseball game. We'd decided to go to a late-in-the-season game, and Erik had gotten us good seats. We each ordered a hot dog with relish, one beer, and shared a little baseball hat full of ice cream. It was a perfectly pleasant evening, until the "Kiss Cam" turned its voyeuristic eyes our way. You know that giant TV screen where they show clips of the audience? And you know how they do that stupid thing where they zoom in on two people who appear to be in love, and wait for them to kiss while the crowd roars and urges them on? Well, I'd kinda always wanted to be on the Kiss Cam. Somehow, that night, we lucked out and the Kiss Cam came straight for us. I grinned, and turned toward Erik only to discover that he was making a disgusted face and exaggeratedly leaning away from me. The whole stadium started laughing, and I went bright red. He laughed, thinking he was Mr. Funny Pants.

The Kiss Cam moved away and got shots of other sweet couples who nuzzled and hugged and kissed and made my stomach sick with envy. I watched them all while Erik chatted about his hilarious performance with the beefy, drunk guy sitting in the seat next to him. After a minute or so, the cruel cameraman swung back around to catch *us* again—everyone obviously remembered us, since they started chanting, "Kiss her! Kiss her!" Some people in our section turned around to stare. My funny man decided to really ham it up this time, pretending I was the last person on earth he'd ever want to kiss. He held his hands over his mouth and shook his head violently. I felt the hot prickle of rejection tears stabbing at the backs of my eyes, and then suddenly, the whole crowd started "aw-ing." I was being pitied by a stadium-full of screaming fans. The tears started flowing and then finally, with the Kiss Cam still trained on us, Erik stuck out his lower lip to pout and gave me a very unromantic kiss as a consolation prize.

He didn't seem to realize how hurt I'd been by the whole thing, since that night he kept talking about how funny and clever it all was. How hilarious *he* was. Several people from work had been at the game and came over to say something to me the next day—I could tell they thought we were one of those couples who insult one another for sport, but the truth is, we weren't. Neither of us was that clever. And the romance and make-up sex wouldn't be powerful enough to handle the joking sting of fake insults. The night after the game was the first night in our entire relationship when I fantasized about Bradley Cooper while Erik and I were having sex. It was also the last time we *had* sex. A weeks-long dry spell followed that made me forget I'd ever had a sex drive.

Then, it was his obsession with the interns. Between Lily at the office and Erik at home, I was fed up with the obsession over youth and promise, and frustrated with my own shortcomings. I started to question my own choices, and began to wonder what would have happened if I'd picked a different path twelve years before. When I realized Erik and his intern-mentee were having a frolicking back-and-forth conversation via Facebook, I was understandably over interns altogether.

Ironically, it was a nimble, red-headed (and innocently unrelated) intern at Centrex that brought on the next wave of trouble.

Centrex had begun to offer a lunchtime yoga class on Mondays and Thursdays, at the recommendation of The Bears. It was good for team bonding, and studies showed that midday fitness boosted moods. I'd reluctantly started to attend, but had been struggling to get any of the moves down. Whenever our "guide" offered child's pose as an alternative to tricky positions, I was the first to creep and crawl down to my mat. I couldn't get the balancing poses, hated the stuff that involved upper-arm strength, and wasn't bendy enough to do a lot of the floor exercises.

But one Monday a few weeks after my dinner with Erik, I foolishly squeezed my mat in between elderly Madelon from accounting and Stacia, the intern. When it came time to do the bridge pose, I looked over at Madelon and saw that she was just laying there, flat on her back. Then I peeked over at Stacia and saw that her body was perfectly arched into a fine, flowing bridge. Her flat stomach rounded up toward the paneled ceiling, fingers and toes perched easily on the floor beneath her.

"I can do that," I thought, glancing briefly back toward Madelon, lying comfortably flat on the floor like a lump of old person. Then I pressed my tummy up and edged my hands and feet under my precariously-perched body. I was so elated my back was off the ground that I ignored the pinching discomfort in my back.

"I'm doing it!" I thought, grinning merrily. "I'm a yoga goddess!" That's when I pushed my stomach further up and came crashing down with a horrible shriek.

"Oh!" Stacia cried, hopping nimbly out of her bridge to kneel next to me. My back was shooting rockets out from the lower vertebrae, and my body seemed locked in a position that was neither flattering nor particularly comfortable. "Are you okay?"

I stared at the intern, wondering if this looked "okay" to her. "Not really," I muttered. By then, the rest of the class had turned to stare, and our instructor was huddled over my body with a horrified look on her face.

She began to rub the area in my back where it felt like daggers were carving someone's initials into my spine. "I offered a modification," she reminded me. "Perhaps the bridge was a bit much for you today?"

"Yes, today it must have been a bit much." I bit my lip as my muscles continued to spasm. "I think I'll just call it a day."

I left my mat on the floor and hobbled from the converted conference room back to my desk. I spent the next hour flat on the floor in a corner of my cube. Lily rescued me after her strategy meeting and set up a floor bed in the corner of her office. I stayed hidden behind piled-up boxes that she ordered interns to carry up from the loading dock. She loaded me up with ice packs and ibuprofen, while I spent the afternoon entertaining her with my complaints about interns and their bendy limbs.

My body wouldn't respond to meds, which meant the gym was out. No endorphins led to next-day depression. Depression led to angry eating. Angry eating helped me pack on a few pounds... so I was feeling fat, depressed, and bitter. And I couldn't even run it off.

I suddenly had too much time to think about things, and had begun to lose perspective and patience. The way Erik breathed as he was drifting off to sleep irritated me, the smell of his body-wash in the shower made me sick, the fact that he never asked me what I wanted to do on the weekend was infuriating. So when I brought up marriage and how much it meant to me again, and Erik just sighed... well, that's when I broke.

I let my engine idle in the parking lot and draped my hands over the heater for extra warmth and maybe a shot of courage. It wasn't even October, but the temperature had already dipped into the forties and I refused to break out my gloves before the official start of fall. I also wanted an excuse to stay in the quiet and question-free environment of my car for a few more minutes. It was Thursday, and I was now ten minutes late for monthly drinks night with my friends.

Eyes closed, I breathed in through my nose, then out through my mouth, wondering if Sherri, my yoga teacher, was good for anything. But instead of my breath shooting calm zen through my system, the moment of solace was interrupted by a thudding knock on my window that scared the bejeezus out of me. I glared out the window and saw Catherine Jenkins' perky face staring back at me.

"Shit, Cat, don't do that!"

I turned the engine off and stepped out of my car to give her a big hug.

"Were you sleeping?" Cat said, flicking her hair extensions over the shoulder of her Burberry trench coat. "That's not a good idea in this neighborhood, Stella." She tapped her cell phone display. "You're late, you know."

"So are you," I said, trudging at a snail's pace alongside Cat as we walked through the parking lot out to the street. Her tottering high-heels kept her from moving fast, and indifference about making people wait made her move even slower. Even though tardy people made me jittery, Catherine had been one of my best friends for more than ten years. She was also Erik's sister, which had made her both "family" and a friend—and the girlfriend I was most dreading talking to that night.

Cat giggled. "I'm always late. It's my thing. You, however, ought to have arrived first."

"I'm turning over a new leaf," I grumbled, not ready to share my news yet. Judging by Cat's lack of panic, Erik hadn't told his sister—or, obviously, his mom—about our breakup yet.

"Oh em gee," Cat said, grasping at my elbow with her tiny, manicured hand. Cat was five-foot-two and tiny, one of those people who made me feel like an ogre. She weighed less than my left thigh. Cat was also a mother of two, and had been known to eat exclusively leftover macaroni and cheese and hot dogs for three days straight. She ate like a child, and had now started to talk like one, too. Things like "OMG" and "natch" and "whatevs" had started to roll off Cat's tongue less than a week after hiring a live-in French au pair who had apparently mastered English watching old episodes of *Gossip Girl* and *Glee*.

"You will *not* believe what Jana Mancini said to Taylor at school today. I think she's putting her on a diet. A diet! Taylor is six. Can you imagine the *issues* that kid is going to have if her starved mother is making her *diet* at six?"

Cat carried on, telling me all the latest gossip from Blythe Day School. I had no trouble keeping up. Cat's girls—Heidi and Pippa—treated me like an aunt, and I'd been around their entire lives. I loved them like my own daughters, and I made a point of dropping them off at school at least once a month. I hoped Cat would still let me be a part of the girls' lives now that I was no longer a part of Erik's.

Heidi was six and in first grade, while Pippa had just started her last year of Montessori preschool. The girls were smart and wonderful, and the gossip that came out of their schools was usually pretty amusing. I listened intently as Cat talked about marital trouble and cheating and whose job was in jeopardy. It was a welcome distraction from the rest of my week, and I suddenly wondered if I could avoid telling my friends anything about my now-defunct relationship all night.

By the time we had walked the few short blocks from the parking lot to the restaurant, we were twenty minutes late and I'd heard all about Melissa Engle's hysterectomy. Lily and Anders were waiting for us at the bar, already halfway through a bottle of red.

"This is mine, girlies," Lily said, gesturing to the wine. "I had a hell of a day, so I'm going to need the rest of this for *moi*." She stood up and squished me into a hug, even though we'd seen each other at the office a few hours earlier. Her suit coat was off, revealing a slim silk blouse that covered her curves like it had been made for her. I could feel my own breasts pushing against the buttons of my shirt, threatening to burst under the pressure of my newfound heaving bosom. I was very comfortable calling my rack a bosom, because it felt huge. My yoga-induced inability to exercise had continued to take its toll, and I'd been self-medicating with food after the breakup that week. The spread had moved from my hips to my thighs to my belly, and was now waging a battle with my bras, too.

Anders Sorenson, who was perched on the bar stool next to Lil, rolled his eyes and swiped Lily's empty wine glass. When Anders hailed the bartender, she rushed over like a dutiful minion and took the glass from his hand. Men and women both tended to respond quickly to Anders. His neat, dark hair and square jaw made him look a lot like a young Pierce Brosnan. Dapper and charming and always honest, Anders was the gay best friend every girl needed—except he was straight. At least, he insisted he was. He rarely dated, never hit on any of us, and gave great advice about just about everything. Even though we were all sure he was hiding a deep secret about his sexuality— from himself as well as the rest of the world—we all simply appreciated the fact that he was all ours.

The wineglass was bussed behind the counter before Lily even noticed it had been taken.

"Might as well drink it from the bottle if you're drinking alone, eh, Lil? Ladies, I've already ordered us our own bottle for the table." Anders was a childhood friend of Lily's, and he had become a good friend of mine and Cat's in the years we'd all known each other. He was laid-back, but had a feisty side that made him a great match for Lily. They only talked about it when they were drunk, but Anders and Lil had dated early in high school. They were strictly platonic now, but talk of their old relationship was always a fun conversation topic.

Lily just laughed and swiped Anders' glass. She filled it to the top, emptying the bottle of wine in the process, and took a huge swig. Cat and I exchanged a look.

"Here's the thing, Sorenson—I know you just want an excuse to talk to the bartender again. She's been ogling you all night, so why don't I take this glass and you can ask sweet ass over there for a fresh one?"

As Cat, Lily, and I followed the hostess to our table, Anders stayed back at the bar to chat up the bartender. This was all part of the usual routine on drinks' night. Since Anders was the only single person in our midst, there was some expectation that he'd flirt on everyone's behalf. We all lived a little vicariously through Anders.

Now that I was officially unhitched, I was concerned my friends might expect me to chat up random people, too. I hoped I wouldn't be expected to start sleeping around, like Lily had before she started dating Chad. Did people still use condoms, or was there some new protection I would have to learn about? Did I have to start getting Brazilians? Would anyone ever actually want to sleep with me? I swallowed back the panic that had been creeping up every few hours since I'd left Erik's house earlier that week.

Anyway, I was getting ahead of myself, since I'd only been single for three days. Three days. It's not like it would be normal for me to just jump back into the ring and start lassoing up men left and right. I was looking for a life partner, not a fling... I wasn't a fling girl. As I sat at the table, adjusting and readjusting my napkin on my lap, I realized all of my friends were staring at me.

"You look weird, Stella." This comment, courtesy of Cat, was accompanied by a nod from Lily.

"I'm fat," I said frankly, as Anders scooted his chair up to join us. "I still can't run, I can hardly walk, and I haven't lifted anything more than a glass of wine in four weeks."

My friends all started to protest, telling me I looked great and relaxed and all the other bullshit friends are supposed to say.

"I didn't mean it like that," Cat said, her eyes wide. "I mean, you look a little vacant."

"You okay?" Lily pushed her giant glass of wine toward me, while Anders flagged down our waiter to get more to the table. "Drink this."

"Yeah, I'm okay," I said, and wondered if it was true.

Anders ordered bruschetta when the waiter came over with our wine, then said, "Have you gotten your back checked out? I can fit you in at the office tomorrow morning, if you want someone to take a look?" Anders was the office manager at a chiropractic and massage therapy center. He loved the job because it gave him time to work on his novel when things were slow, and he was addicted to shiatsu, which he got at a discount from one of the therapists. I wasn't big on alternative medicine, but I was so frustrated by my back that I would try anything. Also, maybe it was time to try a new approach to everything in life. Enough of my life had changed that a significant shift in all my beliefs and attitudes ought to be easier now than ever.

I nodded. "Sure, that would be good." They were all still looking at me, which was making me twitch. When I locked eyes with Cat, I could feel the tears springing up to the surface. "I left Erik," I said, still looking at Cat. "I'm sorry."

This announcement was met with complete and total silence, an unfamiliar sound for this particular group. Cat spoke first. "Left... how?"

"We... broke up, I guess." Do you call it a break up when you've been together as long as we had? It sounded weird.

"Did he cheat?" Lily said, immediately jumping into protector mode. "Oh my god, he cheated with the intern. That skank who wanted him to mentor her—she's a whore, Stella. He doesn't deserve you."

I laughed, waving my hand to get her to quiet down. "He didn't cheat with the skanky intern," I said. I pulled at my earring, remembering when Erik had given this pair to me. It was Christmas, the first year we'd been dating. We went to the winter parade downtown after work one night, and he bought them for me when we'd gone inside to warm up. That was when he still did impulsive things. He hadn't surprised me like that in a long time.

"I guess it just boils down to the fact that I was tired of waiting for him to marry me." When I said it out loud to people other than Erik, it sounded so trivial, so whiny. But it was my reason (the only concrete reason, anyway) and I couldn't question my instincts. It was a big decision, but it wasn't a stupid decision. I needed to do this for me.

Cat had gotten very pale. "It's because of my mom. My mom and the gift exchange." She was staring at me open-mouthed. She looked at Lily and Anders, who were obviously confused. "See, every year my mom puts everyone's name into a bowl and we draw names for the Christmas gift exchange. But to be included, you have to be an official member of the family. She's never put Stella's name in the bowl. Ten years, and Stella sits there at Christmas with no gift under the tree. I told her she was going to drive you away with that effing gift exchange."

"Cat, there are other things about your mom that would have driven me away a lot faster than her Christmas gift exchange. Her 'suggestion' that I find a new hair salon, for one. Or her 'recommendation' that I start to dress myself in more 'winter' colors." I shook my head. Erik and Cat's mom, Laurel, was a piece of work. But since my own mom had died, she was the closest thing to a mother I had.

Anders, who had been casually drinking his wine since I'd made my announcement, suddenly said, "I think it's great, Stella." Cat and Lily turned on him like he'd admitted I was, in fact, getting chubby. "What? I do. I think Erik's fine, but I don't see the spark. You're not even married and the spark is gone? That's not right, sweetie." He squeezed my hand.

"Pardon my logistical questions," Lily said, starting to slur a bit. "But don't you live together?"

"Not anymore." I pulled a piece of bruschetta onto my plate. "I moved to the Holiday Inn on Monday night."

Cat audibly gasped, placing a hand over her mouth to cover up her disgust. "The Holiday Inn?"

"It's less than fifty bucks a night with my AAA discount." I shrugged. "It was my choice to leave, and it's his house, so it was up to me to move out." I'd been desperate when I left on Monday night, and the Holiday Inn was the first hotel I drove past (after stopping for a honey banana milkshake). I probably should have thought it through more carefully, but I hadn't exactly been in a normal state of mind.

I was proud that I had been sensible enough to ask the front desk if they had had any bedbug issues. When they assured me they did not, I plopped my credit card on the counter and told them I'd be staying for a while. That promise had gotten me an upgrade to a room with one king bed and a scabby-looking jacuzzi tub, plus free HBO, all for less than a great meal and a few drinks out. The room itself reminded me of the one my high school friends and I had rented after our senior prom. I only wished I had as much beer as we'd had that night. Instead, I'd opened up the mini-bar, dumped a mini bottle of Bailey's into my milkshake, and found a cleaned up version of *9 ½ Weeks* showing on Lifetime. Tuesday night I'd ordered a pizza and watched old episodes of *Family Guy*. Wednesday, I'd gone home to the hotel, cut slices off a block of cheese that I alternated with bites of a baguette I'd bought in the office cafeteria, and zoned out in front of *Pretty Woman*. All in all, a gluttonous and ugly week, but it had made me feel better. And someone made my bed every morning, which was a welcome perk.

Anders suddenly shouted, "You'll move in with me!"

I had considered that option. Anders actually lived in the tiny, two-bedroom tudor I'd bought before Erik and I had decided to live together. I loved my house, and had wisely decided not to sell it because the housing market had crashed just as I moved into Erik's place. Anders had been looking for an apartment at the time, so for the last four years he'd been renting my house from me. "I'll give you the master bedroom back."

"I can't take your bedroom," I insisted. "But it would be nice to move home. Would you be okay with a roommate?"

"I—well, you—have two bedrooms and I get so bored. It will be fun!"

I wasn't so sure about fun, but I did really want to be somewhere familiar. I couldn't exactly kick him out of my house and I couldn't imagine renting a tiny apartment after spreading out into Erik's house. And I wasn't so sure the lifestyle precedent I'd set that week while living alone at the Holiday Inn was healthy, so maybe it would work out for me to live with Anders.

"Okay, as long as you're willing. I'll cut your rent, obviously."

Cat was shaking her head, and I wondered if she was still thinking about my residence at the Holiday Inn, or if she was back to dwelling on the breakup itself. "This is all very sweet, buddy-bonding roommate business, but I'm having a hard time coming to terms with the fact that you and Erik are separated."

"We're not separated, we broke up," I clarified and took a bite of bruschetta. Through a full mouth, I said, "Separation can only happen when you're married, which we're not." Cat looked at me pityingly, and I knew she understood. We'd talked about this several times in the past, and she'd been pushing Erik to commit for longer than I had. Cat was big on tradition and formality, and I know she got it. I don't think she'd ever expected it would actually drive me away from him. That bothered me.

Lily, who'd now finished her bowl of wine, reached out and put her hand on my arm. "Are you sure it's not about the skanky intern? Please, give me a reason to believe... you guys were just so right together. Weren't you happy?"

I clenched my teeth together and said, "Listen, this wasn't an easy or simple decision. I kinda need your support." Cat nodded slightly, and Lily just looked surprised. Finally, she nodded her head once. "I've been with him since I was practically a child, and I've never really stepped back and considered my own wants and needs. I can't do that when I'm living in Erik's life, wondering if he's ever going to get bored and just take off. For a skanky intern or worse."

"So you're trying to teach him a lesson?" Lily narrowed her eyes at me. She always wanted a clear explanation, and I knew I wasn't going to be able to offer that.

Anders surprised me when he covered Lily's mouth with her hand. "Bottom line: Stella has made a very important decision about her life, and we're going to help her get through this in the best way friends can." How was this guy straight and not taken? I briefly wondered if I could get over the whole mixed-signal-sexuality thing and go after Anders? Nope. Wasn't going to happen. "We will listen, we will tell her she's wise and wonderful, and we're going to help her find a fling that will allow her to forget Erik."

I groaned. "I'm not exactly ready to date. It's been three days. I think I'll take a little time for myself, no guys. Except you, of course," I said to Anders with a smile.

"Girls?" Lily offered helpfully.

"Neither sex," I said. "No sex, that is. I don't need sex."

Lily wiggled a finger at me. "Oh, but you do. You need sex. Sex will make you forget."

"When is the last time you slept with Erik?" Anders asked abruptly. "I don't mean to push, since it's really not appropriate, but it's an important question. Answer honestly."

I glanced around the table and saw that all three sets of eyes were fixed on me. "A few weeks ago. Maybe more."

Both Lily and Anders squealed. "No!"

Lily poured me more wine, while Anders slapped at the table. "It's like you're a virgin again."

"Oh, come on, don't be so freaking dramatic," I said. "A few weeks is not that weird." Under my breath, I muttered, "Or a month or whatever."

"You lived with your boyfriend. Was he doing self-service in the bathroom at night?" Lily snorted. "A little jerky-jerk in the intern room at lunch?"

Cat knocked her on the shoulder. "Hello? You're talking about my brother, pervert."

"First and foremost, he is Stella's ex-boyfriend," Lily argued. "He's fair game. I don't care if he's the Pope's brother, he's getting picked on tonight." Cat nodded, then topped off her wine glass and waved the empty bottle in the air to request another.

I couldn't help but laugh. "I threw my back out, got fat. I don't know, I haven't exactly been feeling romantic."

Lily reached across the table and held my hands in hers. "I will share a little secret with you: sex is not always about romance, sweetheart. Maybe that's what you learned reading Judy Blume, but things change when you grow up. Sometimes, it's nice to fuck someone for the fun of it. To sex!" Lily cried out a little too loudly, holding her drink up, and I knew she'd crossed the line between buzzed and drunk.

Anders cringed.

"I'm going on nine weeks," Cat said suddenly, a little too quietly to really hear over Lily's whooping and laughing. "Maybe ten. Also, Travis and I sleep in separate bedrooms."

The wine arrived then, and we all quieted down. I was the first one to speak after our glasses were all refilled. "Are you pregnant again?"

Lily and Anders both "*oh*-ed," and we all looked to Cat for confirmation. "Nope, not pregnant. Just frigid, I guess." She grinned. "I get it," she told me. "You just get distracted, and other stuff takes over. I thought it was just couples with kids who had this issue, but it makes me feel a little less bad that you and Erik are—were?—in the celibacy club, too. You learn to forget there was once a sex life to be had, right?"

I nodded. That's exactly what had happened. We just started to take each other for granted. Good sex was the first thing to go, foreplay was second, and eventually sex of all variety went away altogether. We'd never been super into exciting and spontaneous sex, but anything that might have been considered hot had cooled down years ago. Bummer, sure, but other stuff took over and mattered more. "I miss that early relationship sex," I said, suddenly realizing I did. I thought back to the night at *Molto*, and to the tingling in my fingers as he'd stroked my hands. I thought about how alive that sensation could make me feel.

"It's not 'early relationship' sex you need—you don't need anything with the word relationship tied to it. You're looking for spontaneous, off-limits sex." Anders grinned, and the look on his face had me worried. "You just need to shake it up a little, roomie."

"I'm not shaking anything until my ass shrinks back down to an acceptable size," I said, laughing. "I'm getting myself put back together and then we can talk."

Lily raised her glass. "I propose a toast… to convincing Stella her ass is in perfect shaking shape and to Cat's comfortable celibacy." We all clinked, and I felt a whole lot better than I had in weeks.

CHAPTER THREE

I stood in front of a locker at the Y, slowly pulling out my swimsuit and towel as naked, elderly women strutted around the locker room chatting. I carefully pulled off my shirt, then wrapped a towel around my curvy body as I discreetly slipped my bra and panties off and pulled on my one-piece. Looking down, I realized I hadn't waxed in over a month. Surveying my surroundings, I quickly decided that just didn't matter. It wasn't like I was at water aerobics to meet men.

I'd been reluctant to meet with the massage therapist in Anders' office, but in the spirit of turning over a new leaf and getting well, I'd gone to see her the day after our drinks marathon. Anders had been right. Forty-five minutes in therapist Sue's tiny, fragrant office had made me feel like a different person. Sue had focused on "muscle release" and stretching, and I was pretty sure I now wanted to marry my therapist, just so I could bring her home with me every night. We'd gotten to talking during the session, and I'd told her my goal was to get back to exercising shape.

"Water aerobics," Sue had said, pulling my foot gently toward the wall. "Trust me. It's going to change your life."

I did trust her, and that's the only reason I was at the Y at seven in the morning the next Tuesday. I'd never been a pre-work exerciser—Erik and I always went together after work because it helped him sleep better if he went later in the day—but old people must have learned life lessons on the value of getting up early and getting exercise out of the way since all the pool classes were offered in the pre-dawn hours.

I stifled a yawn as I stepped into the shower room. I let the water run over my head, matting my dark curls into tight ringlets that clung close to my head instead of staying puffed up like a muffin (the usual morning 'do).

"You don't have to get your hair wet," a raspy voice said from across the tiled room. "Just rinse off the lady bits and you're in business. That's all they really need you to do."

"Thanks," I said, swallowing back a laugh.

The woman who had spoken was no more than five feet tall and weighed much less than Cat. Her swimsuit hung off her wiry frame, and she looked to be in her seventies. She was grinning at me. "You're here for class?" she asked, sizing me up. "Good for you. It's not a grueling workout since half of us have arthritis, but you can make it something if you make the effort. I'm Heather."

"Stella," I said. "This is my first time doing water aerobics."

"No shit, Stella." Heather reached for my arm. "Walk me out to the pool. I can't rely on any of these other old bitches to help me out, so it's good you're here." She and I shuffled toward the pool door together, and I felt her soft arm flesh rubbing against my own. It made me think of my grandmas, who'd both died when I was still a kid, and I suddenly felt a lot happier about my decision to come to water aerobics.

"Are you injured?" She stopped and looked me over. "You look like you work out—you've got a nice figure, and praise Jesus, you don't look like one of those awful, skinny mannequins—but I've never seen you in class before."

"I think I love you," I told Heather, laughing about her nice figure remark. I opened the door between the locker room and the pool for both of us, and we shuffled our way across the pool deck to the shallow L-section of the pool. "I hurt myself doing yoga, and I haven't been able to exercise in more than a month. I needed to find something that won't strain my back."

Heather patted my arm. "This class isn't going to strain much, except your patience. Barbara talks through class—makes it impossible to get a decent workout if you try to listen. I'll introduce you around. The girls are all going to want to set you up with their boys—sons, grandsons, godsons. I'll wait my turn until I figure out if you're normal or one of those shrill gals. Are you single?"

It was the first time I'd been asked this since Erik and I had broken up. Anders, Lily, and I had spent most of the past weekend getting my stuff out of Erik's house (Lily had helpfully emailed him to find out when he'd be out of the house) and moving it into "my" house. It felt good to be home, and I'd been distracted enough that I hadn't thought much about Erik. I was surprised at how little I was thinking of him, actually. I nodded to answer Heather's question, and realized how normal it felt to be saying yes. "Newly single," I said, hoping she'd take that as a hint that I wasn't looking for anyone.

"Perfect. Barbara's got a grandson who seems to only want casual flings, so we'll start there. Barb's pushy anyway, so the sooner we get her little shit out of the way, the better." I stared at Heather. This was what Lily was going to be like in forty years, I realized. Something about the comparison made me feel even more comfortable with Heather.

"I'm not really looking to be set up right now. It was a long-term relationship that ended last week, actually."

"Wah-wah," Heather said, making a squeaky violin noise. "Time to move on. Life's too short for moping, sweetheart. My husband died ten years ago, and I wasted too much time whining about being alone. Learn a lesson from an old lady, and get going now. Your body's not going to look any better than it does right now."

"I'm taking time for me. I've been in a committed relationship since I was twenty-two, and I think I started to forget who *I* was while we were dating."

"You think you need to be alone to find yourself?" Heather started to walk down the sloping ramp into the pool. She let out a little moan as the water hit her belly button. "That's bull-crap. All those self-help books these days tell you to go off and explore the world on your own, eat and pray your way to your soul. Blah, blah, blah. Sex is just as good for finding yourself as this so-called 'reflection' time. And you'll be a lot less lonely." She shook her head, then reached for a pair of inflatable bar-bells that were resting on the pool deck. "It's your own damn fault you let the guy take over. Take yourself back, damn it. Just don't bother doing it alone. You'll just end up feeling sorry for yourself."

I smiled at the advice. I hadn't expected a therapy session at water aerobics. Heather made some good points, but I knew my situation was different. Just as I was about to tell her that, a gaggle of laughing women came through the door from the locker room into the pool area. One man emerged from the hot tub and joined everyone in the pool. There were a total of seven of us, including me, and I was easily forty years younger than anyone else in the class. I started to question this decision again, but I'd vowed to go to at least three classes before giving up. I had to get back to exercise, or I really was going to go crazy. My life felt like it was falling apart, and I knew it was partly because I was depressed and feeling awful about my appearance.

The woman who seemed to be the teacher was in her mid-fifties and heavyset. She was wearing stretchy leggings under her swimsuit, and had on a pair of running shoes. She introduced herself to me as Jean, asking about my experience with water aerobics.

"I'm new to this," I said, and realized everyone was looking at me. I was standing off by myself, and realized they were all huddled together in a circle. I felt as out-of-place as I always did at Erik's office holiday party.

"I'll take things slowly so you don't fall behind," Jean said. "I lead the class from up here on the pool deck so you can see what you're supposed to be doing with your legs under the water."

Before we'd even finished our warm-up, a tall, stately woman (who reminded me of Bea Arthur from *Golden Girls*) lunged over to me in the pool. She didn't say anything at first, but kept smiling at me, as though she had a secret. I smiled back, but tried to keep my focus on Jean. After all, I wasn't there to make friends—I was there for a workout. "Jonathan is thirty-four," Bea Arthur said suddenly, as we all did high-knee kicks.

"Excuse me?" I said, pretty sure I'd heard her correctly.

"Jonathan. My Jonathan, he's thirty-four. Heather told me you were interested in him. He's a musician."

This must be Barbara, I thought. Nothing could be less appealing than a musician. "I'm actually just getting out of a relationship—"

Barbara cut me off. "That's what I hear. Jonathan doesn't mind."

I wonder if Jonathan knows his grandma is pimping him out at Water X Power? I thought, my eyes widening. "I'm sorry," I said. "It's just not a good time. I really appreciate it, though."

Barbara huffed and scooted back toward the circle of women on the other side of the shallow end. I was left alone, feeling like a real jackass. I hadn't realized water aerobics came with so many strings attached. As much as I'd enjoyed talking with Heather before class had started, I realized I would need to keep my distance from these women if I was going to have any hope of making it through class without a bunch of elderly enemies. I could hear them griping and sniping over in their little circle, and Jean reminded them to focus on their workout. Barbara lifted an eyebrow in Jean's general direction and went right back to talking.

The lone gentleman in the class waited for me as we all followed Jean's command to cross-country ski through the water to the deep end, riding atop water-noodles to help keep us afloat.

"You need to hold your own with these girls," he said, looking over his shoulder at the gaggle of women striding slowly through the water behind us. "They'll boss you around until you can't think straight, if you let them. Believe me." He grinned, and as he did, his fleshy chin dipped under the water.

"Thanks for the tip. I'm Stella, by the way."

"That's a pretty name. I'm Jim." He held out his hand to shake, but that sent him under again so he pulled it back. "They just like to feel useful," he said when he'd surfaced. "You're fresh meat. I was the new guy a few months ago, and you can imagine what I went through. It was like they were all sharks, and I was the only fish." He chuckled—at his water metaphor, I guessed. "At least I don't have to listen to them in the locker room. If I were you, I'd take off a little early so you can shower and get the heck out of here before the real gossip starts." He kicked desperately under the surface to stay above water.

I decided to take Jim's advice, so just as we started the cool down I made an excuse about a morning meeting and headed for the locker room. I hadn't exactly worked up a sweat, so I wasn't feeling too bad about missing the stretching part of social hour. Heather gave me a look as I left, and the other women surveyed me suspiciously. It hadn't been a great start to my new exercise routine, but I wasn't going to be scared away by a bunch of angry old ladies.

"I'll see you next week," I said, and waved to show them they couldn't intimidate me. But I wasn't entirely sure that was true.

"I like this Heather character," Lily said later that day, as we walked toward the cafeteria for a coffee. I was trying to convince her to come to water aerobics with me by sharing Heather's comment about rinsing my lady bits. I wasn't sure I wanted to face the regulars by myself again, and hoped I could lure Lily into the shark den. "I also think you should go out with this musician character. It'll be good for you."

"How is a thirty-four year old aspiring musician good for anyone?" I ordered a decaf skim latte, wondering if Erik had been making coffee at home without me there. He usually didn't drink coffee before leaving for work in the morning, but he'd gotten into the habit of preparing it for me every night before bed and I suspected he hadn't yet broken with routine. "Besides, I don't even know this woman. She could be a total nutjob and the grandson could be an Internet stalker, for all I know. Is it really smart to get set up with a stranger?"

Lily moaned. "You really have been off the market for a long time. Perhaps you've heard of something called 'online dating'? It's fairly common. Something relatively new in the last decade, where people get onto something known as the 'Internet' and are matched up with possible partners?"

"You are so funny," I narrowed my eyes at her and swiped my latte off the service counter.

"After you're matched," she continued, smiling smugly. "You meet a relative 'stranger' in a public place and either have an awkwardly fun time or figure out how quickly you can bail without feeling like a total bitch." She grinned. "Bottom line, I think getting set up by a nice old lady you met in water aerobics is as safe, relatively speaking, as an Internet date."

"She's not a nice old lady," I grumbled. "They're mean. And probably *all* chock full of advice."

"Good advice?" Lily bit into her bagel as we walked back through the halls to the elevator. She waved at someone I recognized from the "Winner's Board" that hung in every floor lobby. The Winner's Board was something James had conceived of, a recognition board where peoples' extraordinary achievements were shared with everyone. Every few months the Winner's Board featured photographs of new Centrex superstars, people who had either come up with a way to save or make money, or a creative new way to motivate customers to buy stuff. I'd never been featured on the Winner's Board, and had given up trying. I didn't want to be a winner at Centrex.

"She told me to start sleeping around to get over Erik."

"Sound advice."

"We *just* broke up!"

"You'll just mope if you hang out at home alone."

"That's exactly what Heather said."

"Do you think she'd want to get a drink with us sometime? Heather sounds like a hoot."

"I think it's crass to jump into bed with someone new immediately," I said. I sounded like a prude. Was I a prude? I'd never considered it—I had never needed to.

Lily rolled her eyes as we rode up the elevator. "You're starting over, Stella. You've got to actually *start* somewhere. So maybe you're not going to hop into bed with the first guy that's offered up, but you will—eventually—think about dating. Not necessarily immediately, but probably sometime. That's the first step."

Starting over.

"Oh, my God," I said as the elevators opened onto the twelfth floor lobby. "I'm starting over at age thirty-four. I'm single, out of practice, unwaxed, and unfamiliar with the modern methods of protection, and here I am—" I waved my arms in the air, sloshing latte foam out the little lid blowhole onto the paisley carpet. "Just thrown back out into the single scene, expected to figure out how to start dating as an almost-middle-aged woman." Lily started laughing, which I really didn't appreciate. "It's not funny!"

"You do know both Anders and I are single and in the dating scene, yes?"

"You've got Chad. You're not single."

"Eh, I'm as close to single as you can be when you're 'in a relationship.' We rarely live in the same city. But that's not the point. You're acting like being single in your thirties is the worst curse to have ever befallen anyone."

I shook my head. "You know that's not what I mean."

"That's what it sounds like to me," she said, lowering her voice as we walked past the interns. They all turned and looked at us anyway. "You're in your prime, you're not beaten down from years of crappy dates—"

"Nuh-uh, I have had years of crappy dates. It's just that they've all been with the same person."

"Doesn't count," Lily pushed me into her office and I sat in the chair facing her desk. I propped my feet up on the edge of the faux-wood surface, hoping Lily couldn't see down my skirt. "You haven't been suffering through rounds of bad blind dates and online dates and office romances, so you're not jaded. I think you're going to love dating."

"Maybe you're right," I conceded, thinking about all the meals in my future. I liked eating out. Really, dating was just eating out at interesting restaurants with someone new, right? I would be good at this! "I guess if I really am starting over, maybe I should just get a first date out of the way?"

"Now *that's* the right spirit." Lily flopped down at her desk and logged in, scrolling through twenty minutes worth of emails. "Oh, shit," she said, suddenly paling and looking up at me.

"What?" I was feeling hopeful, and didn't really care what micro-drama James had cooked up today. Surely, the woes of retail marketing and the impending stress of Black Friday (still more than two months away, but ever-present nonetheless) couldn't be as dramatic as Lily's facial expression suggested. "Put on a happy face, Lil. Otherwise, the Bears are going to come after you and eat you up for your bad attitude or something." I laughed. "We'll figure out some punishment."

"Layoffs." She quietly uttered the word every corporate employee dreaded.

"Well, nothing that severe." I looked at her more closely. "Wait, do you have an email that says there are going to be layoffs? Real layoffs, or the performance-based layoffs of last week?" I suddenly felt sick.

"We have a staffing meeting at six to discuss. I don't know when they're happening, but they're coming," she said, licking her lips.

Suddenly, I had the feeling we were no longer alone. I pulled my feet off Lily's desk and turned to look back at the always-open door to her office and saw James Davis leaning casually against the doorframe with his hands tucked into the pockets of his sweater vest.

"What's going on, girls?" James insisted on calling us all girls, despite the fact that it was both condescending and unprofessional. "How were the weekends?" He chewed on something in his mouth. Through his cheek, I could see the outline of his tongue wrap around his back teeth to pull something out of the nether-regions, and the chewing intensified. His hair, which had been pomaded into submission, was artfully messy and intentionally overgrown. I felt the same sickness creep up every time I had to be this close to James. He just oozed eww.

"The weekends were fantastic," Lily said, cool as ever. "Did you do anything fun?"

Our boss tucked his hand inside his pants pocket and jangled some coins, leading me to wonder what else he was touching in there. "Some of the B-school guys went out for a few beers. It's always great hanging out with the old crew." He chuckled, as though inviting us to join his inside joke. James had graduated from business school six years earlier, but he always talked about it as though he'd been out for nearly a century and his memories of it were fading fast. I guess that was his way of trying to add a few years on to his experience to get people to take him seriously.

James was younger than both Lily and I, but had somehow managed to charm his way to the top faster than a regular promotion schedule usually allowed. Even though he'd gotten married in a big, lavish ceremony only nine months before, Lily and I were certain he was sleeping with his boss, the frigid (and close-to-retirement) Chief Marketing Officer at Centrex. It was an interesting and disgusting pairing in every way. "The wife gets a little pesky when I meet up with them, since we all drink like twenty-somethings," James laughed, as though his twenties were such a distant memory. He'd just celebrated his thirty-first birthday that July. "So..." James looked around, suddenly uncomfortable. "Lil, are you going to make it to our, uh, planning meeting tonight?"

"I'll be there."

"Fantastic. And Stella," James pointed finger-guns at me and grinned. He had lettuce stuck between his first and second molar. "Keep up the brave face, got it?" James was gone as fast as he'd appeared.

"What did that mean? Do you think he knows about me and Erik? Is he trying to weasel his way into my personal life?" I squirmed and stood up, thinking it best I get back to my desk. James wasn't big on us loitering or chatting, even though they were two of his own favorite things to do.

"Just his motivational crap," Lily said, smiling. "Now go get back to work. And by work, I mean go back to your desk and fill out your online dating profile. You can submit it through me for approval before you make it public." She gave me her Hardcore Lily stare. "Go, single girl, go!"

It wasn't until the next night, when I got home before Anders, that I finally got the nerve up to check out an online dating site. "Welcome to our community!" I read on the first screen. I had offered up my junk email address, and hoped I wasn't going to start getting even more spam. The emails offering me penis enhancements were already out of control, and now that they knew I was looking for love (or trolling for a decent date), I suspected they had some spambot readying all kinds of new offers for me. "What brings you here today?" The first screen featured an image of a happy couple, about my age, laughing on a sailboat. I hoped I wouldn't have to go sailing on any first dates.

I clicked the box that said, "Just exploring—I'm not sure if I'm ready to do this yet." Huh. That was a pretty accurate description of my state-of-mind, actually. Usually, online forms were an irritating collection of bad answers.

"Relationship status?" Never married.

"Gender?" Didn't I already answer this? I swear I had, but maybe they just wanted to make sure?

"Seeking?" Men, ages... hmm. I might need to ask Lily or Anders about this. Twenty-six to forty? I briefly debated closing the dating service window immediately. I didn't know what I was looking for. I couldn't even pick the age of my future match.

"Where should we search?" My new computer matchmaker asked me. I knew I didn't want to date someone in the suburbs. I liked city guys. Right? I checked "within 10 miles" and moved on.

Call me superficial, but I was also cautious and checked yes when they asked if I wanted to see only matches with photos. I wasn't going to be fooled by some sixty-year-old letch, posing as a thirty-five-year-old, fishing for trophy wives. Need I worry about that? Agh! This was scary. Again, I debated closing the site, but instead clicked "next" to move on to the next page.

As the next page loaded, I heard the front door open and I slammed my laptop closed. I'd been working at the dining room table, and didn't want Anders to see what I was doing. It was so embarrassing.

"What are you up to?" he asked, walking in and throwing his coat on the couch. In the few days we'd been living together, I had discovered Anders was a slob. He left his dishes around for days (or until I picked them up and put them in the dishwasher for him), laid his socks next to the couch while he was watching TV at night, and squeezed the toothpaste from the top. Living with Anders was kind of like living with Erik.

"Just catching up on some work," I said, smiling. "A powerpoint thing."

He narrowed his eyes at me. "Really?"

"Yes, really," I said, patting my computer nervously. "That's all."

"You look guilty."

I sighed, defeated. "Fine. I'm filling out an online dating portfolio."

Anders started clapping. "Excellent! We should open a bottle of wine for this. Can I help?"

"No."

"You're going to sit there, alone, and answer those questions for yourself? Trust me, you need the help of an expert. You don't know what you're doing."

"You're an expert at online dating service forms? Is there such a thing?"

"Just go get the wine and I'll get started." I reluctantly went into the kitchen to pour us both a glass of wine. When I came back out to the dining room, Anders had my computer open and was answering questions about me.

"Curvy?" I asked, peering over his shoulder. "Don't you think 'a few extra pounds' is more appropriate?" I squeezed my belly fat and gazed down at my boobs.

"Curvy sounds a lot better. That's why it's an option."

"But curvy suggests naturally large tits and sexy hips," I looked down at my breasts, which were larger than usual, thanks to the extra pounds, but still not exactly boob-tastic. And my butt was kind of flat. Though I did have nice calves. My calves were curvy and perfect.

Anders looked me over carefully. "Curves can be anywhere. 'Curvy' does not necessarily mean big tits. Trust me, I've gone out with a lot of girls who answer curvy... you fit the bill. You're hot, Stella. Okay, what do you like to do?" He didn't wait for a response from me. Instead, he started checking all kinds of boxes and began to type. "You like sports, right? We'll say running—wait, but then you're going to get one of those self-obsessed running types who spend their weekend training for marathons. How about a more social sport? Are you into biking?"

"Sure," I said, and took a sip of my wine. I'd lost control of the process. "How about hiking?"

"Yes! That's great. Hiking is social, but not too extreme. Yoga?"

I lifted my eyebrows at him.

"Right. Not yoga. Those yoga guys are weird anyway. Remember when I went out with Kelly from my yoga class and she started doing breathing exercises while we were making out?" He shuddered. "So weird. Okay, how about other activities?"

"Eating out?"

"Fine. Ooh, wine tasting? That would be fun."

"Who's going on this date? You, or me?" I grinned at him.

"You'd love wine tasting. Maybe it will get you out of your Malbec slump."

"It's not a slump. I like Malbec. I'm just a creature of habit."

"Exactly, and we're trying to break you out of it. We're trying to break all of your bland habits." He checked the box next to 'wine tasting' and also checked the boxes next to 'coffee and conversation,' 'cooking,' 'movies,' 'camping,' and 'exploring new places.'

"I've been camping three times," I said, dubious.

"Did you enjoy it?" Anders looked up only briefly, still clicking through pages on my profile.

"I guess. I was in Girl Scouts at the time."

"It's not like you're going to go camping on your first date. By the time it comes up, this guy is going to be so into you he'll be thrilled to teach you all about camping. He can teach you how to do it and will feel like a hero." He smiled. "Trust me."

I groaned and drank more wine. "Did you just write that I'm 'active, ready to explore new things, and always eager for a laugh?'" I cringed. "That's so cheesy."

"It'll work. You'll see."

"The last book I read was some sort of chick lit," I said, pointing to the section of the screen that asked what book I was reading. "It was funny."

"You can't put that. It makes you look desperate and dumb." I simply nodded as he wrote that I'd just finished reading *On the Road*. At least I had read it, years and years ago, so it wasn't a total lie.

"I like romance movies, too," I said, feebly trying to re-insert myself into the process as he checked off the kinds of movies I liked. He just waved me off and pressed 'next' to go to the next screen. Apparently, I liked Action, Comedy, and Foreign movies only. We went through a whole bunch of screens about more general preferences, and I discovered Anders knew a lot more about me than I'd ever really realized. "How do you know my dream vacation would be in Italy?"

"Am I right?" He asked, looking smug. "When you and Erik went to London, you really wanted to go to Italy, right?" I nodded, thinking back to how much I'd pushed for us to go to Italy but finally caved at his insistence. "That's when I knew you guys weren't meant to be. It's not cool that he wouldn't go back with you. He's too selfish. You need someone who realizes they would enjoy Italy a million times more than they did the first time, just because you're with them. Not someone who feels like it's a wasted trip because they've already been."

I nodded and sat back to drink my wine while Anders finished my profile. He'd just proven that, in some ways, my friends probably knew me better than I even knew myself. That really needed to change.

CHAPTER FOUR

"Your color is bland. Do you need me to make you an appointment with my colorist?" I stood to the side at the Clinique counter at Macy's and watched as Laurel Wesley dabbed lipsticks on the back of her soft, doughy hand. She looked at me, then turned back to the mirror to test an orange hue on her thin lips. I'd been listening to Laurel coach me on every manner of things for the past thirty minutes, and asked myself—again—why I was still letting her get to me.

Laurel was Erik's mom, and she had played the role of sorta-like-a-mother to me for the past twelve years. Because she'd been a big part of my life while I was with Erik—and was the closest thing I had to a parent of my own—I reluctantly agreed to join her on a shopping trip the weekend after I'd moved out of her son's house. Though she had her flaws, Laurel was the only *real* parent I had gone to in recent years when I needed motherly advice, and I didn't want to just drop her. After my dad died, Laurel had come around at just the right time. When I'd needed it most, Erik's mom had happily given me more mom-advice than any girl could ever need. Granted, it was tainted with Wesley-isms, but that was better than nothing.

"Stella, are you listening to me?" She wiped the orange streak off her mouth and applied a pink coral gloss.

"Yeah," I said absentmindedly. "I have a haircut next week. I'll talk to her about it."

"Good." Then she added under her breath, "Even though your stylist is doing you no favors." Laurel stepped away from the lipsticks and surveyed the free gift that came with every qualifying purchase. "This is a good deal. I might have to buy something just so you can have it. Do you need some new stuff?"

"I'm okay," I said. "They always put the ugly colors in the free gift, you know." I could tell she was disappointed she didn't have an excuse to buy something. "If you really want to buy something to get the free gift, I'd be happy to take it. I'm not that picky."

"It's good stuff, Clinique. Besides, beggars can't be choosers. You take what you can get." She arched her eyebrows at me, and I wondered if we were still talking about makeup, or if we'd moved into the Erik portion of our discussion. "You haven't asked about Erik," she snipped, leading me to wonder no more. "You don't want to know how he's doing?"

I sighed. "I do. I've been thinking about him a lot. I'm just trying not to obsess."

"Have you called him?"

"No."

"Don't you think you're being a little hasty?" We walked from the makeup to the handbags, and Laurel ran her hands across smooth, supple leather on display while I deliberately ignored her. The ugly coral color glowed on her lips like a beacon, which made it hard not to stare. "Did you really give him a chance?"

"Are we really having this conversation, Laurel?"

"He's my son. You're my… Stella. I think you make a nice partnership. Practical."

Practical. "Yeah, I know." I didn't want to offend her and say something I'd regret later. It wasn't *practical.*

"You don't look good." She pursed her lips and appraised me. "Tired."

"Thanks."

"I just mean, it looks like you're having a hard time adjusting. Are you sleeping? Don't you get lonely in bed by yourself?"

I wanted to ask her if she got lonely in bed by *herself.* She and Peter, Erik's dad, had been sleeping in separate bedrooms since Erik and Cat were kids. Laurel took the master suite and

Peter slept on a day bed in his study. "I'm actually sleeping very well. It's nice to be home."

"Home?" Laurel scoffed. "You mean you never considered Erik's house *home*?" She had started to get shrill, and I knew I needed to calm her quickly. Laurel struggled with public-private boundaries, and had no concern for airing her issues in front of strangers.

"Is he... okay?" I asked, not needing to fake the concern that crept into my voice. I didn't really think Erik would be desperately writhing in agony and loneliness (though it would have been nice), but I did worry a little about how he was handling things.

Laurel sighed, deep and low and long. "He's full of regret, Stella." She squeezed her lips together, and I knew she was trying hard to conjure tears. She had her famous blubber-til-you-get-what-you-want face on. She used this tactic when Cat's kids wouldn't give her a goodbye kiss, or when we had a heated discussion at the Thanksgiving dinner table, or when the grocery store was out of her favorite artichoke dip. Like a five-year-old, Laurel used tears to get what she wanted. "He knows he made mistakes."

I nodded, but said nothing. It's not like I'd sprung my desire for more permanent commitment on Erik suddenly. He'd had more than enough chances to take my needs into consideration. He knew what was wrong with us just as well as I did, but he just seemed more willing to overlook the problems out of habit.

I'd had the time and distance I'd needed in the last few weeks to realize it wasn't just his unwillingness to formally commit that had driven me to leave, but also that we'd fallen out of love. I still loved him, of course, but I wasn't *in* love with him. The passion was gone, and only now that I'd stepped away did I realize I wanted that passion and someone who wanted to make me happy. On my terms.

"When are you going to go back to him?" She asked finally, after a few long moments of silence. "When are you going to realize what you left and take him back? We're your family, Stella. You don't just abandon your family."

I didn't bother telling Laurel that Erik hadn't called *me* since the split, either, and the only "communication" I'd had with him had been through her. "I'm not," I said quietly. "Erik and I want different things out of our life together, and there are a few deal-breakers for me."

She *pfft*-ed through her teeth and choked out a laugh. "Such drama, Stella. Frankly, I didn't realize you had all this foolish girl angst in you. I thought we'd taught you better."

Foolish girl angst? My college women's studies professor would have a field day with Laurel's analysis of the situation.

"It was lovely to see you, Laurel," I said, finally realizing I didn't have to be nice to her even when she treated me like a child. She wasn't my almost-mother-in-law anymore. I could just *leave* and I wouldn't have to hear about how I'd hurt her from my boyfriend all night. "I have a date tonight—with a musician! I guess I need to get some rest beforehand since, you know, I look *tired*." I smiled, turning toward the door. Then I looked back and muttered, "By the way, you look like a corpse in coral."

As I walked away, I felt the pang of guilt I always felt when I'd been harsh to Laurel. I was storming out like a teenage girl, and it embarrassed me. After all, she was right: the Wesleys were my family. What right did I have to leave? They were all I had, and they'd been good to me. (Even if my name *still* wasn't in the Christmas drawing. It's not like I wanted a macrame potholder anyway.)

So even if I was unhappy, maybe I'd moved beyond the point of being able to just walk away, free and clear. Cat had always been the first to remind me that you can pick your friends, but you can't pick your family… where did Erik and Laurel and the others fit into that? Had I lost the ability to choose? Was I really prepared to abandon my "family?"

I wasn't lying. I really did have a date. I still couldn't believe I'd done it, but when I'd gone back to water aerobics on Thursday I left my number taped to Barbara's locker with a note to have Jonathan-the-musician call me. I had deliberately arrived to class late and left early to avoid any extended conversation with the regulars, but the note had worked.

Jonathan had called me on Friday and we decided to go out on Saturday.

Initially, I was dreading it. It seemed sort of desperate that this guy had called me based on a recommendation from his grandma, but I was trying hard to be spontaneous and enthusiastic about the possibilities. I wasn't exactly ready to find my next soul mate, but after my morning with Laurel, I was much more excited about having a date. It made me feel like I was moving on, and taking the necessary steps to get over Erik.

Lily came over to help me get ready, and I felt like I looked decent by the time I left home. Lil had tamed my curls into submission, and loaned me one of her cute, long sweater-dress things to go over leggings. The length of the dress hid the size of my thighs, which was a necessity, and I could wear my cute and comfy pumps that were sort of cool (if I squinted and didn't look too closely). I was ready to date a musician!

Unfortunately, the guy who met me in front of the hostess stand at Nina's, one of my favorite neighborhood restaurants, was about as far from Jon Bon Jovi as I was from Reese Witherspoon. The guy who introduced himself as Jonathan was bald, wearing a tux, and when he got close enough to give me a hello hug, all I could think is he smelled like a leaky basement.

"It's nice to meet you," I said, taken aback by the hug.

"It's good to meet you, too." Jonathan twitched nervously as the hostess pulled out my chair at our table. It was sort of cute, actually. Was he nervous? "Wow, you're as hot as my grandma said." He sat in the chair right next to me instead of in the seat across. Erik and I had always sat across from each other in restaurants, and made fun of the people who sat side-by-side at square tables. It always seemed unnecessarily close.

"Thanks," I said, laughing at the awkward compliment. I wondered what Barbara had told him about me. It's not like she knew anything about me, so she would have described me on looks alone. I was oddly flattered that an elderly woman had described me as hot. Apparently, I'd been starved for compliments if that meant so much to me. "So, you're a musician?"

"Yeah, I play in quartets, mostly."

"Oh," I said, nodding. "That explains the tux, huh?" It made sense he was wearing a tux if he'd just come from playing a party or an afternoon wedding or something. For some reason, I'd been picturing a rock-band musician, not a classical musician. Even though he wasn't my physical type, Jonathan suddenly didn't seem quite as lame. Classical musicians were probably pretty sensitive, and obviously had a romantic side. It also took talent to play a tricky string instrument. Could I overlook the basement smell?

"What about the tux?" Jonathan said, puzzling over both the question and the menu. "Have you had the scallops here?"

"Yeah, the scallops are yummy. Were you wearing the tux for a gig this afternoon or something? Did you have a wedding to play? Or a cocktail party?"

Jonathan shook his head. "No."

Huh. Had he worn the tux specifically for our date? I chose not to press on. I could overlook it. "Are you going to get the scallops?"

"I'm not sure," he said, drumming his fingers on the table. "You?"

"I'm going to get the shrimp." I pushed my menu away. I'd been to Nina's enough times to know what I wanted without even looking at the menu.

"That sounds good. I'm just going to order some soup and snag a few bites of yours, if that's cool?" Jonathan pushed his menu away and flagged our waiter over. "Can I get a black napkin please?" When the waiter returned with a black napkin, he explained, "The white ones leave lint on my pants."

"Smart," I said, trying hard not to laugh. The leaky basement smell was starting to get to me again. "So, um, Jonathan, what instrument do you play?"

"Trumpet," he said proudly. Okay, so it wasn't a string quartet... he was in a jazz quartet. Also cool. I don't know why I was jumping to so many conclusions. I vowed to stop making assumptions and give the guy a chance to tell me about himself. "But I'm learning electric guitar to expand the options. I've always wanted to be in a punk band."

I swallowed. Jonathan was not making this easy. I was trying, but there was nothing less appealing to me than a guy my age who was still trying to make it in the music scene. Maybe I was being a little dramatic, but at the moment I couldn't think of anything much worse. My practical side wanted to remind him that if he hadn't made it by thirty-five, he probably wasn't going to be a rock star. Then again, my practical side needed to take a hike, since all my smart decisions and solid planning had left me suddenly single and in a life I didn't even recognize as boring. "That would be cool," I said, even though I didn't think that.

Our waiter came then, saving me from further conversation about being in a punk band. As we waited for our food to come, the conversation shifted to my work (he ranted for a while about Centrex being "The Man" and asked how I could possibly work somewhere that so selfishly promoted a consumer culture), our hobbies (from what I could tell, he played a lot of Wii), and eventually, our meals.

"This is great shrimp," he said, stuffing his mouth full of shrimp that he unapologetically plucked from my plate. "Do you want a bite of soup?"

I almost started laughing. Who shares soup? But Jonathan was serious, and very earnest about his offer, too. "No thanks, I'm going to stick with the shrimp." Based on the uninspiring conversation, it was abundantly obvious Jonathan and I were not a match. So when the meal ended and our check arrived, I figured it would make sense to split the bill and go our separate ways. I might have considered letting him offer to pay if I thought it had been a good date, but as it was, I got the sense this was a divide and say goodbye situation. There would never be a next time. I may have been new to dating, but I wasn't that dim. I pulled out my wallet and slid the check over to my side of the table.

"Oh, awesome, you're going to pay this time?" He was grinning at me and had made no motion to extract his own wallet. "My dinner was pretty cheap, so I guess that makes the most sense." He looked at the check with interest. "Oof, you're not a cheap date, are you?"

"I guess not." This time, I couldn't suppress my laughter. For some reason, Jonathan joined me. I was laughing at him, but I really don't think he realized that. "Well, it was nice getting to know you," I said, hoping to make it home in time for House Hunters.

Jonathan grinned, and leaned forward to hug me, right there at the table. "Yeah, it's been fun hanging out with you, too." The smell of leaky basement was overwhelmingly pungent, and I knew I had to get out of there. "My grandma's home tonight, so is it cool if we go to your place?"

CHAPTER FIVE

A full week later, I sat in the front seat of Cat's minivan, ignoring Pippa kicking at my seat from behind. Cat and I hadn't talked a lot since our drinks night the week of the split, and I'd been missing both her and the girls. When I called to invite myself over to their house the weekend after my date with Jonathan, Cat begged me to join them at some festival they were going to in a local park. It was a Children's Festival, sponsored by Centrex, and the girls' favorite band was playing for free on the big outdoor stage.

I'd happily agreed, looking forward to special time with Heidi and Pippa, but I also longed for something that would get me out of the house. I'd been holing away all week, nervous amidst the whispers of layoffs at work and obsessed with the potential dates they were flagging for me at my online dating site. Anders and I had spent most nights at home that week, searching through the photos of eligible bachelors and laughing. It was juvenile, I know, but after the experience with Jonathan, I was allowed to be picky.

"Do you just get a fresh batch of guys to pick from every day?" Cat asked, peeking in the rearview mirror at her girls. Cat's nanny, a cute twenty-year-old French girl, sat in the back row of the minivan. Even though she had her nanny along to help, Cat was always paranoid and overwhelmed when she was with her daughters. It was frightening to ride in the car with her, since she was constantly interacting with her daughters in the back. Some obnoxious bluegrass music was playing over the car speakers, and Heidi was busy singing along. "Pippa, stop kicking Stella!"

"There have been a lot of profiles to look through," I said, grabbing Pippa's foot behind me to tickle it. "I've only contacted one person, so far. We're going out tonight."

"Whoa, two Saturday nights in a row? You're a real swinging single." Cat smiled, but I knew she was still finding it hard to talk to me about anyone other than her brother. It was definitely weird between us, and that sucked. I wanted to tell her how much I was missing Erik, how much I was thinking about him and wondering what he was doing, but I knew if I opened that line of conversation, she'd just enable me to dwell. I had to make her believe I was coping, in part to help convince myself.

We pulled into a parking spot and I helped lift Pippa and Heidi out of the car. They ran ahead with their nanny while Cat and I dawdled behind. We walked through the grassy pathways in silence, both of us probably thinking about how awkward it would always be for us to talk about my dating life. "Do you want to hear about this?" I asked finally. "Is it weird for me to talk about other guys with you?"

"No," Cat insisted. "I don't want you to think you have to filter yourself, just because of Erik. I'm not going to tell him anything, you know."

"I wouldn't mind if you did, actually. I sort of want him to know I'm functioning without him." I shrugged. "That's normal, right?"

"I'll do my best to slip in some little anecdotes when I see him." She stepped lightly on the grass, balancing on her toes to keep her heels from sinking into the not-yet-frozen ground. "I think he's really missing you," she said. "For what it's worth."

"It's worth something."

"Hey, Stella!" Pippa was calling to me from where she was standing near a stage on a hill. "Look! It's Joe!"

I looked over at Cat, who rolled her eyes. "Both Pippa and Heidi have found their first true loves. Joe is the lead singer— and banjo player—in the Dog Hounds."

"Dog Hounds?"

"This is a Dog Hounds concert, babe. You'll be a groupie before you know it." We had reached Pippa, who was staring lovingly across the stage to where three guys were setting up their stuff.

"So these are the Dog Hounds, huh, Pip?" Pippa nodded up at me silently, staring with rapture at the adult men who were dressed in ridiculous hats and silly overalls. I squatted down next to her and watched the guys warming up, wondering what made a perfectly normal man decide to become a children's musician. I guess maybe you weren't a normal guy, if this was what you did for a living? Were they pedophiles? Overgrown kids? Men who lacked the social skills to talk to other adults? I'd always found the Wiggles to be alarming, but I guess children's stage bands freaked me out just as much. Not so much when normal bands, like They Might Be Giants or Jack Johnson, did kids songs... but men whose goal in life was to play for children? It was an odd pursuit. Not that I was judging.

Pippa and Heidi stood amongst a crowd of children, all of whom were watching the band tune their instruments and get ready for their set. One of the guys sauntered over to the edge of the stage and waved to all the little girls, who literally swooned.

"Hey, kids!" he called out, his voice full of cheesiness.

I felt bad for the guy, really. He was almost like a clown, wearing those ridiculous overalls—and that stupid hat. The poor dude had to wear a cowboy hat. From a distance I could see that under the hat, he'd puffed his hair up so he looked a bit like a dark-haired Ronald McDonald. Or Art Garfunkel, to his credit.

He strummed a few chords on his banjo, and Heidi's shoulders tensed in anticipation. I bet these guys felt like real superstars, getting little girls to fawn over them like this. They couldn't make it in a real band—like Jonathan—so they found poor, unsuspecting kids and sang stupid songs about breakfast and farm animals. Talk about a complex. I bet they all still lived with their grandmothers.

I studied the guy who was playing a little pre-show for us on the stage, and realized he was surprisingly good looking. He was probably in his late-twenties or my age, even, and had adorable dimples right at the tops of his cheeks. When he smiled, I caught myself smiling right along with the little girls, and realized I was being sucked into the vortex of children's band crush right along with Heidi and Pippa and the rest of the crowd.

Overall Guy looked strangely familiar, and I wondered if maybe I'd seen his face on a billboard around town or the side of a bus, perhaps. He tipped his hat at me, then strummed his banjo for the kids. It was almost impossible not to smile back at him, but instead, I squirmed and looked down. I wasn't a mom, so I wasn't about to fall for this crap. Maybe he was used to lonely moms who wanted a little extra attention from the fancy musicians who charmed their kids, but I wasn't going to get sucked into it. Also, I wasn't going to date guys whose faces appeared on the sides of buses—realtors, musicians, weather guys, politicians. That was a rule. There was just something smarmy about a person's mug grinning down from a public transit vehicle or billboard. It was like those people wanted the wrong kind of attention.

When banjo guy started singing, however, I was captivated. He had a beautiful voice, and I couldn't help but wonder why he was wasting it on a song about roller coasters. The kids all screamed and jumped up and down, excited about the pre-show show. Pippa reached for my hand and pulled me down to her level to say, "That's Joe. He's so funny."

Joe caught me watching him, and grinned again. I looked around, and realized I wasn't the only adult woman who had noticed how hot he was under the hat and the fluffed-up hair. Several women had recently reapplied their lipstick (at ten in the morning, mind you), and a few were dancing along (one was swaying seductively in her ass-crack jeans, which seemed way wrong). Joe finished singing, and bent down to talk to a few of the kids who had pressed up close to the stage. He really knew how to talk to kids, and I caught myself smiling.

Even though I didn't want kids of my own, guys who knew how to talk to kids and interacted with them in a normal way always impressed me. Erik had always been so awkward with Heidi and Pippa—he'd always get them all riled up, then got frustrated when they chased him around the house. And it had irritated me when he talked to them like small morons. They were smart girls, and he treated them like dolls or babies.

Heidi rushed over to me, her face flushed with happiness from her brush with fame. "Did you see him, Stella? Isn't he ah-ma-zing?"

Before Heidi could gush more, Cat called to us from across the lawn. She'd spread a blanket on the grass, and had poured little cups of hot chocolate for the girls to help keep them warm. Aurelie, the au pair, was shivering inside her cute-but-chilly shawl.

"So these guys are from around here?" I asked Cat as I settled onto the blanket. Both Heidi and Pippa tucked up against me, cuddling into my armpits. I squeezed the girls, and wondered how much I would see them now that I wouldn't be at any of the Wesley family functions. I hated thinking about breaking up with Erik's family, too, but it was inevitable in situations like mine. I couldn't stay with a guy just because of his nieces, right? And Cat and I would make it work... eventually, both Erik and I would find other people, and Cat and I would be just like any other friends.

"They're both from Boulder or something, but they mostly play shows in the Midwest now. The girls love them, obviously."

"Obviously," I said, rubbing Pippa's soft, blond hair. Pippa was as tiny as her mom, but had gotten her dad's coloring. She was a petite blonde pixie, and absolutely adorable. I couldn't resist grabbing her up into a squeeze-hug, but she squirmed out just as soon as the band started playing.

"Mom, I'm going to take Pip to the stage, okay?" Heidi looked at Cat hopefully, and Cat nodded. She gave Aurelie a look, and the au pair stood and followed the girls at a distance.

"That banjo guy is kind of hot," I said, watching as the band transitioned from a song about pancakes to one about a kid who turned into a tree.

"Yeah, I've always thought that, too." Cat laughed. "I think half the moms who take their kids to these concerts have the hots for one of the guys in the band."

I looked around, and noticed all the women sitting near us were smiling way more than they ought to have been for a kids' concert. "What is it about musicians?" I asked. "What's the deal with these guys? Single? Married? Kids?"

"Ooh, are you interested?" Cat lifted her eyebrows and stretched out on the blanket. The girls were dancing in front of the stage with a few dozen other rabid fans.

"No!" I was not attracted to musicians. Certainly not musicians in costume. But even as my head insisted I not think about Joe, my body grew heated at the thought of what he would look like when he was freshly-showered. And naked. What was hiding beneath those overalls? "I'm just curious."

"Well, the rumor on the mom circuit is that Joe—the real charmer—is a total douchebag. Janell LaMere had a girlfriend who heard he sleeps with anyone within a ten-mile radius. Frank—well, let's call him the ugly one—lives with his parents and has a dot-com day job. Theo—he's the dorky-looking runt—is in a really cool band, but is also married with kids. Probably cheating." She shrugged. "But that's just the mommy gossip. Remember, we make stuff up to keep things interesting."

Cat and I watched the band in silence for a while then. I thought about how uninhibited Pippa, Heidi, and the other kids were up in front of the stage. I envied their complete lack of self-consciousness. I couldn't help but think of all the times I'd been somewhere with Erik, and we'd both been so fixated on how we might be perceived by others that we failed to try something new or have a good time.

Like Justin Frederick's thirtieth birthday party, which had been at a gymnastics center, when Erik and I had stood laughing on the sidelines instead of swinging and trampolining with our friends because neither of us was particularly physically capable. Or Lily's annual Halloween party, where Erik and I had worn the same boring, generic superhero costumes for six years in a row because it was easy and efficient. Or our permanent role as designated drivers at all our friends' and coworkers' weddings, which meant I'd never been even a little bit embarrassed about my behavior the day after a wedding.

I suddenly wanted to dance. So I jogged over to the girls and held their little hands in mine and swayed to the rockabilly beat. They cheered and giggled as we all bounced to the music, and when the set was over, I didn't think twice about joining the girls in line to get CDs signed by the band. When we got to the front of the line, the girls ran forward and hugged each member of the Dog Hounds like they were old friends.

The guys in the band were super-sweet with the kids, and gave the girls high-fives and asked them about school. I stood back, letting Pippa talk all about preschool. As she talked, Joe looked up and me and winked. I furrowed my brow, wondering what the wink meant. Despite the wink, he was *so* hot. Smoldering, sexy musician hot. My insides squirmed as I watched how he stroked his banjo and thought about what his hands would feel like on my body. Why did charming guys always have to be something skeevy, like musicians or investment bankers? Okay, investment bankers weren't charming, but they were rich and, according to Lily, it was the same thing.

I smiled at Joe, and he grinned back.

"Hey," he said, all smooth smarm and charm. "Did you like the show, pretty lady?" Pippa and Heidi were each talking to one of the other guys in the band, allowing him to step over toward me.

I stepped backward a hair. "Yep. Good stuff." I smiled thinly. Not falling for it.

"I recognize these girls," he said, gesturing the Pippa and Heidi. "You're not usually with them. Are you the new nanny?"

I laughed, then realized I had the opportunity to give myself a whole new identity. "Yes, that's right. I'm the girls' nanny."

He nodded. "Well, cool. I hope we see you at another show soon..." He looked at me questioningly, obviously waiting for my name.

"Stella."

"Well, Stella, I'm Joe." He grinned in a way that made it clear he thought he was really something, and then the girls pulled me back toward Cat again. When I looked back as we walked across the lawn, Joe tipped his hat at me, and I felt a lot giddier than I would have expected. Who knew I was the type of girl to swoon over a "rock star?"

"I miss Erik," I announced to Anders as I tucked my curls back with bobby pins for my date. I was going out with someone named Stephen, an accountant, and about as excited about it as I'd been about Jonathan *after* our date. But he looked cute in his online photos, and he and I seemed to be a decent match. His online profile had droned on and on about goals and strategies for his life, and I found the type-A tendencies somewhat comforting. I hadn't yet told Anders who I'd picked for this date. "I haven't talked to him in almost three weeks."

Anders buttoned his shirt and ran his hand through his hair. He and I were both getting ready to go out—he was meeting some girl who had come into the office for a massage earlier that week. Despite all his apparent expertise with Internet dating, Anders refused to go out with anyone he met online. He said the women he met online were often stupid. I countered with the fact that maybe he just attracted that type, and he had slugged me. "You haven't called him, have you?"

"No. But why hasn't he called me? Doesn't he miss me?" I knew he did—both Laurel and Cat had told me so. But without Erik actually calling and begging me to come back, I seriously questioned his misery and loneliness. I wanted him to grovel. I wanted him to beg. I wanted him to tell me his life was miserable without me, and that he was a shriveled piece of shit without someone as wonderful as me in his life. He hadn't even called to tell me I'd forgotten a pair of socks at his house—and at this point, I'd be happy with that. Without any of those things, I wondered if we'd wasted more years than I thought we had together.

Anders sighed and flopped down on my bed. "I'm sure he misses you. But he's a stubborn ass, and doesn't want to admit how much he needed you."

"You're just saying that."

"Yeah." Anders nodded and took a swig of his beer. He flashed his adorable gap-toothed smile at me and I rolled my eyes. "You know I'm not an Erik fan," he said, only slightly apologetically. "I'm not going to give the guy the benefit of the doubt and assume he's sitting at home, full of regrets."

"You don't think he's dating, do you?" I said, terrified my ex was kissing some other woman. What if he had fallen for a spontaneous vixen who had taught him all about sexiness and living for the moment? What if Erik had learned how to have fun without me? "Oh god, what if he's *happy*?" I sobbed, just a little.

"You're actively getting ready for a date. Need I remind you that you've moved on?"

"That doesn't mean I want him to be seeing other women. There's an appropriate amount of time one is supposed to wait before starting to date again."

"Apparently there's a different standard for men and women?" Anders finished off his beer and placed the bottle on my bedside table. I shot him a look and he folded up a tissue to use as a coaster. "Why do you get to start dating after two weeks, and he has to wait—what, a year?"

"That would be best." I stepped into my closet to slip out of my robe and into the wrap dress I'd bought for that night. "The thing is, I was the dumper. That means I am *supposed* to get over him faster than he's supposed to get over me. I had the weeks of build-up leading to the split, but he should still be processing."

"That is completely unfair." Anders gave me a look that was probably supposed to mean something, but I looked away so I could ignore it. "You don't think Erik had any sense that a breakup was imminent? Seven weeks without sex was so normal he didn't suspect something was wrong?"

"Let's not talk about sex," I said. "It's irrelevant."

"I disagree. A multi-week dry spell is very relevant."

"Not for us."

"Are you serious?" Anders sat up, obviously alarmed. "Was he just bad in bed or something?"

"No, he was fine."

"Fine?" Now my roommate looked like he was going to be sick.

"That's not the kind of couple we were. We were very deliberate and predictable in our sex life," I said, holding up two pair of shoes I was debating between.

Anders pointed at the black Aerosoles heels. "Go with those. But honestly, they're both ugly. Get Lily to take you shopping at lunch. You have too many 'sensible' things in your closet."

I sat down on the edge of bed. "Sensible shoes, sensible boyfriend, sensible sex. It's the story of my life."

"All things that are fixable," he said. He sounded alarmingly upbeat. "You'll get there. Erik is out of the picture, so you can finally figure out what grown-up Stella wants out of life."

"What if I can't figure it out?" I said. "I haven't really gotten to act on my own impulses in a while—what if I don't even *have* any impulses anymore? What if Erik was as good as it gets?"

"God, that's depressing." Anders looked at his phone and hopped off the bed. "I'm leaving. Partly because I'm going to be late, but partly because I'm not even willing to get into such a stupid discussion. You're not a needy girl, so don't start acting like one now. Erik may have made most of the choices in your relationship, but that doesn't mean you lost the ability to form your own opinion. Don't fall back on old mistakes because you're scared of making new ones."

If things worked out the way they should have—the way I would have planned them had I, say, made a list—I would have gone off on my date after Anders' motivational speech and met Mr. Perfect. He would have been handsome and charming and spontaneous and he'd smell good and he might have even inspired me to go out with him a few more times that week so we could spend the next weekend frolicking around in our undies between sessions of really great sex.

But you can't plan everything, so instead of Mr. Perfect meeting me at the restaurant that night, I got Stephen.

Stephen was perfectly nice, but also painfully boring. He asked me questions as though he'd rehearsed them from a script, and answered mine in exactly the same way. The way he nodded, just once, after each of my answers felt like some sort of director-style approval. Even his smile seemed canned. I tried, really I did, but then he ordered the only other entree on the menu that cost exactly as much as mine—and I knew, because he told me, it was only so we could split the bill exactly in half and it would be fair.

A few days later, I went out with Marco. Marco spent much of the date explaining the details of his fantasy football spreadsheet. When he actually pulled out a copy of the spreadsheet and showed me his calculations, it was all over for sad, sweet, lies-on-his-online-profile Marco.

Next was Tim. Tim worked in sales, which he mentioned just a few times. Tim had a lot of interesting stories and I actually thought there could be some potential for a second date. Until the dessert menus came, and Tim informed me he wouldn't be ordering anything because he'd already had his one dessert for the week. He wasn't on a diet, but kept a careful food diary to avoid needing to diet in the future. Apparently, he had saved up his week's quota of bread for our date, but wasn't willing to veer off plan for a spontaneous, bonus dessert. I couldn't handle food issues and the excessive planning made me think of Erik. It was a deal-breaker.

As I ate my creme brulee alone, I realized I attracted stiffs. Or sought them out. Either way, it was discouraging. But it told me something about me that I was obviously trying to suppress. I also wasn't entirely sure I was a normal date—why were they all going so badly? What was it about me that made Marco think it was okay to talk about a spreadsheet? Did I look like that kind of girl?

More importantly, had I made a huge mistake? Even with Anders' help spiffing up my profile, I had somehow managed to pull a large lot of losers who looked like crap compared to Erik. Unmarried-to-Erik suddenly felt a lot less horrible than it had a few weeks before. At least his flaws were familiar and he made good soup.

I spent the rest of that night considering the collection of studs I'd been matched with, and convincing myself everything that went wrong with Erik was as much my fault as it was his. The next morning when I got to the office, I wrote Erik an email. Ultimately, I never sent it... but the fact that I wrote it at all says something, I guess. And it also helps explain why, when an email from Erik appeared in my inbox later that same day, I wrote back and re-opened our line of conversation.

I blame it on Jonathan, Stephen, Marco, and Tim. If they hadn't been such dolts, maybe I would have had the willpower to just hit delete.

CHAPTER SIX

I couldn't cop to my email conversation with Lily (who would cringe, then call me something inappropriate, like "pussy"), Anders (who had now admitted to hating Erik and would think I was a spineless sad-sack), or obviously Cat (she'd swell with false hope), so I decided to spill the beans at the only other place I could think of: the Y.

I'd been going to water aerobics for a few weeks by then, and the women were starting to warm up to me—a little. The cluster of ladies still shot me nasty looks when I came late and left early, but no one was *obviously* whispering about me in the pool, and Heather had started dawdling in the locker room before class so she could walk out to the pool on my arm. I'd made an effort to keep my distance, but now I was starting to feel a little lonely at class and wondered if maybe it was time to stop acting like a snobby bitch. I was becoming a regular, so it was probably time to start acting like one.

"You wrote back?" Heather asked in the locker room the next week, after I gave her a brief history of Erik, all the way up to the emails we'd been exchanging for the last few days. She stared at me with her sagging swimsuit pulled only halfway up. I diverted my eyes. I was getting used to the cattiness of the water aerobics crew, but the nakedness had not gotten any easier to handle. "Stupid."

I wrapped a towel around my body and pulled my shirt and pants off, then expertly eased my swimsuit up over my towel-wrapped body. "It's not stupid," I said, shaking my head violently. "He wrote to me. I was just being nice by writing back."

"What good is it going to do you?"

"I don't know. I guess I hope we can stay friends."

Heather made a rude noise and waved her hand in the air. "Bullshit. You don't want to be friends. You're just lonely."

"I've been on four dates in the last two weeks. I'm not lonely."

"I heard about your date with Jonathan—granted, it was his side of the story, told from Barb's point-of-view. If any of your other dates have been anything like that classy piece of work, I'd say you're lonely."

"I'm starting over. It just feels weird."

"Starting over?" Heather hooted as we walked into the shower room to rinse off. "You don't know starting over."

"I'm ignoring you," I said sullenly. "You're judging. Poo-poo to that." Heather laughed harder when I shot her a dirty look. The reality is, I wasn't looking for advice—I just wanted a sounding board. These women were supposed to be supportive, like grandmothers, but Heather didn't look like she was about to offer me hot cocoa and compassion. She was making fun of me.

"Fine," I grumbled. "Judge me. But I haven't done anything wrong."

"Why are you justifying it to me, then?"

She kind of had a point.

"You need to feel the energy of your partner, extending up into your hand and through your power center. Let it energize you. Can you feel it empowering your creativity?" I looked around at the select group of coworkers who were huddled together in the Conference Room. We were smack-dab in the middle of yet another on-site offsite, which was being held in the conference room on the twelfth floor James had temporarily renamed "The Giving Tree."

We'd been talking about bonding and spirit and creative juices all day, but I knew they were just buttering us up to give us bad news. Lily had told me layoffs were finally imminent, and that meant James had been pouring all of his resources into building up everyone's spirit and teamwork, so the people who remained after the bloodbath would be more positive about our shit-bag company.

Even though none of us would ever call our wonderful employer by that name aloud, we were all thinking it deep down. No amount of Care Bear-inspired cheer could get people excited during a time of bad sales.

I held my hand against Gina Kriesel's back, pretending to listen to the motivator guiding our session. I felt nothing but nerves as I sat there in the conference room, wondering if I'd be part of the group that would be laid off. Lily swore she had no idea if I was on the list or not. I didn't report to her, and she only knew which of her own direct reports was on the chopping block. I'd noticed James looking at me with increasing frequency in the last few days, and I had been the one who had found him with his hands and lips on his boss's neck a few weeks after his wedding. He'd sort of had it out for me since then.

After a game of sharing circle, where we all had to reveal a secret about ourselves—mine, obviously, was a lie—we all were sent back to our desks. When I arrived at my cube, I found a green folder sitting passive-aggressively on the seat of my rolling chair. My name was typed on a peel and stick label affixed to the bottom right corner.

"You're fucking kidding me," I heard Gina mutter from two cubes down.

I opened my folder and found a letter that informed me I was to report to Conference Room B at three o'clock. There was no other information contained in the folder. I walked past Jennifer Hutchins' cube, and noticed she'd sat down at her desk and was not obsessing over a letter or a folder. This was not a good sign. I stepped into Gina's cube, and saw she had a red folder. Her folder also contained a letter, directing her to Conference Room C at two o'clock. She had also been given a package of coupons for Centrex products, as well as a dollar-off coupon for the frozen yogurt place in the skyway, a free pizza voucher from Papa John's, and a fifty-percent off one-day U-Haul rental.

I continued down the hall toward Lily's office. "What does this green folder mean?" I pulled the folder out of my sweater, where I'd hidden it from my coworkers' prying eyes. Carrying it around felt like wearing a scarlet letter.

"Oh, thank God," she said, looking harried and horrible. "Green is better than red."

"What does it mean?"

"You're being cut back to eighty percent."

"Cut back?"

"Instead of laying off fifteen-percent of the staff, they're only laying off ten-percent, then cutting costs further by reducing a chunk of employees to eighty-percent employees. You'll still get your benefits and everything." She chewed on her lower lip. "And you'll get more details at three."

"I don't want more details at three," I said. "I want more details from you."

"You get to take one day off every week."

"And they pay me twenty percent less?"

"Yes." Lily pushed a fresh latte across her desk toward me. "James just brought this for me. You want it?"

I nodded. "Yeah. I can't afford lattes anymore."

Sullenly, I left Lily's office with my charity latte and green folder in hand. She called after me, but I hustled off and into the elevator before she could catch up. I rode the elevator down twelve flights and stepped outside into the pleasantly-warm October afternoon. Nicollet Mall was crowded with people shopping at the last Thursday farmer's market of the season. Everyone looked so jolly, carting their pumpkins and squash down the sidewalks. I was busy eyeing up a bakery stand when I felt a hand on my back.

I turned, and Erik's face stared back at me with a mixture of hope, fear, and… happiness?

"Hi, Stella," he said, trying a smile.

"Hi." Even though we'd been exchanging casual emails for a few days, it still felt weird and sudden and alarming to run into Erik like this. I wasn't ready to see him. I was feeling hurt and angry and frustrated about work, and I was planning to look blissful and happy when I saw him again. I clutched the green folder to my chest, hoping he wouldn't ask about it. "I'm just getting lunch."

"Isn't it kind of late for lunch?" He asked, looking at his watch.

"I eat when I'm hungry," I snapped, eager to show him I didn't play by the rules now that we were broken up. I was a new, spontaneous, self-directed woman.

"You look beautiful," he said, as I reached for a muffin.

I deliberately chose a pumpkin muffin—which I'd never ordered in the history of our relationship—and handed it to the woman taking money.

"Thanks. You look good, too." He didn't. He looked stiff and old and unhappy. Was his chin fatter than the last time I'd seen him? It was probably impossible, but I was going to hope. I wanted him to look a little worse.

"Three dollars," muffin girl said, and I reached for my wallet.

"I don't have my purse," I clutched the latte and my folder desperately. I'd left the office without my Centrex ID, without my purse, without my wallet. "I'm sorry, I'll have to come back later." I moved to put the muffin, with its one tiny bite, back on the table with the others.

Erik quickly pulled a ten out of his pocket and offered it to the woman. "Let me." I thanked him, and we walked together down the crowded sidewalk. I picked at my muffin, wishing I could have picked the time and the place to see him again. I just had to make the most of it.

"So you're dating…" Erik shuffled awkwardly beside me, and I had this sudden reminder of him as a twenty-three year old. I remembered the first date we'd gone on—he'd been all arms and legs and awkward self-confidence.

I'd been so won over by this scrawny, sure-of-himself guy. Even though he was only a year older than me, he'd treated me like an adult when I was fresh out of college, and that had made me feel important. We'd skipped the crazy, drunken first dates and gone straight to visits with Grandma and family dinners. I wonder if Erik knew how to do crazy, drunken first dates? I made a vow to have one of those of my own, just to prove I could do it.

"Anders and Lil signed me up for an internet dating service," I said, stretching the truth. "There are some real winners out there."

"Which site are you using?"

Oh, God, was Erik dating, too? What if I accidentally got matched with my ex-boyfriend? I'd heard about that happening—hopefully Anders had tweaked my profile to make me seem enough unlike me to prevent that from happening. "Why? Are you hoping we get matched?"

"Yeah, I was going to sign up just to find you and hope I could convince you to go out with me."

"Are you making fun of me?" I asked, irritated. I looked at Erik and realized he was being serious. "Why would you do that?"

"I miss you, Stella. I want you back."

In every novel and movie I'd ever read or seen, this is the line the heroine is waiting for. But instead of Erik's words making me giddy or filling my head with cheesy guitar love ballads, my first instinct was to run away. "You don't want me back." I thought about my conversation with Anders just a few days earlier, and how I'd wished this was how Erik was feeling. Suddenly, confronted with his admission, I was disgusted. It just seemed so *sad*.

"Can I try again?" He looked at me with his deep brown eyes, pleading without looking like a baby. Erik was a guy who knew how to get what he wanted. He'd just fooled me enough times that I wasn't going to fall for it so easily again. "I know we weren't perfect, but we were happy. I was happy—weren't you? Let's try again."

"You tried again. And again. And again." I ran my hands across the small flowers on an autumn-blooming plant. "I'm happy now, Erik. Please, can you just let me move on?"

He grabbed for my hand. "Maybe if we do things differently?"

I looked at him, curious. Erik didn't do things differently. "How...?" I could hear Lily's and Anders' voices ringing in my ears, but then I also thought about Pippa and Heidi and Cat—and even Laurel. Things would change between all of us, eventually. They were Erik's family, and I was just an outsider.

I couldn't help but yearn for everything I'd given up. I could hang on to all of them for a while without Erik, but probably not forever. Erik was my link to *family*, the only family I'd had in recent memory, and leaving him meant leaving it all. "I have to go," I said and turned back toward the office before I said something stupid.

I wasn't a stupid woman. But faced with the offer of comfortable companionship of my ex-boyfriend, I suddenly felt like I had the capacity to be very, very foolish indeed.

CHAPTER SEVEN

Lily's annual Halloween party was always held on the Saturday night closest to Halloween. Various people from work, college-remnant-friends, and a few people from her church gathered in Lily's gorgeous downtown loft for an amazing party and far too many drinks.

This year, without Erik, I was planning to get pleasantly drunk and crash in Lily's spare bedroom. Erik and I had always come to the party a little late, mingled for a short while, then left before things got out of hand. This year, I was going to be the person who got out of hand. I deserved to get sloppy drunk. I'd missed that phase of my twenties, and there was no time like the present to make up for lost time.

To prepare for my night of drunken debauchery, Anders and I did a couple of shots together while we got ready for the party, then jumped in the cab we'd called to take us downtown. I was excited to show off my costume—since I didn't have to coordinate my costume with Erik, I finally got to try something new.

I knew I didn't want to dress in anything slutty. The year before, Lily had worn a sexy cat costume and her boob accidentally slipped out when she tried to do a somersault late in the night. I don't know why she was trying to do a somersault anyway (Erik and I had already gone home), but I knew her biggest regret was that she was wearing a costume that had failed her in the late-night hours. I had no control over what I might do after all the drinks I planned to have, so I wanted a costume that was full-coverage.

Lily opened the door when we got there and stared, horrified, at my costume. "You're trying to meet men and you chose *that* for Halloween?" She was dressed as Stripper Nurse or something equally tasteless. "Are you a scarecrow?"

"I'm one of the Dog Hounds," I said proudly. "Joe."

"You look like a dude. An ugly dude."

"I love it." I was proud of the overalls I'd found at Goodwill, and thought I looked kinda cute in my cowboy hat. I'd ratted my hair into a poofy ball and slapped the hat right over the top. It was a good costume. Clever, I thought. Most of the men who would be at the party were either gay or married, so it wasn't like I was worried about scaring off all the single men at the party with my sex-less costume. "We brought vodka," I said, thrusting a bottle toward Lily.

"It's half empty," she said, leading me inside the apartment. "Did you guys drink this?"

"I'm a good influence," Anders said, laughing, then set off in search of other people he knew.

"Is Chad here?" I asked Lily, looking around her apartment. Her loft was open-plan, the kind of space where the kitchen, dining room, and living room all blended into one. She'd painted the walls varying shades of gray, and had hired a fancy decorator to come in and infuse the place with pops of color. All of Lily's furniture was from Room & Board, and much of the apartment was set up so it looked exactly like the Room & Board showrooms. It was mid-century modern with a romantic twist. Lily always had bunches of fresh flowers scattered around the room, creating a softness that her overly-designed space needed.

Lily grabbed me a wine glass, but I reached past her and grabbed a martini glass instead. "Chad *is* here. Do you want him to make you something?" Chad was a cocktail expert—he even hand-stuffed his olives with blue cheese before serving.

"Yes, please. I'll take a Bombay martini, extra olives, please."

"Hitting the hard stuff?"

"Yup." I waved, noticing Cat and her husband, Travis, had just walked through the front door. They were dressed as Mickey and Minnie Mouse. Cat obviously recognized my costume, since she gave me an exaggerated thumbs-up. "I think I deserve a night of drunken irresponsibility after my week of winner dates."

Lily called Chad over to order my drink, then pulled me aside to quietly ask, "Do I have any bra line spillage?"

"Excuse me?"

"I'm going to turn around, casually, and I need you to take a quick peek to see if my back fat is spilling out around the edges of my bra line."

"Lil, you don't have any back fat."

"When Chad hugged me earlier, I felt his hand linger near my shoulder blades, and then there was some definite squeezing. The bad kind."

"He was just being affectionate."

Lily wriggled uncomfortably in her skin-tight nurse costume. "Just check, okay?" She spun around, and I was forced to admire her enviably tight backside. I could never understand how someone who looked the way she did could ever grapple with self-consciousness. Chad pushed my drink across the kitchen island and winked.

"Your lines are clean," I whispered.

Lily beamed at me. "Thanks. It's just been a while since Chad and I have been together, and I want him to want me, you know?" I did know. And when Lily headed off in the direction of the front door, I thought about how, early in our relationship, I'd wished Erik would look at me like I was desirable or sexy. I'd forgotten to want that after a few years. It just never happened—we were too practical for passion—and I never really thought it was worth wishing for anymore. Well, now I did want someone to want me... but maybe not *immediately*. After all, I was dressed like a male rockabilly band member with fluffy hair. Anyone who was inclined to hit on me had pretty bad taste.

I recognized a few people from work, and saw Cat and Travis making their way toward me in the kitchen. As I waited for them to finish chatting with a couple wearing matching bathrobes, I felt someone pluck my hat off my head.

"Hey!" I said, turning to find one of those vinyl gorilla masks staring back at me. "A band leader needs her kick-ass hat. Can I get it back please?"

Whoever was wearing the mask ignored me, and placed the hat on their furry head instead.

"Who's in there?" I asked, annoyed at the gorilla's juvenile behavior.

Silence. I could tell it was a man—his slim hips and muscular thighs were perfectly wrapped inside a pair of Levis. The legs didn't look familiar—I'd remember those legs—and the strange plaid shirt didn't look like anything one of my coworkers would wear. Was it one of Lily's ex-boyfriends? Unlikely, since she only dated hipsters, investment bankers, and guys who were far too obsessed with their own image to wear that specific style of plaid.

"I'd appreciate my hat back," I said again, a little more insistently this time. I knew how stupid my hair looked without the hat, and it kinda just looked like I'd picked an ugly outfit instead of attempting a real costume if I wasn't wearing the hat.

"Greg?" I asked, wondering if maybe it was Greg Kling, from HR. He had a tendency to act like a sixth grader on occasion, and he'd been laid off yesterday. Maybe he was expressing his anger by annoying me.

The gorilla grabbed a beer off the counter. He stuck a straw in the top of the bottle and pushed the straw inside the vinyl gorilla mouth to take a swig.

Just as I was starting to get weirded out, in addition to annoyed, Cat extracted herself from the conversation she'd been having with the Bathrobe couple, leaving Travis behind. She gave me a big hug and said, "You *have* to come trick-or-treating with the girls tomorrow. They'll die when they see you dressed up as a Dog Hound. That's what you are, right? It's fabu."

That's when gorilla-man finally spoke. "I think you may owe me royalties or something. At the very least a little fee for intellectual property theft." The gorilla mask came off, and Joe—star of the Dog Hounds—stood in front of me. His face was flushed from being tucked up under the mask, and I immediately noticed he was so much better looking than he had been at the concert the weekend before. Without the ridiculous overalls, silly hat, and puffed up hair, he looked like a relaxed, super-cute guy with a full head of sandy-brown waves. "Nice costume."

"Why on earth are you at this party?" I asked, taken aback. "That is an impossible coincidence. Isn't it?"

"I have to agree with you. You are dressed as me, after all." Joe smirked. He nodded at Cat, who was staring at him like a superstar had suddenly appeared at the party. I watched his ego inflate, right there in front of us. "I can't imagine when you put on that outfit, you thought you'd run into *the* Joe." He patted his muscled chest proudly.

"How do you know Lily?" I ignored his ego, and tried to change the subject. It couldn't hurt to chat with him, even if he was a prick.

"I went to college with Chad. Frat brothers."

Great, a frat boy *and* a musician. He was getting less appealing by the second.

Joe handed me my cowboy hat, and I dropped it back on my head. His eyes scanned me from head to toe, lingering near the curvy bits that were mercifully hidden under my overalls. His mouth curled into a lazy smile as he met my gaze to say, "You look cute dressed as a Dog Hound. It helps that you're dressed as the best-looking Dog Hound. You even got my show hair down."

"Your hair looks normal tonight," I quipped, rolling my eyes at Cat. I couldn't keep myself from wondering if this man-child thought his self-promotion was charming. Cat gave me a look, then excused herself. I was left alone with Joe's hot thighs and smug attitude. She had told me he was a player— why would she leave me with him? He and I were not going to happen. But I figured it couldn't hurt to flirt, as long as I stopped short of jumping him. Which, three or four drinks in, was a real possibility. "I'm Stella, by the way."

"Joe." He obviously hadn't paid attention or really noticed me when I'd introduced myself the first time. Not that I would have expected him to, but it just verified all the rumors about him and women and showed he hadn't actually been that interested in me.

"I know you're Joe." I gestured to my outfit. "Obviously."

We looked at each other in awkward silence for a few seconds, and then I quickly swallowed down the remnants of my drink. I popped both of my remaining olives in my mouth, chewing slowly to savor the yummy blue cheese. I sort of hated olives, but they were okay when they were bathed in liquor and stuffed with blue cheese. Eating the olives also gave me an excuse to not talk for a few more seconds. Why the hell was I so attracted to someone everyone knew was a player?

"Are your kids fans of the band or something?" Joe asked, taking another swig of his beer. He twirled the gorilla mask around and around his left hand. "I remember now… you were at one of our shows."

"I brought my nieces—I mean, not my nieces, but my sorta-nieces." I didn't really want to get into the story of how I was linked to Pippa and Heidi. Joe didn't ask any questions. I hadn't expected him to, since he was probably just trying to find the fastest path into my overalls. "It was a good show."

"Are you a regular at kids' band shows?"

"No, not exactly. It was my first time."

"Did you enjoy it?" He puckered his lips into a smug half-smile. I think he was trying to be cute. It worked.

"You guys are really good," I said, trying to remember how to flirt. I was buzzed and faced with a cute guy who I would surely never see again. This was my chance to test my single-girl skills out in the wild. I decided I could let myself act stupid with a guy for one night. "Do you practice a lot?" Okay, so I sucked at flirting. Wasn't I supposed to say something coy or suggestive that meant something other than what it actually sounded like I was asking? Instead, I sounded like a journalist.

Joe leaned against the kitchen island casually, obviously accustomed to crappy flirts. He was used to hitting on married moms—some of them had to be out of practice, too. Was it obvious I thought he was hot? "Yes, we practice a lot."

"So do you, um, have a real job?"

"Yeah, I'm a musician."

"What kind of musician?"

"I play the banjo in a band called the Dog Hounds."

"That's your real job?"

"Yep. Sometimes I tend bar for friends at events—weddings and whatever—but it's not a moneymaker or anything. I just do it to help out friends if they need it."

"Oh." I felt like a real ass for pressing on the band thing, but it seemed impossible that was his real job. Was being in a children's band an actual profession?

"People ask me about the band a lot—most people assume you can't actually make a living in a local band. I'm not rich, in case that's something that matters to you, but I do make a decent enough living to do what I want to do with my life."

"Cool," I said, feeling like even more of an ass. "That's fine."

"I'm delighted you approve." He smirked again. I hated smirkers. He finished his beer and leaned in close to me to say, "Even though I make a decent living playing kids' birthday parties and stuff, I do rely on miscellaneous income to pay my cell phone bill. Royalties, for example." He reached out and wrapped his fingers around my overall strap. My breath caught in my throat. "Can I get some cash for your use of the costume?"

I blushed because his hand was so close to my boob. I suddenly felt like I was seventeen. He wasn't actually touching my chest, but I was responding to his hand like he was. In fact, I was acting like my friend, Tina, had when the lead singer of our high school talent show band told her she could give him a blowjob backstage. It was like she'd been honored with a real reward.

"Are you serious? You want me to pay you for use of your likeness?"

"No, I'm not serious." He laughed and narrowed his eyes at me. He let go of my overalls, letting his hand drop back by his side. "You, however, are a very serious person, aren't you, Stella?"

"I'm not a serious person," I said, even though it was probably a bit of a lie. "Hey, if you're a bartender, how about making me a fresh drink?" This was better. Talking to a banjo player-slash-bartender about alcohol was probably a better way to flirt.

He threw his gorilla head onto the floor and rubbed his hands together. "You got it. What do you like?"

"Surprise me," I said, and impressed myself with the flirty undercurrents in my voice. I wasn't terrible at this. Even though Erik had always laughed at me when I'd tried to seduce him, I had obviously learned something through years of watching cheesy romance movies.

Joe stepped around to the other side of the kitchen island, and pulled a few bottles away from where Chad stood, mixing drinks for guests. The rest of the party was in full swing now, and I looked around while Joe energetically mixed a little of this and a little of that into the cocktail shaker. I spotted a few people from work lounging around the couch. I knew at least one of them, Fiona, had lost her job when I lost my Fridays, since she was in the same row of cubes as me. Fiona had always been fondly referred to as "Happy Bear" at work, but now she looked anything but—she sat sullenly on the couch holding an empty beer bottle and wearing a pair of vampire teeth. I grinned at her and she nodded back.

"You know a lot of people at this party?" Joe asked, pulling my attention back toward him.

"Yeah, a few coworkers and some mutual friends. I came with my roommate." I pointed to Anders, who was animatedly chatting up Corinne Andrews from work. If Corinne was interested in someone like Greg Kling, who was built like a football player and had soft, ebony skin, she certainly wasn't going to go for Anders. He was pretty, but he also looked like the kind of guy who got regular manicures. I suspected Anders wasn't really planning to go home with anyone that night anyway. He flirted like a professional, but always came home alone.

Joe waved at Anders, and Anders tentatively waved back. "Your boyfriend?" Joe asked.

"Not even close," I answered. "A good friend."

"How does your boyfriend feel about you living with a guy who looks like that?"

"You think Anders is cute? Your type?" I was flirting!

"Sure, he's a good-looking guy. I would guess the kind of guy you would date wouldn't be too psyched about you living with someone who looks like, um, Anders. Am I right?"

"What do you mean, 'the kind of guy I would date?' What kind of guy is that?"

"A serious guy." Joe shrugged. "Corporate type."

"You are quite wrong. I am currently single." I said this proudly. "And I am offended you think I only date stiffs."

"I didn't say stiffs. I said 'corporate.' Though I guess they're the same thing." He smiled and passed me a drink. It was bright pink and had curls of lemon rind floating on top. "Do you date stiffs?"

I took a sip of the drink and let the delicious, pink-flavored goodness wash down my throat. "Yummy!" I said, forgetting he was annoying me. "And no, I don't date stiffs. Stop using that word."

"You brought it up!" He laughed. "Who *do* you date, then?"

"People," I said haughtily. "I date people."

Joe rubbed his hand through his thick, wavy hair and moved back around the kitchen island to stand close to me. I could feel heat radiating off him, and I wished his hand was on me again.

"Interesting. You date people. Do you have a type, Stella?"

"No—I'm open," I said, and wondered if he would take that the wrong way.

"Well then, I guess you'd be open to going out with me." He said this plainly, casually, like it was such a natural segue. He obviously had some practice in asking women out. It sounded pretty good. "Can I take you out?"

"Oh…" I stammered, caught off guard. I'd certainly realized we'd been flirting, but I hadn't actually expected him to ask me out. He wasn't my type. At all. Why on earth would he think I was his? "Um…"

"Here's how I see it: You owe me a date for making fun of my Dog Hounds outfit. If I can take you out to dinner—and maybe a show or something—then we're even. You don't have to give me royalties for use of the Halloween costume."

"I thought you were joking about the royalties."

"Let's pretend I wasn't. In which case, you owe me a date."

"Fine."

He laughed. "It will be fun! I promise. I like to have fun." He stepped away from me and lifted his eyebrows. "You can take that look off your face."

"What look?" I'd been trying to look sultry—apparently, it wasn't translating.

"I'm a good date. I promise. We'll have fun. Unless you don't like fun?"

"I like fun. And I think it will be fun. I'm sorry my face looks… whatever."

"Your face looks beautiful." He smirked. Again.

"Can you stop smirking? And please don't say stupid stuff like that. You sound cheesy as hell."

"Cheesy is better than stiff, right?" He kept smirking. "And you are beautiful. That's why I'm asking you out."

"You're asking me out because I'm beautiful?" Okay, it was flattering. But that line also made me wonder what kind of player I'd just agreed to go out with. "Or you're asking me out because you think we'll have a good time?" I wanted to ask if he just thought I was going to be next in his long line of sexual conquests, but that seemed a little rude and presumptuous. It also sounded pretty tempting.

He laughed aloud, which wiped the smirk right off his face. I loved the way his dimples moved up his cheeks and settled in under the outer corners of his eyes when he laughed. He was so cute. Dangerously charming, but still cute.

"I think we'll have a good time, but I guess that'll be partially up to you, too." He lowered his voice to a whisper, forcing me to lean in close to him. He smelled like beer and cinnamon, and I was drunkenly tempted to reach out and touch his hair. "And I do think you're beautiful." This time, he didn't smirk. But then he said, "But that must be because I'm a narcissist. You are, after all, dressed up as me. You're me, except with breasts. What guy wouldn't think that's cool?"

"I'm walking away before you blow it. Get my number from Lily," I said, tipping my cowboy hat at him. I could feel myself getting drunker by the second, and I was a little worried about what I might do in front of all my friends. Getting drunk was one thing, but getting drunk in the company of a hot guy who had called me beautiful and knew how to mix drinks was another thing altogether.

"I'll call you," he promised. Then we went our separate ways for the rest of the party. I seriously doubted he actually would call. But even through my drunken haze, I realized I really hoped he would.

CHAPTER EIGHT

Almost a week went by, and I heard nothing from Joe.

"He's an ass," Lily declared when we met up for drinks the next Friday. "He did ask me for your number, then... nada? Obviously an ass."

"A player," Cat agreed.

"But also hot," Anders said, and we all looked at him. "What? I've had to listen to Stella talking about him all week. Don't give me that look—straight guys can analyze other guys without wanting to sleep with them."

"I shouldn't be surprised," I said sullenly, chewing at my pizza crust. We'd decided to try out a new wood-fired pizza place downtown, and I ordered an extra pizza and an order of shallots "for the table" when Lily had offered to pay. I was still bitter about my reduction to eighty-percent at work, and I was going to milk Lily for all she was worth as long as she was still full-time and high powered. It was childish of me, but I knew she could afford it. "He's not the kind of guy who's going to call when he says he will. He's a musician, for God's sake, and he smirked too much, and all the moms say he's a player, right?"

Cat nodded ruefully. "True dat."

I groaned. "All of that's bad." But Joe also smelled like cinnamon, and made delicious drinks, and made me feel a little giddy and silly and attractive and fun. "I'm not looking for a player. I don't need a player. I need husband-material."

They all sighed.

"You need to have some fun," Lily said, waving the waiter over to order another bottle of wine. It had been another saturated week, where Anders and I had spent many nights drinking too much wine and looking through online profiles. We'd formed a little tradition in the last few weeks—he was teaching me about new varieties of red, and I was happily drinking everything he put in front of me. "Transport yourself back to college and focus on just having a good time."

"I didn't do that in college," I said. "I spent college studying or looking for a husband."

"You didn't have any regrettable one-night stands?" Lily asked. "No mornings where you woke up and thought, 'oh shit, that guy Vic from my cultural anthropology lecture is half-naked in my bed?'"

"Um, no. Did you?"

"More than a few times. Everyone did." I looked around the table. Cat, Anders, and Lily were all nodding.

"You all had meaningless one-night stands in college?"

"That's the whole point of college," Cat said primly. "You get it out of your system."

"You don't get it out of your system," Lily protested. "College is a practice round, where you get all of your worst *performances* out of your system. But things are supposed to get a whole lot better once you leave the twenty-year-old premature ejaculation boys behind." She took a sip of her wine and looked around the restaurant. "Unfortunately, some thirty-year-olds are just as guilty of bad performance as the younger boys. The only difference is, the big boys are always pretty confident about their quality."

"Women are just as responsible as men are when two people are in bed together." Anders stared Lily down.

As they discussed the merits of good sex and the flaws of bad sex, I thought about my own experience. Apparently, I was a sexual pariah. I'd made it through college with a 3.8 GPA and a total of three boyfriends, none of whom had attempted anything more significant than quick, missionary sex with me. In comparison, Erik had seemed like a sexual deviant with his new positions and ability to help me figure out how to have an orgasm. He really was pretty great in bed. Neither of us was ever up for anything risky or crazy, but that was normal. You didn't need a secret pair of handcuffs to have great sex.

I was still thinking about sex with Erik when I felt Lily jab me under the table with her fork.

"Oof!"

"Sorry, sweetie, but look who's here—" She gestured across the room to where the hostess was seating the object of my only decent sexual memories and some dumb-looking blonde. "Who's the bitch?"

I stared at Erik and the blonde. I could feel Cat squirming in her seat next to me. I'd just seen him last week. He'd told me he wanted me back. And now he was at dinner, at a new restaurant, with a new girl? My stomach made its way up my throat, and nearly emptied its contents onto the partial pizza sitting on my plate. It hadn't felt so weird that I was dating, but seeing Erik with another woman made me sick.

"I'm leaving," I said, hastily dabbing a fresh coat of lipstick over my lips. "I'm not going to sit here and watch his date. I understand if he wants to have one, but I don't have to be mature enough to sit within spitting distance of it."

"Don't leave," Cat urged. "I'm sure it's not a date. He hasn't said anything about dating—honestly, he only talks about you."

I kissed her, leaving a dull pink print on her smooth cheek. "I appreciate that." I smiled and shook my head as Anders moved to put on his coat. "I'm leaving alone. Seriously. I just need to get out of here. I'm not freaking out or anything— there's no reason for me to be freaking out." Obviously, I was freaking out. The blonde was pretty. I hated her.

"I'll drive you home." Anders stood. "Please."

Erik still hadn't seen us, and I was eager to get out of there. "Sit down. I'm thirty-four years old. If I want to leave alone, I get to leave alone. I promise I can handle it." I stuck my chin out, stubborn, and dared them to disagree. "All righty then. Lil, thanks for the meal."

I'd be lying if I said I walked proudly out of the restaurant. What I actually did is skulk. I skulked timidly past the tables that ran alongside the outer edge of the restaurant, and kept my head dipped low. I was not going to be a cliché. I refused to have my ex see me ducking out of a restaurant because he'd suddenly appeared with a date. I had made a choice and I was proud enough to stick to it. I had to know he'd be out with other women and Minneapolis was a small enough town that it would happen soon, and it would happen often.

In my obsessive pre-sleep hours over the past few weeks, I'd already fretted about our first run-in at Target or Kowalski's. I'd inevitably be eating a bag of Goldfish crackers from the dollar section and he'd catch me with my mouth full of crumbs. I don't know why I was so opposed to seeing him tonight, since I actually looked good. I was out with friends, pleasantly buzzed, and wearing a new sweater that hadn't yet stretched out in all the wrong places.

But I was also feeling vulnerable. I was waiting for Joe to call, I'd yet to find a normal person online, and I was having serious doubts about letting go of the guy that had been perfectly *fine* to love. I didn't want to see Erik now. I didn't want him to reject *me*—I wanted to keep the memory of him telling me he missed me in my mind, and pretend the blonde had never happened.

I stepped out onto the sidewalk, and realized why Anders had been so insistent about giving me a ride home—I didn't have a car, and he was my ride. Feeling stupid, I walked into the street and looked for a cab. But this was Minneapolis, and cabs didn't just dart up and down quiet neighborhoods like the one I was in. It was cold, I was stranded, and if I walked a block in either direction I'd run into strip clubs and perverts. When a bus pulled up in front of me and the doors sighed open, I stepped up and in. It was an escape route, and I just needed to escape.

I slipped a five into the cash slot, irritated I had to pay a mini-fortune to take the bus just because I didn't have small bills.

"I'm paying for this guy, too," I said, gesturing blindly at the man stepping up and into the bus behind me.

"Thanks," he said, giving me a funny look. "But I have a bus pass."

"They don't give change. I don't want to pay five bucks for only me."

The man ignored me and walked toward the back of the bus. I watched him as I waited for the driver to give me my transfer.

I didn't even know how to get home on the bus, so my plan was to keep requesting transfers and switching buses until I ended up somewhere near home. I'd done this with my roommate in college a few times, and had always thought it was fun to take the bus wherever it led. Now, tonight, I hated the uncertainty of it. I just wanted to know where I was going, and *get there* already.

"Oh, God," I said aloud. "This bus is a metaphor for my life."

The driver lifted his eyebrows at me. "You need to step back behind the line, ma'am. Please take a seat."

I muttered incoherently as I wandered toward the back of the bus. A woman sitting in one of the handicapped seats looked pointedly at me, challenging me to sit next to her. She gave me a look, like "sit here, bitch, and I'll knock the crazy out of you." I had become *that* woman. I resolved to stop muttering to myself.

Plunking down into one of the seats across from my bus-fare-partner, I pulled my phone out of my purse and plugged headphones in. Even though my new friend was pretending to read a magazine, I could tell he was keeping a close eye on me. Was it so weird to try to pay for someone's bus ride? What happened to good old-fashioned chivalry and the courtesy of strangers? *Don't worry, buster,* I thought, smiling to myself. *I'm not nuts. I'm perfectly respectable.*

My Pandora station pulled up a random Neil Diamond song, and I closed my eyes, letting the lurching of the bus lull me into an Erik-free trance. As Neil Diamond hummed his way out of the song, I peeked my eyes open and saw we were driving through the center of downtown. The lights of the empty office buildings shone bright, and the sounds of teenagers shouting at each other outside shot through the bus door every time it eased open to let people in and out. I could feel the last glass of wine soaking its way into my system, and when the next song came pouring through my headphones, I was pleasantly drunk and feeling good.

Oh hey! I thought, reveling in my buzz as I stared out at the bright lights and busy streets. *Pandora is playing that Journey song!* It was the one that made me think of baseball games, since they played it between innings for the sing-along. I never sang along, but I liked watching other people make fools of themselves.

Just a small town girl, livin' in a lonely world. She took the midnight train going anywhere.

Oh crap, was Journey singing about me? *I* was going anywhere! *I* was a small town girl! This bus really was my metaphorical destiny. *I* was living in a lonely world—well, not really, since I had my friends and the girls and all, but I'd go with it—letting the fates take me where they might. It was beautifully symbolic. My eyes popped open and I looked around the bus. I felt so free, listening to Journey as I journeyed.

A bald man, the woman wearing three scarves, two kids fighting over the fourth McDonald's apple pie… these were the people who were witnessing my big awakening! I was in a musical of my life.

Just a city boy, born and raised in South Detroit. He took the midnight train going anywhere.

"Excuse me," I said, startling my bus friend. He looked up from his magazine. "Are you from Detroit, by any chance?"

He shook his head slightly, then rolled the magazine, grabbed his man-purse, and moved to the front of the bus. So this guy wasn't my city boy—frankly, that was a relief since I wasn't big on blondes. Besides, this specific one was wearing a tan trench coat and they always made me think of lawyers and flashers. Both yucky and unappealing.

I began to sing along, quietly, under my breath.

She took the midnight train going anywhere…

"Girl, this is a bus." The lady wearing three scarves said, *tsk*-ing at me. "And we're going to uptown. You need some help?"

I grinned at her and stared out the window, watching everything go by.

Strangers, waiting, up and down the boulevard. Shadows, searching in the night… People, living just to find emotion. Hiding somewhere in the night!

I was being inspired by Journey!

Fuck Erik!

Fuck the blonde.

And fuck Joe—there were a million wannabe rock stars out there. I didn't need him to call. I would make my own happiness, la di da!

Don't stop believing...

I wouldn't stop believing! Hallelujah—I was being saved by Journey!

I popped up and rang the bell to stop the bus. We were on the outskirts of downtown now, near First Avenue, and I was suddenly inspired to walk to find my emotion hiding in the night. I practically pranced down the steps at the back of the bus and walked out into the dark, chilly night. The fresh air hit me hard, like the sight of James Davis in yoga pants, and suddenly my buzz was a lot less powerful. I realized I was still singing along to Journey, and calling the wrong kind of attention to myself. I grinned sheepishly at the cluster of punk kids slouched on the wall outside First Ave. "Who's playing tonight?" I asked, trying to look like someone who might be interested in that sort of thing.

They eyed me suspiciously. One of them muttered the name of some band I'd obviously never heard of.

"Oh, cool. They're awesome."

"Right, lady. *Awesome.*"

I cringed, realizing how uncool they thought I was. If they had seen or heard me singing Journey a few seconds earlier, they probably would have realized I was truly rad. Choice. Coolio. Or any other phat words that made me seem totally not awesome and old. I skulked around the corner onto First Avenue—my second time skulking that night!—and ran into one of the concert-goers. "Oh! I'm so sorry!" I stumbled and pulled at my headphones, trying to tug them out of my ears. Kenny Rogers was now singing through the wires, which really upped my cool factor.

"Well, hey there." I looked up and saw the person I'd run into. Joe. Dog Hounds Joe.

"Wassup." Cringe. I had just said wassup.

"Are you..." He gestured to the club we were standing outside of, obviously surprised to see me there. "...going to this show?"

"Yeah, I'm really into this band," I said, kicking myself for not listening when the slouchy teens had told me who we were here to see tonight.

Joe's face broke into a slow smile. "Really?"

I wrapped my headphones around my cell, laughing nervously. "Yeah, totes." *Totes? Who am I?*

"What are you listening to?" He grabbed my headphones before I had a chance to hide my phone inside my purse. One ear bud was tucked inside his left ear within seconds. He lifted his bushy eyebrows. "Phil Collins. Nice."

"It's Pandora. I didn't pick that."

"Baby, don't you lose my number."

"Sorry?"

"Oh, I'm just singing along." There was the smirk again. "Phil Collins is a true inspiration."

"Are you being sarcastic?"

Joe handed my headphones back to me. "Absolutely not. I would never be anything but completely serious with you, Stella."

I guess it was my buzz, but this made me laugh. I should have been insulted, but instead I started cracking up. He laughed along with me.

"You seem to have lost my number," I said lightly. "I guess you should have listened to Phil, huh?"

"I didn't lose your number," Joe walked alongside me as we moved toward the front door of the club. "I've been out of town."

"Ah, yes. Those long distance charges on cell phones are a real bitch. Wanted to wait until you were back in town to call so it would be toll-free?" I realized I sounded like a nag, and vowed to stop being so annoying. I was trying to flirt, and this time it was coming across as bitter and bitchy instead of coy and clever. "I'm teasing," I said, hoping to lighten my comments.

"I wanted to wait to call until we could actually go out," he said defensively. "I'm not big on leaving messages back and forth until we figure out a day three weeks from Tuesday when we're both available. It's ridiculous."

"Did I touch a nerve?" I asked, smiling at the little rant that had just come out of Captain Cool. He had seemed so laid back both times I'd seen him, it felt weird to have him upset about a little teasing. "Guess I'm not the only one who seems serious sometimes…"

He chuckled and gestured to the tattooed guy standing in front of the door at the First Ave main entrance. "Do you want to see the show or would you rather grab a coffee or beer or something? Like…" he checked his watch, "…right now?"

I nodded and we walked down First Avenue, back in the direction I'd come from on the bus. I told him I'd been out with friends, and decided to take the bus home. How it was pure coincidence that I'd run into him.

"I'm rarely in this neighborhood," I said. "Do you live around here?"

"No," he said with no further explanation. "Sorry I got a little snippy about not calling you."

"It's fine—I was trying to be funny, but I guess it came across as naggy?" I looked at him out of the corner of my eye, trying to appear coquettish.

"I'm not the kind of guy who says I'll call and then doesn't."

That struck me as funny.

"It's fine, really. I wasn't actually expecting you to have left me three or four messages by the time I got home after the Halloween party." I paused. "In case that's the kind of girl you thought *I* was."

We'd reached a small, dim, relatively un-crowded looking bar, and Joe held the door open for me to walk inside.

"I actually considered calling you that night," he said as we settled in at a tall bar table nestled up against a window, a safe distance from the cold air that flew in every time someone opened the front door. "It's all games, isn't it?"

"What is?"

"Dating. It's like playing a game."

"I'm not really sure yet," I said. I ordered a Guinness, a nice sipping beer. I didn't need anything that would go down too easily. I really should have ordered a coffee, but I didn't get the fresh-coffee vibe from this particular bar. "I actually just got out of a relationship. I'm not really an expert at dating." I paused, gauging Joe's reaction. Did he want to be out with someone who had the issues of a long-term relationship? I realized I didn't really care. It's not like I could hide the last decade of my life. "Actually, I seem to be really, really bad at dating."

The smirk was back, then Joe asked, "Now what makes you think you're bad at dating?"

"Maybe it's not so much that I'm bad at dating. It's more like, I seem to have some challenges choosing the right people to date."

He looked offended.

"This isn't a date," I insisted. "This is a random meeting."

"Oh, excellent. I love meetings."

"Do you ever have meetings?" I asked. "Don't musicians get an exemption from corporate thrills, like meetings?"

"I was a lawyer until about five years ago."

I nearly choked on my beer. "A lawyer?"

"Technically, I guess I still am. I've kept up on it, just in case, but the music gig is a lot more fun. I'm a recovering attorney." He wiggled his eyebrows at me. "So I really could sue you for identity theft or intellectual property usage for that Halloween costume. It would be a very sad case, and I would probably lose, but I could represent myself and save on legal fees."

"What made you stop practicing?"

"Meetings," Joe chuckled. "Actually, I decided to leave my practice when the Dog Hounds started to take off. We'd been playing mostly local shows, but then we began to get some national recognition—got invited to festivals in other states and stuff, and I realized one of us was going to have to focus on the business end of the band if we wanted to have any hope of making it." He pointed to himself. "I was happy to volunteer to quit the day job and go for it."

"Do you ever have any regrets?" I asked, wishing I had the courage to leave my own carefully crafted life and find a job and existence that was actually interesting. "Do you ever think about going back to it?"

"I think it's every little boy's dream of being in a band when they grow up. So no, now that I'm doing what I love and making it work most of the time, I don't ever long for suits and client dinners and office politics." He put his hands behind his head and stretched backward, a "look how relaxed I am" pose.

"God, I'm so jealous."

"Do you want to be in a band, Stella?" He was teasing me. The smirk was back, but this time I wanted to reach my fingers out and touch the little dimple that appeared every time he made his charming smirk-face. He was such a bad choice, but there was something so tempting about him. So unlike *me*.

I laughed. "No. No bands for me."

"You don't like musicians?" He pouted.

"I didn't say that. I don't know how I feel about musicians." I nibbled on my lower lip, then took a sip of my beer. A tiny sip—I was starting to feel sort of floaty again, but I suspected it was from Joe this time, not from the beer. "I guess we'll see what I think of musicians after tonight."

"Ooh, am I being interviewed?"

"Yes," I said, grinning. "Isn't that how dates work?"

"I thought this wasn't a date. It's a meeting, remember?"

"Yes, a deposition." I laughed. "A deposition would be more interesting than a lot of the dates I've had in the last few weeks."

"Dates? Plural? You've been on multiple dates with multiple people in the last few weeks?" His eyes were wide. "You're a busy girl."

Embarrassed, I admitted, "I've recently signed up for an online dating site."

"Which one?"

"I'm not going to say."

"Why not? I'd like to find you and wink at you or high-five you or whatever they do on the site you're on."

"You can just wink at me here. In person."

Joe closed both eyes deliberately.

"Was that a wink?" I asked, laughing.

"I don't know how to wink."

"Here," I reached out and put my hand on his face. His skin was soft and warm, and all I wanted to do was let my hand run up his cheek and tug at one of his soft, wavy curls. Instead, I held one of his eyes open and commanded, "Blink." He did, and I cracked up. "That was the scariest-looking wink I've ever seen." After I took my hand away from his face, Joe kept blinking.

He took swig of his beer and rubbed at the foggy outside of his pint glass. It was a nervous gesture. "So how long ago did you break up with whoever it was you were dating?"

I stared into my beer when I said, "A few months ago now."

"It was a long relationship?"

"Twelve years."

"Shit. That's longer than my marriage."

I looked up. "You're married?"

He laughed, but it wasn't a particularly happy sound. "Not anymore. Divorced."

"I'm sorry."

"Don't be. We're much better off."

"How long were you married?"

"Five years—she left when I went full-time with the band." He smiled sadly, and my insides squirmed, just a little.

"That's horrible."

"Divorce is fun!" He said sarcastically. "Really, it feels like it all happened in a different life. I'm not the same person I was then."

"That's good, I guess?" I wondered, briefly, if he felt like a different person because now he could sleep with a different woman every night. Then I realized I was being judgmental, and tried to keep an open mind. This was fun, just fun, and I could loosen up and enjoy it. At least, I hoped I could.

"Definitely." Joe nodded. "I regret not being able to make it work. There's probably something satisfying about figuring out how to keep it together, even as you drift apart, you know? It feels like such a failure to put that kind of time into something, and then you just... give up." He was still smiling, despite the topic. It almost made him look a little naive, but I knew he wasn't. "I mean, it's not that we just gave up, but a part of me wonders if it's better to hold onto something you've taken time to build than to just start over at the beginning again." I swallowed, his words hitting hard. "You want another beer?"

I was still feeling the effects of the wine and now had the Guinness layered on top, and I was not eager to turn this into the drunken first date I'd vowed to have sometime. I didn't want to ruin it. I was having fun, despite the fact that Joe had just dredged up a lot of the things I'd been fretting over for the last few weeks.

"No, I don't think another beer is a good idea."

"Right, yeah," Joe started to pull out his wallet to pay. "Can I give you a ride home? Your bus transfer is probably expired by now."

I realized he must have misinterpreted my reluctance to have another beer as a way to end the conversation and our night. "I didn't mean I wanted to get out of here this second or anything. I just don't want another beer. Maybe I'll order a coffee?"

"Oh," he looked embarrassed. "Yeah, sure." He spun his empty glass in his hands, fidgeting. "I thought…"

"I don't care that you're divorced," I said quickly. "In case that's what you were thinking…"

"No, no," Joe said quickly, but I could tell I was right. He grinned sheepishly and pushed his hair back away from his face. "Well, yeah, maybe I did. Sometimes when I talk about it, I wonder if it looks like I'm still dwelling. Like I'm still hung up on her or something? Because for the record, I'm not. I got over it a few years ago, but you always wonder a little bit what might have happened if you'd stuck it out back when it all went wrong." He laughed humorlessly. "Agh, I'm blathering. You're making me ramble. I sound like a lawyer—can't stop talking. But you know what? I don't want you to get a coffee here. Maybe we should call an end to this 'meeting,' and I could ask you out on a real 'date' date?"

"I'd like that," I said, and meant it. Joe surprised me. I'd originally agreed to a date with him because I thought it would be fun, different, amusing maybe. But now I realized there was more to him than the dopey guy dressed up in a costume trying to make it in the world of children's music (not that I was judging). I was intrigued. But he'd also given me a few things to think about. Hearing from someone who had done what I'd done—left something decent and not quite right behind and headed out into the wild blue yonder—made me wonder if maybe I was being a little selfish for leaving Erik.

Not for the first time, I worried that maybe I'd made the wrong decision.

CHAPTER NINE

I sailed through the next few days on a Journey- and Joe-inspired high. I was feeling better about myself than I had in a long time, and I was finally starting to feel like maybe I had some sense of self back. Unfortunately, with my new self-satisfaction came a renewed doubt about my decision to leave Erik.

When I brought it up with Anders, he asked me to stop watching Oprah specials.

I decided I wasn't going to discuss anything with Lily at work, since I'd never hear the end of it. I would keep my newfound happiness to myself and just revel in the fact that I felt fabulous—if a little lonely. I realized it was a little strange that my woo-hoo moment had come courtesy of Journey. If I ever got an award for successfully figuring out my life and finding my way back to me (yeah, I'd been reading self-help), I would be more than happy to thank them for their contribution to my life.

After getting a ride home from Joe on Friday night, we'd agreed to go out a full week later. He was headed out of town to play a few shows at public libraries in Iowa on Saturday and Sunday after our "meeting," so I suggested the next weekend. He'd offered to plan something, and I was eager to see what he'd come up with.

When I got to the office on Monday, I was greeted with a huge bouquet of tulips (my favorite!) in a pint glass vase. I'd sworn I wouldn't get all dopey about Joe, but I couldn't help but swoon a little at the romantic gesture. Erik had never done anything like this. There were no sudden impulses, no random acts of romance. I hadn't even realized I was the type of person to fall for this kind of thing, but giddiness bubbled up when I saw them contrasted against the drab gray of my cubicle.

I opened the card, and my stomach squeezed when I saw the note: "Stella, I miss you. Erik." That was all. The card was even written in Erik's distinctive, looping handwriting, which meant he'd taken the extra step to actually go to the florist and fill out the card. Most people just called in their order and had the lady behind the counter write a dictated message. The card, the flowers, the message, it was all so unlike Erik that my body went a little cold at the significance of the gesture.

"Pretty flowers," Lily had snuck up behind me, and was peering over my shoulder to try to see the card. "Booty call offering?"

"Ha ha. No." She was probably right. Did Erik just want to get some? I suddenly realized that wasn't actually that terrible... hadn't I always wished he was more impulsive, more romantic, more *exciting*? Would I have broken up with someone who sent me flowers for no good reason at all, except to tell me he missed me?

"Who are they from? The mouth breather or stat boy?"

"Neither. They're from Erik."

"What did he do wrong?"

"The card just says he misses me."

Lily scoffed. "He's obviously feeling guilty about something specific. I bet he slept with the blonde. Erik isn't the kind of guy to send tulips just because."

"I know he isn't. But he did. So maybe he is, and maybe I just never inspired him to send tulips before. It's not as if we've seen how he acts as an adult man trying to woo a woman. We got together when he was still sort of a kid, and he never had to woo me."

"Don't let him fool you. You can't fall for it." Lily sat in the guest chair that was squeezed into the corner of my cubicle. "Might I remind you of the time you brought home that bouquet from the Farmer's Market and Erik told you you'd wasted twenty bucks because you were going away for the weekend, and they'd be dead before you got home to enjoy them?" I nodded slowly, and she nodded along with me.

"You're not enough of a sucker to fall for this, are you?" She adjusted her suit coat, and I caught a glimpse of something red and sparkly underneath.

I shook my head and laughed, but I could hear Joe's comments from Friday night taunting me. Was it stupid to give up on something I'd spent so much time building up?

"I won't fall for it. Why are you wearing sequins?"

She grinned mischievously and leaned in to whisper, "Because it makes me feel like a Barbie doll. Corporate Barbie."

"Don't let anyone else here hear you say that. You sound a little less fierce when you're comparing yourself to Barbie. She's not exactly a model of professional success."

"Maybe I'm tired of being a model of professional success," Lily grumbled.

"Coffee?" I asked, and stood up. We walked together toward the elevators, then emerged into the skyway. In Minneapolis, you could go an entire winter without going outside if you wanted to. I liked that. "What's wrong?" I asked, when we were finally away from Centrex offices.

"I'm just a little messed." She put on her usual Lily veneer, and made a funny face to play it off as nothing. "I don't know—just thinking about things lately."

"What kinds of things?" Lily was often dramatic, but I'd never seen her get really down. She almost looked like she was going to cry.

"I think I fucked up."

"Lily Sparrow does not fuck up." That was true. I'd never known Lily to do something she regretted. She made mistakes, but never actually considered them mistakes—just changes of course.

"I slept with a married man." She stopped suddenly and faced me. "Multiple times."

"Who?" For some reason, that's the only thing I could think of to say.

"He has kids." She looked horrified. "I'm a bitchy, slutty whore. I know. Please don't say it."

"Of course I wouldn't say that. You're my friend. I'm on your side—I don't care what you did."

"I slept with a married man, Stella. I'm the 'other woman.'" She was starting to get loud, and we were still in the skyway. We were far too close to Centrex headquarters for her to get shrill. I pulled her toward the pizza place that was notorious for giving people food poisoning—I knew we wouldn't run into anyone we knew there. We bypassed the bored-looking kids working at the counter and settled into a booth in the back without buying anything. "I don't know what I was—*am*—thinking."

"It's still going on?" I asked, a little surprised.

"Yes. And I think I'm in love with him."

I tried hard not to show my reaction on my face. As confident as Lily always seemed to be, I knew she was really vulnerable and would read into my facial expressions. "Does Chad know?"

"Of course not."

"Does the guy's wife know?"

"No," she cringed and looked straight at me, scared. "I threatened to tell her. I had a psycho moment last night, and just went off on him. I told him I was going to tell his wife."

I stared at her, seeing a whole different Lily than I'd ever seen before. "God, Lil, don't do that."

"Well I won't, obviously. I'm not a psychopath. But I just kind of freaked out, and said it. We were sitting there, eating Thai take-out, nothing significant. I watched him take a bite of spring roll and it was like I was possessed by bad lemongrass. I just went off. Afterward, when he went home, I started to think through what I was doing and realized how *stupid* I am. What right do I have to take someone's husband, someone's father. Am I the reason Daddy doesn't come home in time for bed?"

"That's the guy's problem. He's the reason his family is fucked up. He made choices, too. It's not like you forced yourself on him and made him have an affair." I didn't want to say out loud that I doubted this was the guy's first affair. I supposed she wanted to feel special, somehow, but I'd never really had a lot of faith in guys who cheated. What had caused Joe's divorce? Was he the kind of guy who would do that sort of thing?

Was Erik? I knew the answer to that was no. As much as I hated the way Erik fawned over interns, I knew I'd never had to worry. Honestly, Erik didn't have the confidence to pursue an affair—he'd never assume anyone adored him enough to go for it. It's part of what I loved about him.

Lily sniffled, and it almost sounded as though she was crying, but there were no tears. "My dad had an affair. That's why my parents got divorced. I always assumed it was that bitch's fault. My dad would never do something so horrible, so it must have been some slut who came in and ripped our family apart. She was the bad guy, not my dad."

I didn't know what to say. Uncomfortable, I ended up saying, "I take it this means things aren't going so well with Chad?"

She laughed. It felt good to hear her laugh, but I knew I'd just put a temporary band-aid on her real feelings.

"Unlike Cat, I prefer to sleep in the same bed as my partner. I'm not sure why that inspired me to hook up with a married guy who can never sleep over, but at least he's a warm body I can touch more often than once or twice every few weeks." Her laugh transitioned into a giggle. "He has so much chest hair. I've never been with anyone hairy. Do you realize how sweaty chest hair gets during sex?" She shuddered. Suddenly, her Blackberry buzzed and Lily pulled it out of her pocket. "Fuck. I have Strategic Planning. If I'm late, James is going to stick me with the three-year-plan formatting project. I hate doing powerpoint over the weekend."

"Lil, you can't go back to work." She was a mess. At least, she seemed that way to me—but to everyone else she would probably seem as hard and emotionless as always. It was her image, and she had perfected it over the last five or six years. Her success was a direct result of her stony image. "Are you okay?"

"I'm fine. Erik's tulips threw me."

They had thrown me, too. But I wasn't about to admit that. "Don't you think James is going to put you over the edge at Strategic Planning? You seem a little... shaky. Care Bear Davis has the ability to push people into the abyss."

"Work soothes me." She pecked me on the cheek as we walked out the door of the pizza place, and I could smell her lavender perfume and the vanilla traces of her shampoo. Lily was far too good to be with someone so terrible. She was too good for Chad, and she was certainly too good for a married man trying to fulfill a need. She always seemed so perfect, but was absolutely crippled by her own insecurities when it came to guys. "Do I smell like pizza or anything?"

I shook my head. "You smell pretty."

That made her smile. "I need a haircut. Mine is starting to look a lot like Miranda Hopkins' hair—from accounting?"

"Miranda Hopkins uses a crimping iron."

"Is that how she gets it to look like that?" Lily pulled out her Blackberry and I knew I'd all but lost her to Centrex again. "I should borrow it from her."

When we reached the security desk at the Centrex offices, Lily headed inside, but I just didn't have it in me to go back. She waved goodbye absentmindedly, already drowning in a mess of emails and distractions. Meanwhile, I couldn't stop thinking about the flowers, and I couldn't stop thinking about Erik and what I'd lost when I left him. I didn't know if I could sit in the drab, uninspiring cube and look at his romantic gesture all day. I had an idea in my head, and the longer I stood there, the stronger the urge to follow through on that idea grew.

I walked through the skyway, acutely aware of everyone I passed as I headed over streets and past salons. As I walked, I took in the pungent odor of cheap lunch deals and the enticing sweetness of fresh-baked brownies in the cookie cart. I could probably have walked this route with my eyes closed, following only scents and sounds to get to where I was going. But I wanted to make sure this choice was deliberate, and I had to do this with my eyes open.

Joe's words from that weekend had been bothering me, and I owed it to myself and to Erik to see if maybe I'd been too hasty.

Erik's office was in a huge tower stuffed with lawyers and accountants and consulting and design firms, everyone mashed together behind semi-transparent glass. I waved at the security guard and made my way to the bank of elevators that would take me up to my ex-boyfriend's office in the Zoom! headquarters. I stood numbly, watching as the numbers flew from one to twenty in just a few seconds, and realized I had less than ten seconds to change my mind and go back to work. I could throw the tulips in the garbage, or give them to one of my coworkers, or simply keep them and appreciate what they represented.

But instead, I was sucked toward the comfort of my past. After all, Erik had never been truly cruel to me, he'd never cheated, he'd never done anything offensive or intentionally hurtful. My heart was telling me I was about to make a bad choice, but my head had convinced my heart to shut up and stop being so irrational already.

I knew I deserved happiness. But I'd begun to realize that it was possible I was walking *away* from happiness by leaving Erik. Maybe we could both dig deep and find those parts of ourselves that had been squashed, and become something fantastic and new together.

As I walked through the lobby of his office, I detected the smell of chemical orange hand sanitizer, a scent Erik had carried home on his hands every night. My stomach flipped, and then I was in front of his office door, and suddenly I stopped.

His door opened, and I realized my hand had reached out and turned the metal handle. He was sitting at his desk, his glasses folded and hung over the top button of his shirt. He was wearing the shirt I'd bought him last Christmas, the one I told him looked nice with his eyes. I hadn't been wrong. When he looked up and saw me standing in his door, his eyes lit up and I felt the comfort I'd known for the past twelve years come whooshing back in a flash.

"Thanks for the tulips." I said. He stood and brushed the wrinkles out of his pants before walking toward me. He had tiny creases in his lip and I saw him subtly slide a breath mint out of his pocket and into his mouth.

"It's so good to see you," he said, studying me. I could smell his body wash and the hand sanitizer, and I wished he didn't smell so much like antiseptic. He broke into a huge smile. I hadn't seen Erik look so unabashedly happy in a long time. "God, you look great." He leaned back against his desk, resting in a half-sitting position on the corner of the factory-scuffed wood tabletop. There was silence for a few seconds while I continued to stare, absent of any thoughts or emotion of any kind other than nerves and worry.

I bit my lip, and noticed his eyes darted to my mouth—just briefly. He stood and walked behind me to close the door again. His office had three solid walls and one wall made entirely of glass that overlooked the streets below. Once, I'd suggested Erik and I make love on his desk, but he'd scolded me for being crass. "We aren't exhibitionists," he'd said, and I was quick to agree.

Once the door was closed, Erik walked back to the desk, his shoes scuffing on the rigid nubs of the cheap berber carpet. As he passed me, I felt his hand brush against my lower back. It was the first time he'd really touched me with any meaning since long before I'd left him. It made me think of the times we'd been together back when everything was new. The uncertainty, the vulnerability, the buzz of exploring new things. I wanted that back. I wanted him, and the comfort he represented.

Before I could say anything or think about what this would mean, he grabbed me and his hands wrapped around my hips. I felt his fingers dig into the soft contours of my waist, and I let him pull me hard against him. He murmured, "Oh," as his mouth found mine and we fell into the comfortable rhythm of our kiss—the only real love kiss I'd ever known.

His cheeks were rough, and I knew he hadn't shaved that morning. I could taste the breath mint on his lips, but also the undercurrent of sugared coffee and the lingering sweetness of his morning blueberry muffin. The smells and tastes and positions were familiar, but the passion felt new, reckless. My hands hung limply at my sides, and I melted in against him as we thumped backward against his office door. He let out a small, quiet laugh and pulled me toward his desk.

We were a mess of body parts, flailing and rubbing against each other. Me, propped up against his desk, and him, leaning over me as he kissed my neck, my collarbone, the hollow of skin between my breasts that he knew was like a trigger. I shuddered, kicking at my shoes as he lifted me onto the desk and lay me back to work his lips down my chest. He lay his head against my stomach, his chest heaving against my thighs, giving both of us a moment to breathe.

"I want you back," he said quietly, between breaths.

"We can't," I whispered, trying to get myself to pull away. I couldn't. "I shouldn't have."

What had I been thinking? Why had I come here? As the regret began to wash over me, Erik took my hips in his hands and moved in toward me. He swayed between my thighs and I could feel him harden in the space between us. His eyes locked on mine, and everything inside me melted again.

Within seconds, he'd pulled my tights down and tossed them onto the floor next to my shoes. He fumbled with his belt, so I reached out and helped him pull it open, grabbing greedily at his pants. Before I even realized they were open, he was inside of me and it felt so right, so good, so warm. He held my legs around his waist and pulled me in closer, leaning over me to kiss my breasts through the thin fabric of my shirt.

My fingers worked at the buttons, pulling it open so he could push my bra up and out of the way. His lips found first my left breast, then my right, and I heard him moan as he pressed himself further inside of me. I let my head tip back, and relished the crisp whiteness of a fall sky, wondering if anyone from the building across the street could see us, wishing they could. We'd never been so good, and I wanted to stay like this forever. With Erik inside of me, and his hands all over me—with the passion of knowing someone so well holding us together.

We'd been together long enough that I could sense his climax and he waited, making sure I was with him. We came together, both of us quietly, and then he collapsed on top of me while stroking my hair. It was a routine, the hair stroking, and I found it both comforting and chilling. I loved how it felt, but I hated the sense of tradition combined with the exciting newness of what had just happened. Erik and I had never been together like this before—*never*—and I wanted it all to feel new. I wanted it to feel like the first time, but I knew it never could.

"Thank you," he murmured, standing up to button his pants and refasten his belt. He held his hand out to me and I stood, pulling my skirt back down to cover my knees, and settled into one of his office guest chairs to put my tights on. Erik moved around to the other side of the desk and took a seat facing me, appraising me. It felt suddenly formal, like he was my boss, and I squirmed under his gaze.

"Do you want some water?" He reached under his desk and pulled out a bottle from the private stash he kept there for when the office water cooler was empty. I knew he didn't like to replace the empty jug with a full one, so he found an alternate source of water until someone else came around to deal with it.

"I'm okay," I said, and he cracked open the bottle to take a long swig. "Listen, Erik..."

He looked up, wiping a drop of water from the corner of his mouth. "So you got the flowers? My mom dropped them off at your office front desk this morning. They wouldn't let her come up to put them on your desk in person."

"Your *mom* dropped them off?" I felt the lust that had been there moments before screech to a halt and swiftly change into something else, something sour. Did it make the gesture feel less significant, now that I knew Laurel had been involved? "Thank you," I said, clearing my throat. My mouth was dry and I wondered why, especially after what had just passed, I was nervous to see him. "I love them."

"We knew you would." Ugh. There was the "we" again. I desperately wanted to get Laurel the hell out of the middle.

"So I should have said this before—um, well, before *that*." We grinned at each other, and I felt like a teenager who'd just gotten away with doing it in the back of my parents' car. Not that I'd had sex in high school, since I was too busy planning and preparing for the life that was now so dull, but I'd seen that scene in TV shows. "What I wanted to say is, we should talk about what this means."

"Isn't it kind of late to talk about what this means, Stella?" He looked so proud, so satisfied, so in love.

"It's not, and we need to." I looked into my lap at first. But then I stared straight at him, knowing I had to stick to my convictions or I was going to hate myself by lunchtime. "This wasn't us getting back together."

His eyebrows went up. "Okay…"

"I haven't changed my mind." It just spilled out. "I'm happier without you."

Erik blinked rapidly a number of times, making it look like his contact was stuck somewhere up in his eyelid. It was his classic stalling tactic.

"I'm not sure I get this, then." He gestured to my open blouse and messy hair.

"I don't get it either." I didn't get it. It had felt so good, but part of me wondered if maybe it felt so good because it was wrong. It felt like something illicit, scandalous, secret. "Maybe we could talk later this week?"

"Do you want to come over?" he asked, taking another drink of water. His lips were still puffy, and I wondered how long he would stay hidden in his office before facing his coworkers. Ten minutes? Was post-sex glow a source of pride for most people? Not for Erik, I could be sure.

"No, I can't come to your place." I thought about the sex, and how if we met at Erik's house, there might be opportunity for more. It felt so good, but… "Or maybe—" I stopped. What was I doing? I had to get out of there before I committed to something I would later regret. "No, I'll email you, okay?" I stood and slipped my shoes on. As I looked down and wobbled my way to the door with one shoe on and one still half-off, I realized Anders was right. I really did have a lot of sensible shoes. That needed to change if this was the new me.

I opened the door, walked out, and closed it behind me without a look back.

CHAPTER TEN

After I left Erik's office, I trudged shamefully back to my cubicle. I spent the rest of the day waffling, alternately reveling in the incredibleness of the sex and kicking myself for having done it. What was I going to say when we "talked" later that week—that I still didn't think he was perfect for me, and I still resented his inability to commit, but I liked the way he made wild rice soup? That his thighs were always nice and warm at night, and that was maybe enough?

Why couldn't I just let go?

James came by my desk around noon to drop a small Care Bear figurine on my cube wall. "Found this at a garage sale this weekend," he explained proudly. "Made me think of you. Always upbeat, aren't you, Stella?"

I glowered at him, unwilling to stay upbeat in the midst of a salary cut and my own grumpiness.

"Forget to take your happy pills this morning, sweetheart?"

"Don't call me sweetheart," I spat, irritated by his false cheer and emotion-marketing messaging. "Save it for your boss."

James reddened, nervously dancing the figurine around on the top of my cube wall. "Excuse me?"

"Nothing," I grumbled. It wasn't wise to wage a war with my boss over his crass and inappropriate relationship with his boss. After all, I was one red folder away from losing my job altogether, and then I'd have no choice but to go back to Erik. Laid off, desolate, and with Christmas on the horizon. I could think of nothing more depressing, except being alone, too.

James strode off, all coiffed hair and snazzy suit, and I grabbed the Care Bear off the ledge. With a laugh, I chucked it ceremoniously into the trash.

"I hate this job," I muttered, and as I said it I realized it was true. Professionally, it was everything I'd ever achieved to be in life, and now I was here and it sucked. What kind of stupid teenager makes her ultimate goal a meaningless job marketing Soft Scrub and mops to the masses?

I'd seen this happen to other people—they get everything they've always wished for, and then they realize even that sucks. Like my cousin Aria, who spent years getting advanced degree after advanced degree in her pursuit to be some kind of medical specialist (something that involved penises, that's all I knew), and when she finally graduated and got a high-paying job, she left it all because she had no work-life balance. Her lifelong goal had let her down, and now she owed more money than I'd make in my entire life but she had no idea what to do with herself.

I shut down my computer at two and went looking for Lily. The interns outside her office informed me Ms. Sparrow had gotten called into an hours-long advertising review, so I left. I went home, put in the first of the *Alias* Season Two DVDs, and poured myself a glass of wine.

I drank two glasses of afternoon wine as I wondered what right I had to be depressed. I had a date the next weekend with a guy who seemed totally decent, and who smelled like cinnamon rather than antiseptic. But even still, I couldn't stop pitying myself.

Just as my buzz kicked in and Sydney Bristow started kicking some serious ass, my cell phone rang. Foolishly, I picked up without looking at the caller ID.

"Stella?" Laurel Wesley's sharp voice rang through the phone and I inadvertently released a loud, exaggerated sigh.

"Hi, Laurel." This was going to be hard. I found Laurel difficult to deal with when I was in a good mood, but in this state I worried about what I might say. I'd grown comfortable enough with her that I treated her much like I might treat my own mom if she were around—though we'd always had a few extra layers of the tension that tends to exist between a mother and her only son's significant other. She was the closest thing to a mother I had, and I was going to have to let her go, or this situation would get really awkward. As I realized that, my mind flashed back to that morning, to the feeling of Erik's hands confidently gripping my thighs in that comfortable grasp and I wondered if maybe she knew we'd been together. "How's it going?"

"I'm fine, Stella. I hear you saw Erik?" My stomach churned. Erik had already called her? "Cat mentioned she was out with you on Friday and you ran into Erik at his firm's intern farewell dinner?"

"We didn't get a chance to talk," I said, relieved Laurel didn't seem to know about that morning. "But yeah, I saw him from afar. That was an intern farewell dinner? Awfully intimate, Erik and just one cute blonde."

Laurel cleared her throat. "Well, yes. Did you notice how good he looks?"

I rolled my eyes and paused *Alias*. "Yes, Erik has always been good looking."

"He looks better than ever, Stella. He's been on a new soup diet, and I took him to get his hair cut at my salon."

"Laurel?" I said, attempting to cut her off. I didn't want to listen to her prattle on about the merits of her son.

"It's all for you, you know." I could tell she had mustered up her courage to tell me this. "He loves you, Stella. I just wanted to know… should I put you in the Christmas drawing this year? I can add your name to the gift exchange, if you want to come spend the holidays with family."

I sat on the line silently, listening to the click of Laurel's iPad as she dragged letters around on her Scrabble game. "I appreciate that. But I won't be at Christmas this year."

"We're your family! If you don't come to my house, where will you go? I don't want you to be alone for the holidays." I knew she meant it well, but instead her reminder that I'd dropped my whole family, along with Erik, really stung. I hadn't thought about Christmas. My parents were both gone, my friends all had families of their own, and I hadn't sent gifts to my extended family in more than ten years. "I'm cooking lamb. I know it's your favorite." That actually wasn't true. It was Erik's favorite, and I always thought it tasted gamey. But I'd never said anything, so I suppose it was fair that she thought he and I were both lamb-lovers.

I said, "I'll be fine for Christmas. Listen, Laurel, I have to go. Did you need anything else?"

"I was hoping to get your Brussels sprout recipe—I'm entering the Foodie Channel Home Chef competition, and I was hoping to include them in my audition video."

"Sure, I'll email it to you." Laurel tried out different hobbies the way some women experimented with new hairstyles— often, and frequently with disastrous consequences. She'd been on a cooking kick for a few years, and had entered every single contest the Foodie Channel had offered. She'd yet to win any of the competitions, but was determined to get one of their fancy chefs to visit her state-of-the-art kitchen to film her fifteen minutes of fame. "Please say hello to Peter for me."

We hung up, and I felt even worse. I poured myself another glass of wine and clicked play. If only I could transform myself into a new existence with something as simple as spandex and a purple wig, a la Sydney Bristow. But my thighs would never fit into catsuit, so I guess that was out.

The next morning, I was up early, ready to face the ladies at water aerobics. For once, I arrived on time and got myself stripped down and dressed amongst the scuttle of everyone else's bare bottoms. The gang was downright cheery around me now, and I had begun to find their random musings on life comforting in a weird sort of way.

The women of Water X Power rarely had conversations, per se, but stacked stories on top of stories as they talked at one another. Fran muttered crabbily about the way the garbage men always left her garbage can in the middle of the alley, and she had pulled her hamstring dragging it back to its place in front of her garage. Lydia often had the latest on some sale or another. Rae was quick to share recipes and gossip from a dinner party she'd attended sometime in the few days prior.

Barbara always told tales of her grandson—the famed Jonathan, my favorite date yet—and his escapades with ladies in his life. Had I stuck around after that first water aerobics class, I would have heard enough to convince me to never go out with him in the first place. But now, Barb seemed to have forgotten we'd ever gone out, since she hadn't brought it up since.

Barb also talked often of her husband, who had passed away earlier in the year. Apparently, he left a mysterious collection of chewing gum under surfaces throughout their house.

"It's hard to speak ill of a dead husband," is how she prefaced most of her comments. "But that bastard has me hunting on hands and knees for dry, chewed-up wads of old gum. It's as though he never threw them away—must have known he'd knock off first and stick me with the messy job of cleaning up after him. I keep hitting on them accidentally. Last week, I got my good church pants stuck on a chunk of mint gum. That bastard left chewed up wads until the day he died, and probably laughed his ass all the way up to heaven." She crossed her hand over her chest and added, "Bless his heart."

Heather, still my favorite, stayed relatively quiet. From time to time, she'd insert comments under her breath only I could hear. I'd learned she had several grandchildren, but she didn't talk about them in great detail, the way the other ladies did. Mostly, she just judged the rest of us and uttered strange wisecracks and comments about everyone else's life.

I hardly ever said anything at all. I was still trying to fly under the radar and find my place amongst the group. After class on Tuesday after my Monday o' Erik, I hustled into a private shower stall like always. But then I dawdled, wondering if maybe someone would have some good advice for me on what to do about Erik, and Joe, and my life in general. It wasn't as if I could talk to my friends about my "office incident" with Erik—I could see the expressions on each of their faces, and it made me a little weepy. I decided I had nothing to lose, and that if anything, telling the water aerobics girls something about myself would help me feel more a part of things in class. Then, maybe I could slough off and chat during intervals, like they all seemed to do.

The confession, once I decided to come out with it, slipped out easily. I found once I'd begun to speak about my personal life, the women encouraged me and asked questions and egged me on, until I didn't even realize I was spilling far more than I wanted to share. I told them the things I'd already shared with Heather… a brief history, the why of the split, the highlights of dating since.

"I think I may have met someone I'm interested in," I said, moving into the more recent history. "Joe. He's in a band."

Everyone was wearing at least underpants by now, which made looking around a little easier. Barb was still wearing *only* underpants, but I'd take it.

"A band?" Rae scoffed. "What kind of band?"

"Don't be quick to judge, Rae. My Jonathan is in a band, and he's a good kid."

"He's not a kid, Barbara. He's thirty-four and lives in your basement." Fran knocked gently at Barbara's head. "Stella, you should meet my son—he doesn't live in a basement and he's got a whole head of hair. Forty-five and not bald at all! Eh?"

"No more set ups," I said, as kindly as possible.

Fran blew air through her lips. She sat down and her bare thighs slapped noisily on the wooden bench. She fixed Barbara with a firm glare when she said, "Kick the man out already, and tell him to get a life. Your Jonathan is—"

"It doesn't matter," I said, cutting her off and trying to move things along. "The point is, I like Joe, the musician, but he's not my type and then this weekend on our first… well, our first date, I guess, he started talking about his ex-wife."

"Still in love with the ex-wife? Get out of there *now*," Barbara had moved on. "That's not gonna change."

"No, he's not still in love with her. He just said some things about trying to make it work, and how maybe it's better to stick it out with what you know and have spent time on than to start over. Like me."

Heather was sitting on the bench, trying to get her left sock up to her knee. "Bah. That's what I say. You weren't happy. Get the hell out of there."

"Right, so that's what I did back in September, right?" I ran my fingers loosely through my curls while the other women gathered in a circle around me. I felt like prey. Mom prey. "Well, when Joe said all that, I got a little mixed up, and then Erik sent me flowers at the office and all of a sudden, I went to see him and we just sort of slipped back into some old patterns. But just once."

Lydia looked at me over her glasses. "How do you 'slip' back together? You're not stupid. You know there aren't accidents when it comes to nookie."

"The point being," I said, and took one of the cookies Rae was passing around to everyone in the locker room. Wait—did they always have cookies after exercise class? "The point is, it was fun and exciting and very different from the old us. I don't want to be *with him* with him again, but I did enjoy *that*." I suddenly blushed, realizing I was spilling my sex secrets with a bunch of retirees. They probably thought I was a harlot. That would be the word, right?

"I'm sorry, I don't know what got me talking about this. It's just my friends all hate Erik now, and I can't really talk to *Erik* about Erik, and the only other person I've got is Erik's mom and, well—"

"Have you heard some of the shit these women talk about?" Heather asked, patting my arm. "It's a relief to get some variety in the locker room. Don't worry about shocking us— we've gone through a few things in our years." She looked around at the other women, all of whom were nodding. "Except Lydia. She married her high school sweetheart and is still with him to this day. They're as sweet as French silk pie, but spending time listening to her talk about him gives you the same kind of bloat in your belly. It's sickening."

Lydia just shrugged. "There's something to be said for consistency. But that doesn't mean things were always great." Lydia sat down and gestured to the cookie bag. She grabbed a second and a third, and started talking. "When we were just out of high school, young and foolish—"

"Here we go again," Heather muttered. Lydia threw a cookie at her and Heather wasn't nimble enough to duck. It chucked on her the shoulder.

Lydia continued, "As I was saying, there was a time when I was still young, when Gray was traveling a lot for work. He'd spend nights away, on the road, and I was lonely. I began to fantasize, noticing other men out at the shops, and there were a few times I wondered if maybe I'd taken the wrong path."

Barbara cut in. "Get to the point, Lyd. There's a sale at Nordstrom Rack you need to be getting to."

"Anyhoo," Lydia said, grinning like someone who'd certainly made the most of her life. "I stuck with him and we've got two beautiful children to show for it. He's always been kind to me, and wants me to be happy. He'd give me the world, if I asked for it. That's the one thing I'll say about Gray. He's a good man who makes me feel like a wrinkly old princess, even to this day, and that counts for something."

Was Erik a good man? I wondered. I suddenly had a memory shake loose from a few years before, when Erik had been on a conference streak. He'd convinced Centrex to send him to several marketing conferences in one summer. He'd gone to San Francisco, New York, and Chicago all within a matter of a few months. I'd never been to San Francisco, and suggested I join him.

"I'll be busy," he'd said, making excuses. "You have work."

"I can use vacation days—or call in sick," I'd said, rubbing his feet that were resting on my lap beneath a blanket. "Isn't it worth it?"

"Too impulsive," he'd said. "The flight will cost a fortune—it's less than two weeks from now."

"But I want to go," I'd argued, getting frustrated by his curmudgeonly attitude. "I've never been." I'd saved enough money over the years that I could afford it, so money wasn't the issue. Other things stood in the way.

"I've never heard you talk about wanting to go to San Francisco before—where is this coming from?"

"I've never mentioned it because it's never come up. It's not like my life's goal is to go to San Francisco, but that doesn't mean I don't *want* to go. Sometime. And now seems like a perfectly reasonable time. We have a free hotel room, we can share meals, it will cost us virtually nothing." At the time, we'd been saving for a house we never bought—instead, we moved into Erik's place, the one out in a suburb I despised, decorated with all his mom's old furniture hand-me-downs.

"We'll plan a trip, somewhere else we want to go. Just you and me, no work obligations."

"Really?" I asked, realizing then that we'd never planned a trip together. Early on in our relationship we'd been young and poor. Then, work had gotten in the way. Eventually, it just wasn't part of the plan. "That would be amazing. I've always wanted to go to Italy."

"I've already been to Italy," he'd said, flipping the TV channel, away from *House Hunters* and onto *Sports Center.* "Somewhere new."

"But Italy is my dream," I'd said, sulking. "And I was watching that show."

That night, we kept watching Sports Center and a few months later, we had booked a flight to England, with a short jaunt to Paris. I was still waiting for the trip I'd always wanted.

I turned my attention back to the ladies in the locker room, who were all dressed now and bundling up in their winter jackets.

"Do you want to come for a coffee, Stella?" Rae asked. She crumpled the plastic cookie bag in her hand and threw it away, empty. "We usually grab some lunch after class."

"It's eight-thirty in the morning!" I laughed.

"Well, I for one ate breakfast before class," Lydia announced sourly. "That makes the next meal lunch. I don't care what time it is."

"Next time," I promised.

As we walked out of the locker room and into the front lobby of the Y, Heather held my arm and said, "Do what feels right. Doesn't matter if you look backward or step forward, just make sure you're living for you."

I squeezed her hand. "That doesn't really help."

"I may be old," she said. "But I don't have all the answers. I've made too many mistakes myself to be coaching anyone. But I do know life is usually long enough to screw up a few times without it biting you in the ass." Heather pressed the button to open the front doors that would let us out into the chilly winter air. I felt my hair freezing into tight, crispy ringlets as we walked toward our cars.

"Sometimes, life can't be planned. You strike me as the kind of girl who needs to be reminded of that from time to time. Just let it happen, and see how much fun you can have. Eventually you'll have to decide where you want to go next, but not today. Not today."

CHAPTER ELEVEN

I was in no condition to make any decisions immediately. Obviously.

Instead, I pretended the oopsie-sex with Erik had never happened and actually went so far as to automatically forward his emails to my junk mail folder (for a few days). I didn't have to think about my date with Joe until closer to the weekend, so instead I focused my emotional energy on trying to get Lily to open up about the man who had made her a mistress. Not surprisingly, private Lil wasn't talking, and she refused to show even a shred of emotion about the current state of things after her breakdown on Monday morning.

Anders was no help through any of this, since I couldn't tell him about Lily, refused to spill about Erik, and had exhausted our analysis of Joe-as-potential-lover. Anders was eagerly urging me to carry-on with the internet date-a-thon, insisting a banjo player in a children's band was not a good reason to stop the search. If he only knew it was actually Erik who had me rethinking things.

I finally made it through the week, and when Friday came around, I convinced Lily to take me shopping during lunch. She took me to Saks downtown, forcing me to buy a dress that cost something close to my monthly salary.

"It's perfect," she'd insisted, tucking my wild hair behind my ears. "When's the last time you bought anything for yourself? Really?"

"I got some winter boots on sale last week. Now that I have to shovel for myself."

"Make Anders do it. He's your tenant—write some manual labor into the lease. He's getting a little doughy anyway, and could probably use the exercise." She pushed me back into the dressing room, and I heard the click of her Blackberry as she checked emails. "Besides, winter boots don't count. Anders told me you have a closet full of ugly shoes. Should we get you something less sensible to go with this dress?"

"Thanks, Anders," I muttered. Good to know my friends were talking about my lack of fashion. "My shoes might not be flashy, but at least they get me around in the winter. I'm not buying something stupid that I'll wobble around on in the snow."

"You're going out with a rock star," Lily chuckled. I knew she was being facetious calling him "rock star"—she'd made it clear all week long that Joe's job would be an endless source of ribbing. "Do you want to get something a little edgier? I won't force you into high heels if you insist on buying them from Aerosoles. But I will make you get a fabulous pair of boots. Something with noisy buckles, so when you're rocking out to the banjo beat everyone will hear you. In honor of *Nashville*." Lily and I had always loved TV dramas, and anything about fictional celebrities or actual, spoiled-rotten rich people were our favorites.

"Yeah, boots would work," I agreed, refusing to laugh at her stupid banjo crack. In fact, I'd always sort of wanted a pair of amazing cowboy boots, the kind you could wear with jeans or floaty dresses. But I'd always felt they didn't really fit the image Erik and I had designed for ourselves. Even still, there was this pair of turquoise boots I'd been coveting for years "I'll buy impractical boots that totally do *not* suit me if you'll tell me more about this hairy lover you've taken on."

"I don't want to talk about it," she insisted, and when I peeked out of the dressing room, I could see she had her chin raised defiantly. "I'm serious, Stella. It's embarrassing. Not that he's hairy, but that I'm sleeping with a married man."

"It's not embarrassing." What was embarrassing was the vision I'd started to replay in my mind of myself walking the walk of shame through Erik's office after our little reunion on

Monday. "It's not the best decision anyone ever made, but you're really not the one at fault here."

"I knew he was married before we had sex."

I breathed out, hoping the dressing room curtain would prevent her from hearing what was obviously a judgmental sigh. I was trying hard not to judge, but it was tough.

"Who is he?" I asked, zipping up my no-work-day jeans. I was excited I had the whole afternoon to prep for my date—I guess that was one of the pros of losing twenty-percent of my job. "Anyone I know?"

Lily groaned. "No, I don't think so. He's the creative head for one of our agencies. We went out to lunch a few months ago, after they'd pitched us their ideas for the Easter campaign. We'd been in meetings together before, and I guess I'd noticed him flirting, but I never thought anything would come of it. It just happened to be the week Chad decided not to come home because he wanted to go to his friend's broomball tournament in Chicago." She sighed. I opened the dressing room curtain and we walked toward the cash register. "I was feeling slighted, and depressed, and self-conscious because I'd found two gray hairs in my *eyebrows* that morning."

She stopped talking while I paid. The Saks clerks always seemed so eager and nosey.

As we walked out, back into the skyway, she continued. "When he put his hand on mine during dessert, I didn't really think it would lead to anything. Just a little innocent flirting. But we ended up staying at the restaurant most of the afternoon, and then suddenly it was happy hour, and we had a few drinks, and then his hand was on my thigh, and under my skirt. It all made me feel so good about myself. Chad was gone, but at least someone wanted me. Gray eyebrows and all." She laughed, but it was that same hollow laugh that didn't sound right at all.

We passed the sandwich place, and my stomach rumbled. I wanted lunch, but I knew Lily probably had a Lean Cuisine waiting for her back in the pantry.

"Can you ditch work for the rest of the afternoon? We can see a movie, or get some coffee, or just shop some more or something?" I knew the answer was no. For Lily, work was like an off-switch for everything else in her life. "I'll let you approve my boots."

"I can't. Ironically, we have an advertising meeting."

"With the guy?"

"Brad. No, he won't be there."

"Brad? You're sleeping with a Brad and a Chad?" This was too good to ignore.

"I guess you owe me for all the banjo cracks?" She elbowed me as we walked through Macy's, back to her office. I could feel palpable relief that I didn't have to go into the office. I was really digging this new four-day workweek. It helped me forget how mundane the day-to-day at Centrex was. Lily stopped outside Caribou Coffee. "Do I have to tell Chad?"

"You owe him nothing," I said, and believed it. Chad was an ass who put Lily last, no matter what else was on the list. She deserved way better than him, I'd thought so for years, but I also knew single life would not serve Lily well. She'd be crippled with self-loathing and loneliness if she knew she had an empty house to look forward to every night—and it wasn't as if this Brad guy was going to leave his wife and kids to keep her company. "You don't have to tell Chad, but you do need to end things with Brad. You already know that…"

"I do. It's just, I really like him."

"Because he's off-limits," I said, following as she started to walk toward the Centrex offices again. "You're not allowed to fall in love with him. But the fact that you're into someone else at all suggests there are some flaws in your relationship with Chad."

"Yeah," Lily pulled out her Blackberry as we passed the pizza place. "I know. I just don't want to be alone, and it's easy to stay with Chad. He's never here, but he's always there, you know?"

"Good God, Lil, that's depressing." I groaned. "You're gorgeous, you have perfect, symmetrical breasts, and could drink any intern under the table. I think those are all qualities that make you a perfectly suitable mate… on top of the fact that you're the kindest, most selfless person I know."

She hugged me. "I love you, you know?" She squeezed tighter. "Maybe we should just vow to stick together? We'd be good partners."

"I think not," I laughed, just as we came up to Centrex security. "I'm not looking for a life partner, remember? I had that with Erik."

Lily tsk-ed. "I am *so* not Erik. I am much more fun than Erik. Let's not compare me and your ex again, okay?"

Still laughing, I said, "Done. It'll never happen again."

"Have a good date! Don't forget to get the new boots. Not Aerosoles, right?"

"Not Aerosoles," I promised, and then she was gone.

Hours later, as I stood on a Welcome Winter! float squeezed between Dancer and Prancer and their excrement handlers, all I could think was: Thank goodness I bought new winter boots. The edgy, turquoise cowboy boots I'd bought for my date that night went unworn. So did my new dress from Saks. Instead, I was wearing my winter boots, borrowed furry snow pants, a velvet dress ringed in green tinsel, and a big floppy hat.

When Joe had come to pick me up that night for our date, he sheepishly asked if I'd be up for a slight change in plans. "Those boots are unbelievably sexy," he'd said. "But they may not have the heat you're gonna need."

The Dog Hounds had been called late that afternoon and asked to fill in for a local high school jazz band in that night's Welcome Winter! Parade. Flanders High School's jazz band had to back out because of an especially intense case of head lice that had hit the entire trumpet and trombone line the day before. The kids in the band weren't allowed to wear their marching hats, and the band had to back out. Lucky enough, the parade people had thought of the Dog Hounds as they were searching for a replacement musical act to perform on the reindeer float.

The Welcome Winter! Parade was a huge deal with Minnesotans, sort of like Groundhog Day, I guess. The parade was always held a few weeks before Thanksgiving, either to

celebrate the snow that had already fallen or to summon some
to get here already, and it was a huge honor to be invited to
participate. All the local news anchors hosted a float, and the
mayor walked alongside the Butter Queen from that summer's
State Fair. High school marching bands from around the state
were invited to participate, as well as popular Minnesota
musical acts.

"Come along," Joe had prodded, begging me to join him on
the float. "We'll have fun."

"No, no," I'd said, feeling certain. After all, Centrex people
brought their families to the parade. Cat usually brought her
girls to the parade. For all I knew, Erik could be with them on
an Uncle date. I thought about all the people I might know who
could see me up there, and shriveled down into my new boots
from the anticipated embarrassment. "I'll just meet you after,
okay?"

"Please come," he'd pleaded. "I know this is an
unconventional first date. But I promise it'll be fun." He could
see I wasn't tempted. I was giving him my skeptical face, and
on top of that, I could hear Anders chuckling in the living
room. Besides, it was obvious from the cute floaty dress and
fabulous boots that I wasn't dressed for a parade. "You'd get to
stand next to a reindeer."

Looking at Joe's adorable, puppy-dog face, all thoughts of
embarrassment and ridiculousness and foolishness drifted
away, and I realized maybe it *would* be fun. Why would I say
no? Had I ever been in a parade? No. Not once. So why not
start now? On a float with a band! It was kind of cool.

"Okay. But I need to change." Now Anders was laughing
heartily. One should not have a roommate at my age. It was far
too annoying to have to listen to their years of judgment.

"Yes!" Joe jumped up into the air, and I recognized one of
his band moves. "And yeah, you do need to change into
something a little warmer. But I thought ahead, and I've got it
taken care of already. My friend Mandy had something I could
borrow for you."

Mandy? As if I wanted to hear about *Mandy* on our date.
Whoever she was. Probably one of his many mommy-
conquests. I'd tried to forget about his reputation, but it came

flooding back at the mention of one woman's name. I decided to give him the benefit of the doubt, and smiled instead of getting irritated. "Can't I just wear my own warm clothes?"

"Nope."

"Okay. Do I have to wear anything embarrassing?"

"We have to get going—it might be better if I just show you when we get there."

And that's how I'd ended up first in the staging area, and eventually the reindeer float, at the Welcome Winter! Parade. I was wearing something that made me look like an elf in drag, or Mrs. Claus after a really, really wild night out. Also, I was having an amazing time. It was surprisingly fun to be on a musical float, and the Dog Hounds' songs were really catchy. I found myself singing along more than a couple times.

I'd been assigned the simple job of swaying along to the music and ringing a set of bells that resembled a giant snowflake. Unofficially, I'd also taken on the responsibility of alerting the poop scoopers every time Dasher and Donner (or was it Dancer and Prancer? There were two generic looking live reindeer wearing little sweaters beside me) eliminated on the fake snow next to my feet. But I was warm, Joe and the other guys in the band were charming and funny, and I felt a little bit like a local celebrity because I was associated with them.

What would Erik think of this? I thought back to all the times we'd done anything out of character or a little silly or embarrassing or (God forbid) inappropriate, and could count them on one hand. There was the one time when, drunk off too much wine from a box his Grandma had had for who knows how long, we'd gone skinny-dipping in the nursing home pool. It had been much more tense than fun, since Erik insisted on holding his hands between his legs and shouting, "Jump, will you? Just get in!" the whole time I was doubled-over with laughter on the side of the pool.

Then there was the time we'd stolen a bag of oranges from a luggage cart outside a swanky hotel in Paris. They looked sweet and delicious, and Erik had just had his wallet stolen. He was crabby and frustrated, and we were both hungry, so I'd secretly snuck off and taken them from some obviously wealthy traveler to save his mood. I guess, in retrospect, that one was all me, but since we eaten them together, I considered it a joint effort.

The only other thing I could think of was the weekend after he'd quit his job at Centrex, before he'd started the new one, when we'd gone away for one night to a small B&B that was a few hours' drive from our apartment. We'd had champagne and chicken cutlets and a wild rice pilaf, and then gone back to the room and tried a few positions from the sex book that had been left in the B&B's bedside table. We picked the three that looked the least complicated, but even still Erik had been frustrated and embarrassed the whole time. Finally, we reverted to our usual position and finished things up quickly, neatly, and efficiently. Erik had been so sore in the morning, he swore off sex for two weeks. Not a lot of guys would stick by that vow, but he hadn't had any issues with it.

Not that any of those things had anything to do with me standing next to a pile of reindeer dung on a winter parade float, but I felt so out-of-character that I couldn't help but compare then to now. When the parade ended, and we said goodbye to Comet and Cupid (or was it Donner and Blitzen?), Joe and I shuffled away from the float in our matching furry pants and he asked, "Do you want to stop back at your place to change? You get to pick the rest of the date, since I commandeered the beginning." He ruffled his hair, which was still poofed up into his Dog Hounds 'do. "Unfortunately, I'm going to have to wear a stocking cap all night, or you'll have to look at this. It takes a shower to make it flatten down again. So maybe we should save the fancy meal for next time? Do you like Mexican food?"

"Sure." Erik and I had tried both of the new, talked-about Mexican restaurants a few times, and I hadn't been impressed. But I was so hungry I'd eat almost anything. I glanced briefly at Joe's outfit—overalls and a cowboy hat. Hmm.

"I'm just going to get out of these overalls," he said, as though he'd read my mind, and I picked up a hint of the southern twang he used on stage.

"Okay. Where are you from, by the way?" We walked together toward a coffee shop just a block down from the parade route. Joe magically produced a pair of normal-looking jeans from under his overalls as we walked down the street. "I keep picking up a little hint of something southern..."

"That's all for show," he grinned. "We put on a little southern twang for shows, tell people we're from Boulder for the rugged credibility, but it's all lies. We like to shroud ourselves in an air of mystery. I'm from Detroit—which isn't as exciting as Nashville or Boulder, sadly."

He walked off in the direction of the coffee shop bathroom, while I stood in the door letting Journey flow through my head. *He was a city boy, born and raised in South Detroit.* I wasn't opposed enough to the concept of fate (versus planning) to reject the idea that Joe *had* been waiting for me after my bus moment the previous weekend. He was the city boy Journey had been singing about, just for me!

As excited as I was by this new discovery, I swore I would not, could not, tell anyone about my Journey awakening. Especially not Joe. He would think I was a giant kook. Of course, I was wearing furry snow pants and a velvet dress, so I wasn't entirely sure how much lower I could go.

When he returned from the rest room, I saw he was still wearing his checkered Dog Hounds shirt, but now his lean hips were wrapped inside an especially flattering pair of Levis. He'd put a brown stocking cap over his puffy curls and the whole look made me think of a rugged, Lands End model. I was suddenly tempted to buy a puffy vest and a pair of fleece-lined jeans and suggest we take a dog out hiking in the woods.

"Ready?" he asked with a big smile. Oh man, he was hot. I was on a date with a sexy lumberjack. I wanted to curl up in front of a fire with him.

"I'm just going to pull off these snow pants," I said, while trying not to stare.

When I returned from the restroom wearing the jeans I'd worn under my costume, along with the velvet, tinsel-trimmed mini-dress, he said, "You're still very sparkly. I appreciate your efforts to dress so fancy for our date. The tinsel looks particularly fine with your hair."

I bowed, and we walked together out into the crowded streets toward Joe's car.

"So, Stella, what do you want to be when you grow up?"

I gave him a funny look. "When I grow up? I hate to say it, but I am grown up. I'm there."

"You're doing exactly what you want to do for the rest of your life?" he asked, pulling his parking ramp ticket out of the overalls now draped over his arm. "Doesn't everyone have big plans? Hopes for the future?"

"Well, yeah, I guess," I said, wondering if it was unusual that I'd only planned my life out through age thirty or so. "I had goals, but I completed most of them already."

"What do you mean, 'completed them?' Like, you have a list hidden under your mattress?" He laughed, sounding smug again.

"Yep. I do."

We were in the car now, and Joe turned his key to start the ignition. He didn't drive anywhere, just sat there waiting for the heat to kick in while he stared at me. "You have an actual, physical list of life's goals?" He was smirking again, and it pissed me off. What right did he have to make fun of my list?

"Yes, I do have an actual list. I made it when I was fifteen."

"The list hasn't changed since then?"

"Not really. It was a very well thought out list. I'm thorough."

He reached his hand behind my seat to reverse out of his spot. Before he shifted the car back into drive, he stopped and looked at me. "Was dating a medium-sized, handsome man in overalls on the list?" He asked this very seriously, but then laughed.

"Actually, no," I said, laughing along with him.

"Then I guess it's good I changed out of the overalls, eh?"

"Your fate would have been sealed if you'd left them on," I teased. As we pulled out of the parking lot, I asked, "So you mean to say you don't consider yourself grown up yet?"

"Not in the least. I play songs for children. It kinda keeps you from growing up in a lot of ways."

"But you're also an attorney. And divorced. Don't both of those things have a tendency to age you?"

"Sure," he shrugged. "But then you rinse them away and start again. It feels good to start fresh, rewind a few years, shuffle hopes and dreams and all that funny business. If I'd had a list, I would have rewritten it about thirty times by now. The life I wanted when I was fifteen would have left me stoned on someone's couch, testing Playstation games for a living. Oh, and there would have been Cheetos. Lots of Cheetos."

"You had big ambitions."

"I've changed a lot since then." He broke off, and I felt like there was something more he wanted to say. But it went unspoken and a moment later, we turned into a parking lot attached to a small, ramshackle-looking Mexican restaurant. "This okay?" Joe asked, noticing I was eyeing the restaurant warily.

"Sure, it's fine. I've never been here before."

"Best Mexican food north of Kansas City," he said, opening his door. "So, Stella, how are you so confident you knew how your life should go when you were just fifteen? Don't you ever wonder if maybe you sold yourself short?" He held the door for me, and we both stomped our icy, muddy boots on the mat inside the door. The inside of the restaurant was minimally-decorated, with plain wooden booths surrounding a few tables covered in vinyl tablecloths. The lighting was dim and sparse, and I was immediately reminded of a truck stop restaurant Erik and I had once stopped at while we were driving back from somewhere. When I was with Erik, we had promptly left any restaurant that looked like this. He refused to eat anywhere that appeared even a little bit sketchy. This place was definitely sketchy.

"I didn't sell myself short," I said finally. "My mom died when I was fifteen, and it gave me a lot of time to think about what's important in life. For a couple months I dwelled on the things she never got to do, and it got me thinking about what the must-haves were for me."

"What are some of the highlights?"

I thought through my list, and realized there was nothing worth sharing. "Sadly, there aren't really any highlights. I didn't really give myself very lofty goals." As I said it, I recognized I was coming across as a real whiner. "I guess I've always just been realistic—I never asked for much, just a good job, good friends, maybe a trip to Italy..."

"A trip to Italy is on the list?"

"No, it's not on the original list, but that's one of my later-life addendums. A P.S., if you will. I didn't recognize the allure of Italy until I realized Italian food was more than just a jar of red sauce poured over spaghetti with a little dried parmesan sprinkled on top."

Joe cringed. "Sounds delicious."

"That was my dad's idea of ethnic cooking."

The waitress came and took our order. I picked enchiladas mole, and Joe ordered fajitas. We both ordered Jarritos soda since the restaurant didn't appear to have a beer and wine license. Obviously, Joe wasn't trying to get me drunk tonight. Chalk one up to class.

"So," Joe said, as soon as our drinks arrived, along with paper-wrapped straws. Joe paused, ripped off the top of his straw wrapper, and blew the rest of the wrapper at me. It was oddly amusing, rather than juvenile and annoying. Maybe it was just the expression on his face, one of simple glee and unwarranted pride that went along with the action. "A good job, good friends... that's it? That was—is—your life list?"

"There's more to it than that. Like I said, those are the highlights."

"Is there anything you haven't accomplished? What's your big regret?" He put his chin on his hands, and his elbows on the table. His eyes were fixed on mine, and my stomach fluttered. His lips were still red and a little dry from singing outside on the float that night, and he licked them quickly as we looked at each other. Inadvertently, my eyes flickered to his mouth. Joe must have noticed, since he pressed his lips together, then smiled in that coy way he often did.

"Getting married," I said, and instantly regretted it. We were on our first date, and I'd just come out with the fact that my biggest unfinished goal in life was to get married. Hello, potential lover, would you like to get married and have my children in, say, forty-five minutes? "I mean, not that I need to get married, like, now. But I would like to. Someday. Maybe. Kids weren't on the list, though. I never felt a desperate need for kids."

He laughed, obviously aware of my discomfort. "Glad we got that conversation out of the way on the first date." He was still chuckling. I reddened and took a huge swallow of my soda. "You said you just broke up with someone?"

"After twelve years, yeah."

Joe whistled. "That's a long time."

"Yep."

"He wasn't into the idea of a wedding?"

"Nope."

"This line of questioning is making you pretty uncomfortable, isn't it?"

"A bit." I grinned. Blessedly, our food finally arrived, and I took a big, gulping bite so I could stop talking. I was sure the cheese hanging off the side of my mouth was every bit as sexy as I'd always wished I would be on a first date. Not that I'd really imagined a lot of first dates, seeing as how I wouldn't have expected to be on any more of them at this stage of my life. After I swallowed, I said quietly, "I'm sorry I brought up the marriage thing—"

Joe cut me off. "I think I brought up marriage, actually. Last week, I seem to remember talking your ear off about my own crooked concept of happily ever after."

I did remember that. In fact, his notion of sticking with your ever after through bad and worse is the reason I'd left Erik's office earlier in the week with my tights in a bunch.

"Yeah, I've been thinking about what you said a lot," I said aloud, not copping to the fact that my idea of a reconciliation was a quickie on my ex's desk. "Do you really think it's better to stick it out and try and try and try again, even if you're not really, truly happy, in the hope that maybe you can change a person? Isn't that a stupid notion?"

"Yeah, it's very stupid."

"So why did you say it?" I didn't want to believe I'd misheard him. His words about regretting his divorce were a big part of the reason I'd had amazing, new-feeling sex with Erik. "Didn't you say it's better to keep building on the foundation than to start over completely?"

"Did I?" Joe shrugged. "Yeah, that sounds like me. But I go back and forth a lot."

I seethed as he wrapped sizzling meat and veggies in a tortilla. It bugged me that he was being so wishy-washy. You can't just up and change your ideals on a whim! He had told me he wished he had spent more time working through his marriage, that he regretted leaving something established for the great unknown. I had heard what he'd said, and it had led me to reconsider a future with Erik. It had led me to let my ex into my undies.

"You're giving me looks," Joe said, gesturing at my face with his fajita.

"What kind of looks?"

"Weird looks." Wow, that was flattering. "Did what I say really have that much impact on you? You know I'm not some kind of relationship expert, right?"

"I don't know. You have been married and divorced. That should give you some amount of savvy."

"It just means I've made bad choices, then adapted accordingly. I firmly believe you can't plan life, and you have to go with the flow. We sing about it."

"In the band? You sing a song about divorce?"

"About going with the flow." He sang a few bars of a song, and I was reminded of his charisma up on stage. Why was that charisma morphing into ignorance and immaturity in a one-on-one situation? As an adult, I would fully expect Joe to have stronger plans in place for himself. Like… well, like Erik. Erik had plans and goals and a road map. But he wasn't acting on them. Unlike Joe, who'd apparently had no long-term goals for himself, but had just up and quit everything to be in a children's rockabilly band.

"Do you ever think about the future? Like, five, ten years down the line? Don't you feel like you need to put plans in place to get yourself to the next hurdle?"

"Hurdle?" Joe leaned back against his booth seat and set his fajita down on top of the salsa and sour cream-laden plate that sat in front of him. "I don't really see life as something filled with hurdles to get through. I like to map my course with lots of blank spots, and see what lies around the next bend. Like hashing—you've gotta get somewhere eventually, but there are plenty of stops for fun along the way. Have you ever been on a hash?"

"Are you talking about drugs?"

He laughed, short and loud. "No. Hashing is basically running while socializing, with a little beer thrown in. One of the guys in my hash group once called us drinkers with a running problem, or something like that."

"Running with beer?"

"If you're going to run, there might as well be something good keeping you going. That's my theory, anyway. We drink a little before, during, and after. Keeps you going."

Now I was sure I was dating a child. Drinking before, during, and after running sounded a lot like hazing at a frat house. Grown men went out for nice dinners with their friends, they served on neighborhood association boards, they volunteered with their mother at the soup kitchen on Christmas Eve. At least, that's what Erik had led me to believe.

I gritted my teeth. Once again, I was letting Erik's opinions and views on life dictate my own. Instead of dwelling on how strange and juvenile this hash thing sounded, I let myself wonder if Joe wore the brown stocking cap while he was running. He looked hot in that cap. I knew he had great legs, too. The little bit I could see through the jeans had gotten me really curious, and I wished I had an excuse to see him in shorts—or maybe those tight, shiny running pants Lily always made fun of. Or nothing at all.

"Do you think I could go with you sometime?" I had not planned to say that, but there it was, and now I couldn't take it back. I didn't run. I only went to water aerobics. I hadn't even tried to step foot on the treadmill since a few days after the yoga incident—and now I was thinking of downing a beer and hitting the pavement?

"We love newbies," Joe said, and suddenly my only hope was that the date would go so off track from here on out that I wouldn't ever have to do this hashing thing. "Come with me on Sunday. I mean, if you really want to. It's going to be totally different than anything you've ever done before, I can pretty much guarantee that."

I nodded hesitantly.

"If it's not your thing, just speak up," he said earnestly, "You never have to come again. If you're not a runner, that's cool, too. We have a big group that walks the route. It's really just about hanging out. No competitions, I promise."

"Okay, I'll try it."

"Excellent. Does this check off another box on your list?"

"Strangely, hashing didn't make it onto the list." I laughed.

"So we're veering off plan? Is that allowed?"

"Come on!" I said, still laughing despite the fact he was making fun of me. "It's not like I refuse to do things that aren't on my list. It's just that I want to make sure I *do* do everything that *is* on my list."

"I can't stop thinking about the logistics of this list," Joe said, leaning in toward me across the table. "Does it actually exist? Be straight with me. Is it, like, written in purple marker and hidden in a diary somewhere? Or is it just a vague thing that lives in your head?"

"The list is hand-written, and I keep it under my bed." I pushed my plate away, and relaxed back, watching Joe finish his entire skillet of fajitas. "Inside a yearbook. It's written in a slim, black sharpie marker."

"I'd like to see it."

"I don't show it to people." I narrowed my eyes flirtatiously. Even though I was acting coy and speaking playfully, I was actually very serious. I'd never shown anyone my list—not Erik, not Lily, not Cat. It was sort of sacred. Like the wedding dress I had stuffed inside a garment bag behind the business suits I hoped to someday be able to fit in again. The wedding dress had been an accident—a spur-of-the-moment mistake I'd foolishly swept into my arms at a trunk sale I'd snuck off to one day in my late-twenties. I hid the dress inside the winter clothes' box in my trunk for almost a week before I had the nerve to sneak it into my closet where I hoped it would stay hidden from Erik.

"Fair enough," Joe eased up. "If it makes you feel better, I have a list of my own."

"You do? Where do you keep it?"

"In my head," Joe reached up under his hat and scratched at the hair behind his ear, as if saying the word "head" had reminded him of an itch that had been nagging at him. "But I know what's on it. It's a list of things I've done and never want to do again."

"What's on *your* list?" I was curious to know more about how he ticked. We obviously weren't a great match in any of the traditional categories, and I still couldn't figure out why he'd asked me out in the first place. There was no way I was his type, and even though he was hot, funny, and made me feel relaxed and comfortable, I didn't know that he was mine. "Can you give me the highlights?"

"Marrying a lawyer is definitely on my list of things to never do again," he said, cracking himself up. "Practicing law is on there, but I guess I have to scratch that off if I'm ever really hard up for cash again. Dating Tara Gayle would be on the list, as well."

"Who's Tara Gayle? Your ex-wife? Did she make the list twice?"

"High school girlfriend. She really messed me up."

"More than your wife?"

"That's a tough call. One messed with me as an adult, one fucked me up as a vulnerable, stupid teenager. But you'll notice they're both at the top of my list, so each was traumatic in one way or another."

"You seem to have an issue with the women in your life," I teased, hoping he wouldn't take it the wrong way. "Maybe you have a tendency to choose bad ones?"

"Maybe so," he said with an adorably crooked, cocky smile. He studied me in the dim light of the Mexican restaurant, and it took every bit of willpower to keep me from reaching over to wipe off the dab of sour cream stuck just under his lower lip. "We'll see how this goes. Here's what I'm hoping: I'm hoping *I* make your list instead of *you* making it onto mine. That would be a better way for all of this to work out, wouldn't it?"

CHAPTER TWELVE

"So do you really like him?" Anders asked, reminding me, as he always did, of a very good girlfriend rather than the straight man he claimed to be. "Are you going to sleep with him to find out if he's a little less childish and immature when he's in bed?"

I slapped my roommate hard on the shoulder, despite the fact that he'd gone out in the sub-zero temperatures to bring us fresh baguettes and steaming lattes from our neighborhood bakery before I woke up. I had discovered there were a few perks of having a roommate who wasn't Erik. Anders couldn't make coffee, but he was kind enough to go out and get it for us. Buying it fresh each morning kept the house from reeking like a coffee shop, so I was finding I didn't miss Erik's morning brew. For some reason, even my panties had smelled like roasted coffee when I'd lived at Erik's. Coffee crept into the pores of a house and stunk it up, but my own house smelled like lemon fragrance sticks instead.

"I do like him, but he's just so different from—well, different from Erik. I don't really know what to make of him."

"Did he kiss you?"

"No," I thought back to the end of the date the night before, and how Joe had just promised to pick me up at one on Sunday afternoon for the hash. Then he'd given me one of his smirking grins, told me he'd had a fun time, and politely waited in his car at the curb to make sure I made it inside my front door. All signs of a decent date, but there had been nothing physical, nothing even remotely related to physicality. "I can't figure out what he thinks about me," I said. "Cat said he was this huge player, but I don't get the sense that he's trying to mack on me—"

"Mack on?" Anders cut me off, laughing hysterically. "When was the last time you talked about guys and hooking up?"

"So my slang is off," I waved my hand in the air, baguette held high and proud. "At least I'm trying! Anyway, I don't feel like he's trying to be super pervy with me or anything."

"What a glowing recommendation. 'He's not trying to be pervy?' Does he seem like the kind of guy who might be pervy? Because I think we should talk, if that's the direction you're headed."

"No, he seems really nice. Kind of commitment-phobic, but very fun. A good fling."

"Except there's no macking," Anders cracked himself up. "Isn't it a little tough to have a fling if there isn't any macking?"

"You suck." My cell phone started to ring, and I reached over him to grab it. "What I'm saying is, there's potential, but I'm not sure yet." I peeked at the caller ID before answering. Cat. I had been avoiding Cat all week, ever since I'd flinged— flung?—with her brother on Monday. I didn't want to talk to her, after getting the third degree from Laurel the afternoon it had happened. I never thought I'd be in a position where I had to avoid one of my best friends.

"Hey, Cat," I said, trying to act cool. "How's Er—I mean, how's everything?" God, I was not cool.

"Hi, Auntie Stella," Pippa's voice shouted through the phone. "Can you come for dinner tonight?"

"Oh, hi, Pip," I said, missing her desperately.

"Can you?"

"Sure, Pippa, I can come over for dinner. Does your mom know you're inviting me?"

"Yeah, Mom knows. She said I could invite you. She told me to tell you it's a party. Will you be my date?"

"Absolutely. Can I talk to your mom?"

Cat breathed, "Hey, Stell," into the phone, and I heard her dictating instructions to the au pair and her daughters in the background. For someone who didn't work, had live-in help, and a weekly housekeeper, Cat seemed awfully stressed all the time. I imagined half her life was spent managing Laurel's whims and wonderings. "You're sure you're cool with this?" she asked, sounding hurried and harried. "The girls have been asking to see you all week. I wouldn't ask, but—"

"It's fine. Great. I miss them, Cat. It will be good to see you, too."

She paused. "Okay. Six, okay? We're eating early so we can get the girls fed and put them in front of a movie. You can hang out as long as you want, 'kay?"

"Okay," I agreed.

"You rock. Bring a bottle of wine if you want, but you can just bring yourself if that's easier."

"I'll see you tonight—and I'm on the wine."

"Later, babe."

"Later," I said to a dead phone. I turned to Anders and said, "I'm not sure where this thing—or whatever it is—with Joe the singer is going, but my, oh my, is he hot. So I'm not saying never. I'm just saying, I'm still treading lightly."

"But if he macks on you, you'll be up for it?"

I stood up and made my way to the shower. "Mack away," I said, acting like it was such an easy thing to say. But even as I thought about kissing Joe, I was thinking about Erik and how it had felt to touch him again on Monday. Why was it so hard to just let go?

When I arrived at Cat's house later that night, I ran into the girls' au pair, Aurelie, outside in the driveway. She had been dispatched to fetch a box of Annie's shells and cheese, since Pippa was apparently refusing to eat the spaghetti Bolognese Cat had prepared. I let myself inside assuming everything would be so frantic, no one would hear the bell.

As I pulled off my shoes and placed them neatly on the shoe rack near the front door, I should have realized it was far too loud for a regular Saturday night at Cat and Trav's house. I should have noticed the spare adult voices, and should certainly have recognized all of them. But I guess I just wasn't paying close enough attention, because when I walked through the dining room and toward the large, Italian-style kitchen, I was shocked to see Erik standing at the stove, his back to me.

I paused in the doorway, tucking into the shadowy space between the dining room and the kitchen's pantry area, and surveyed the scene. Erik was stirring something, and was wearing his classic chinos with a striped blue and white shirt that he was convinced gave him an edge. Really, it just looked like a heaping portion of Gap stirred into a side of Banana Republic, but that was thrilling for Erik. The buttons were in unconventional locations on the sleeves, allowing him to roll them up to three-quarter-length and strike a casual-yet-chic pose.

As I stared at him wearing his marketing uniform, I couldn't help but notice his arms looked more cut and his rear end looked the teensiest bit more tempting than it ever had before. I'd never been tempted to squeeze it, but I suddenly wanted to stride right over there and give it a little rub. I bit my lip, realizing I was thinking about Erik-from-Monday instead of Erik-from-the-last-twelve-years, and I hated how I'd started to replace my old memories with a better, fresher option. He was not one morning of sex. He was years worth of regret and lost independence. I broke up with him. It wasn't a hasty decision. There were reasons, and I was finally almost able to recognize myself—digging out from under years of someone else's dreams—emerging from beneath an easily-influenced shell.

He wasn't cute.

He wasn't spontaneous, or passionate, or, for that matter, really all that fun.

He made me believe my life was as good as it was ever going to get.

But because he belonged in the family I wanted to continue to be a part of, I would have to learn to coexist with him without it being weird. I knew I was going to have to talk to him about what had happened on Monday, and then I simply needed to move on. Because he was the same tight-assed, self-centered, stuck-in-a-rut ex boyfriend I'd left months before—and I needed to remember we were over. For good.

I stepped into the kitchen. Pippa noticed me first and came charging over to say hello. I bent down to give her a hug, and Heidi yelled out, "Stay away from Pip, Stella. She's pukey."

But I had already squeezed her and had her tipped halfway upside down when I heard a disconcerting gurgle. Suddenly, I felt a drizzle of something warm hit the back of my neck, and felt wet stickiness seeping down my shoulder and soaking through my shirt.

"Sorry," Pippa said when I had her upright again. She grinned apologetically, then chirped, "I feel better."

"Oh, Stella, I'm so sorry," Cat said, rushing over. "This started about half and hour ago—I thought it was something she ate, but I called a couple of the other moms and found out there's a bug going around this weekend. She feels fine otherwise, but it has been hurl, hurl, hurl for the last half hour. We have a towel set up for her over there in the corner. She's supposed to go there if she feels any more coming on."

I reached up and felt my neck, which was covered in a thin, hot, runny goo. My shirt was stuck to my back and I could smell the putrid acidity of booze-free puke wafting around me.

"S'okay," I muttered, trying to put on a brave face for Pippa's sake. I could see why the girl didn't want to eat spaghetti Bolognese—I could only imagine what that would look like coming back up. Of course, little macaroni shells wouldn't be much better, but at least she wanted to eat something. "It will wash out."

Erik walked over and dabbed at my neck with a damp kitchen towel. He gave me a timid smile, and I did my best to shoot a casual, hey-you grin back at him. But there was something about the tenderness and generosity of wiping vomit from my neck that made my stomach twist, and not in a sick sort of way. Seeing him again, up close, in familiar surroundings, made me want him. I wanted to touch him and feel that comfort and security in the way he touched me again.

I grabbed the towel from his hand and muttered, "Thanks."

"No problem." He walked to the sink to wash his hands, and I could see him watching me as everyone bustled around me cleaning remnants of Pippa's puke from the floor. In my attempt to avoid his gaze, I looked around the kitchen, and only then did I notice Laurel and Peter were sitting on bar stools at the kitchen island, watching everything with great interest.

"Hello, Laurel," I said, trying to hide my surprise. What I'd mistakenly thought was a quiet night at home with Cat, the girls, and Travis had turned into a full-family affair. "Hi, Peter."

They both raised their wine glasses at me and muttered their hellos.

"Would you like a glass of wine, dear?" Laurel said, pushing a bottle of Malbec toward me. It was one of my favorites, a variety I hadn't had in quite some time—since I'd left Erik's probably. "You look like you could use a glass or two of wine." She laughed, and waved her hand in front of her nose. "Perhaps it would be nice for all of us if you could find a fresh shirt first?"

"Oh, yeah, absolutely," I said, only then remembering the two bottles of wine I'd brought. A Cabernet and a Tempranillo—two of the new wines Anders had been educating me on. "I'll change, and then I think I'll open one of these."

Erik looked at the wines, and hastily said, "I'd like to try one. I never have anything other than Malbec. I'd like to give the Tempranillo a try." He was obviously waiting for me to notice his big, rebellious wine moment. Erik took the wine bottles from my hand and set them on the counter. "Let me help you clean up first."

The last thing I wanted was for him to come upstairs with me to clean up. But I also knew we needed to talk, and I didn't want to sit through an entire dinner without having talked to him about what had happened on Monday. It was awkward, I was dwelling on it, he was probably embarrassed about it… we had to talk.

"Okay, that would be great. Cat, can I use any towel from the linen closet?"

"Of course, of course," she muttered, pulling a loaf of burning bread from the oven. "Take your time. Dinner is a shit-show. We might be ordering in." She bustled around the kitchen, and Travis helpfully followed behind her swatting at her butt with a kitchen towel every time she bent over. "I've royally fucked this up. Shit! Sorry, girls. You didn't hear that."

Erik and I walked upstairs in silence, and I tried hard to think about Joe, the cute guy Lily had introduced me to from legal, anything to keep me distracted from thoughts of Erik, his office, and Monday. Finally, when we got upstairs, he followed me into the bathroom and I turned to him. "I'm really sorry about what happened on Monday. It was a mistake."

He looked at me, and I could see frustration, disappointment, and hurt in his eyes. "It wasn't a mistake," he said. "Monday was amazing."

"It was amazing, but it was a mistake. We're not getting back together, and how are either of us supposed to move on when we do something stupid like that?" I began to unbutton my shirt, momentarily forgetting I didn't do that in front of Erik anymore. I paused, and opted against buttoning up the two buttons that were already open. "I have to get this shirt off. Can you give me a sec?"

Erik paused, his eyes glancing briefly toward my nearly-exposed chest, but then he stepped into the hallway and closed the door behind him. As I pulled my shirt off, I looked at myself in the huge mirror that lined one whole wall of Cat's guest bathroom. I could tell the water aerobics were starting to melt away some of the weight I'd gained after the yoga accident. I'd sworn off scales years ago, gauging my weight only by the fit of my jeans and the feel of my bras. I was never going to be a rail, like Lily, or have a boyish figure, like Cat, but I was back to feeling and looking pretty good for me.

I dropped my shirt in the sink and grabbed a hand towel from under the sink. I turned the water on to fill the basin so I could soak my soiled shirt. I wet the towel and began to dab at the skin hit with Pippa's puke missile. After a few seconds of scrubbing, I could tell I wasn't going to be able to reach most of my back, where I'd been hit the hardest. I thought briefly about hopping into the shower, but decided to just suck it up and wrapped myself in a towel before calling Erik in from the hallway.

"Can you get my back with the wet towel?" I asked.

"Oh, yeah, sure," he muttered, obviously as freaked out about the situation as I was. "How far did it go?"

"Pretty much all the way down," I said, shivering from my bare skin, the cool water, and Erik's touch.

I could see Erik's reflection in the mirror. He was staring off into the distance, blinking rapidly, trying hard not to stare at my exposed shoulders. I never thought of my shoulders as sexy before, but they suddenly felt like the bazooka of sex weapons. Powerful, strong, and succulent. I could almost feel Erik's lips on them when I noticed his eyes flick to the bare skin peeking up over my towel.

"I think you're going to have to unwrap your towel a bit," he said quietly. "Maybe you can just hold it up in front of you? If you're uncomfortable about taking it off in front of me?"

I laughed nervously. I knew my very put-together ex-boyfriend could handle himself around my well-covered breasts. I let the towel slip to the floor, and felt Erik's hands wrap around my chest just as quickly as it lost its towel covering.

Someone—me?—sucked in a quick, startled breath, and then my body melted against him, my skin instantly soaking in the warmth coming through his shirt. I looked up, into the mirror, and watched his eyes on mine as I felt his hand slip up under my bra. My eyes closed momentarily, and I moaned despite my head telling me to stop what was going on with my body. But instead of listening to reason, I reached over with my foot and kicked the door closed. Erik pressed himself against me and buried his face in my neck.

"We're doing it again," I whispered. "This isn't like us."

"It is now," Erik muttered back. "I forgot how sexy you are. I feel like I've missed years of these gorgeous breasts. I have to make up for lost time." He grinned, something I'd never really seen Erik do, and turned me around so he could put his lips between my breasts and work his way up. I leaned against the countertop and felt the water—still running in the sink—spilling out across the vanity. While Erik took my bra off and ran his tongue over each of my nipples, I shuddered and tried to keep enough control over my body to turn the water off.

"Do you think you need a shower?" he murmured in my ear. "It might help get you clean."

I'd never heard Erik talk like this, I'd never heard him suggest something so... hot... spontaneous... tempting. Ever.

"Yes, I think you're right," I said, making my way down his chest, pulling at his shirt buttons, and kissing a trail down his body. When I got to his pants, I pulled them open and eased the fabric past his hips. I reached around and squeezed at the butt that had been so tempting in the kitchen earlier in the night. He groaned and tugged at my hair. Slowly, deliberately, I pulled his boxers down, inch by inch, until I could feel him pressing against the fabric holding him in. I slipped the boxers down past his knees and made my way back up again with my mouth, kissing first his knees, his thighs, his hips. Until finally, I took him in my mouth and felt his body relax when he pressed into me.

I was only there for a few seconds before he stepped away and helped me take off the rest of my clothes and together we stepped into the shower. He turned on the water and it flowed over us, the water loud enough to drown out every bit of doubt and worry that crept into my mind. It felt good, and my body desperately wanted to be there. I wanted to be with Erik like this, I wanted to know him like this. I wanted him to know *me* like this.

He pushed my hair out of my eyes as water streamed down from overhead, soaking us. I'd never felt this kind of intensity with him, and I could only imagine part of the reason this was happening was because it was wrong. I was cheating. Cheating on my new life with my old life.

When my mind finally broke through to remind me of this, I stepped back and stared at Erik through the curtain of water that poured down from above us. "We have to stop," I said, but my body was screaming at me to continue. "I can't."

"You can. We are," Erik said, and his gentle touch felt like a million kisses on my cheek. "Enjoy this. We deserve it."

We did deserve it. Erik and I deserved the opportunity to look back on our lives together with this as the grand finale. If he was willing to carry on with no consequences, mindful of the boundaries, knowing this wasn't going to go anywhere, then I could, too.

"Maybe you're right," I said. When I smiled, he took me in his arms again. His skin was hot, and he was wet and slippery from the shower. Still, something felt wrong. It was impossible to let myself relax when I knew I was cheating on myself. I pushed away and said, "No. We really need to stop."

Erik stepped back. He nodded, then we sat together on the floor of the bathtub, letting the water run over us while I relaxed into his familiar chest and felt his breath rising and falling beneath me.

Though it felt like we'd been upstairs for hours, only about fifteen minutes had passed while we were in the bathroom getting me cleaned up. Even still, I wasn't looking forward to going back downstairs to face the family and the curious looks on everyone's faces. While Erik dried his hair and re-dressed, I sat on the closed toilet, wrapped in a towel. I watched him style his hair and put himself together, impressed at his ability to make himself look precise again in less than five minutes. No one would ever know what he'd been up to just moments before. The thought made me smile, and he turned to me, his expression curious.

"I'm just thinking about your mom," I said, laughing. "What if they knew what we'd been doing up here?"

"No one will know," he assured me, coming over to place a kiss on top of my head. "They just think we're up here talking."

"We're not."

"No, we're not." He stopped preening and gazed at me in the mirror. "Do you want to talk?"

"Not particularly."

"I'm not going to make you do anything you don't want to do," he said, and I wondered where *this* guy had been during the last ten years. "I want you back, for good, but we can talk when you're ready. If you want."

"Thanks," I said, standing up to put on my clothes. "I don't have a shirt," I said, only then realizing that even though I was clean, my shirt was still soaking wet in the sink.

"You could come to dinner in that," Erik teased. He leaned over to kiss my bare shoulder. Oddly, the gesture felt cold and awkward outside the heat of the moment. I pulled the towel tighter around me. Erik stepped back and began to unbutton his own button-down. "Here," he said. "Wear mine. I'll just wear my t-shirt." Erik always wore a plain, white t-shirt under his dress shirts. Always. He said it extended the life of the nice shirts. I was glad he had offered me the top shirt and not the undershirt—wearing his undershirt felt too intimate. I could come *this* close to fucking my ex in his sister's shower, but wearing his shirt felt too intimate. There was something wrong with this picture.

I took his shirt and began to button it over the bulky towel still wrapped around my body. It didn't really fit, but I was relieved to find I could at least close the buttons over my breasts. He and I weighed roughly the same, and I'd always worried someday his clothes wouldn't fit me anymore. It was some stupid measure of femininity that had led me to believe a girl should fit in her boyfriend's clothes.

I suddenly wondered what I would look like in Joe's overalls. I bet they'd be cute, in a rural sort of way. I'd sort of like to see them *off* him even more than I'd want to see them *on* me. Ack! I was thinking about another guy five minutes after nearly having sex with my ex. Maybe it was the sexual tension I'd felt building up the whole night before with Joe that had led to what had just happened with Erik.

"Are you good now?" Erik asked, and when I nodded, he smiled and slipped out the door to let me finish dressing alone. I could hear his footsteps in the hall and then on the stairs, and I knew I was alone.

I breathed out and studied my wet hair and my body inside Erik's shirt in the mirror. I tried hard to smile at myself, but found I couldn't. I wasn't proud of what had just happened, and it sickened me to think of how good it had felt. I wondered, for the millionth time in the last few months, what right I felt I had to leave Erik in the first place.

A timid knock at the door pulled me out of the dumps, and I opened the door to find Pippa grinning at me.

"Dinner's ready, Stella," she said. "Mom ordered pizza. You can have a bite of my mac and cheese, if you want."

I grinned at her and took one last swipe at my hair to try to put it in place. "You know what, Pip? I'm not sharing anything with you. You puked on me, remember?"

"You look cute in Uncle Erik's shirt," she said, fingering the fabric around my wrist. "Grandma says you miss him. Mom told her she was reaching. What's reaching?"

I ignored the question and changed the subject to ask Pippa about school. She told me stories of her classmates all the way back down the stairs. When we got to the dining room, everyone was seated around the table and the only two spots that were left open were on either side of Erik. I guess that took away a bit of choice. Looked like this was going to be an awful lot like old times. But in old times, there was a zero-percent chance Erik and I would have ever had a quickie in the bathroom before a meal. So I guess that changed the stakes a bit. I was feeling strangely relaxed and also increasingly awkward as I settled into my seat at the table.

The whole family was looking at me—were they all giving me a *look*?—and Erik was grinning at me like a fool. His hair was dry and put back into place—the only thing different about him was his missing shirt (perfectly reasonable explanation there)—but he was also wearing that stupid, sex-induced grin. *Stop grinning.* I twitched involuntarily and glanced around. I realized Laurel and Peter were focused on the texture of the cheese atop their pizza and Cat was fully-focused on forcing Heidi to put something other than candy corn on her plate. No one was looking at Erik except for me.

Still grinning, he slid a piece of pizza onto my plate. "Plain cheese, right?" he asked.

"Actually, I was going to try the olive and pepperoni," I said, slipping the slice back into the box. I replaced the pizza on my plate with a thin sliver from the other box.

"You don't like olives," Erik said. He was still grinning. "I mean, you never liked olives before. At least, not olives without blue cheese stuffed in them."

"I think I do now."

"You think?" Erik teased. "Or you do?"

"I do. I do like olives." This was ridiculous. I was trying to pick a fight with him about what kind of food I liked. I did *not* like olives, but for some reason I was hell-bent on showing him I'd changed since I'd left him. I wanted to show him I'd moved on. Olives were symbolic of other things.

"In fact, I love olives. They're my favorite." I took a big bite and smiled through the salty grossness. It wasn't as bad as I would have expected, and it wasn't as hard to pretend I was really digging the pizza as it could have been.

Erik watched me closely as I took a second, then a third bite. His brow was pinched together, obviously concerned my palette had evolved in our days apart. That this should bother him said something about the nature of our relationship. I could change. I *should* change. Why hadn't he ever let me change?

As I chewed my way through my first slice, Laurel looked around at everyone gleefully and said, "I have news!"

Knowing Laurel, this announcement could precede anything from, "My colorist has contracted a case of herpes," to "I've been diagnosed with cancer, and you'll all need to rest at my bedside for the next three weeks while I die." Laurel got great joy out of imparting any kind of information she had and no one else did.

"I've been selected," Laurel spoke slowly, pausing for effect. "I have been *chosen* as one of the featured participants in Cooking Circle, a new series on the Foodie Network!"

"You're kidding!" Cat said, putting down the spoonful of Macaroni and Cheese she'd been trying to shove into Pippa's mouth. "Mom, that's amazing."

"No, I am not kidding," Laurel said snippily. "They chose me, out of hundreds of thousands—possibly millions!—of applicants."

"So what are you going to have to do? Will they fly you to New York?" Erik looked proud of his mom, which reminded me he really was a good man, deep down.

"Actually, they'll be sending a film crew here, to our house. They're going to film me making a family dinner." She paused, took a sip of her wine, and looked directly at me. "They asked that both of my daughters be on hand for the filming."

Cat glanced at me, and I thought I saw a smile tugging at her mouth. Erik cleared his throat. Meanwhile, Pippa said, "Gran, you only have one daughter."

"Stella, it's your Brussels sprout recipe that won them over. I can't claim them as my own. It wouldn't be decent."

I shook my head. "No," I said quickly. "I don't think that's a good idea."

"I think it is a great idea," Erik said, patting my arm. My skin itched where his hand rested like a hot, heavy lump. I didn't want him touching me. It felt like he was trying to possess me, and like Laurel was trying to guilt me back into the family. I couldn't go on cable TV, acting like a member of the Wesley family.

"You can make the sprouts your own," I said, pushing my pizza around on my plate. "Add some extra herbs or bacon or something that will make it your own special recipe."

"I want you there," Laurel said, her voice as smooth as honey. "We all know Cat can't cook, and I expect you to be there for me. I need you, Stella. You're family."

I looked desperately at Cat, who didn't seem to be taking her mother's insult all that harshly. "I'm really busy," I lied. "I'm sure they don't want to work around my schedule."

"Cat tells us you've been downgraded at work?" Laurel smiled at me mournfully, full of pity and judgment. "Hours cut back a bit?"

"Yep," I shot a look at Cat. *Traitor*. "I'm really enjoying the extra time off, but it's amazing how quickly the hours get filled right up again."

"What are you doing with all that extra time?" Laurel's napkin was pressed to her slice of pizza, dabbing at the grease that had pooled on top of the cheese. "You must have plenty of time alone these days—aren't you bored?" She seemed to have forgotten about the cooking show momentarily, and had moved on to general criticism. If she thought picking on me would make me run back into her arms, she was sorely mistaken. "Don't you get lonely?"

"Nope, not at all." Her judgment no longer bothered me. I was not going to let her get to me. She was only a tiny little sliver of my life now. "I um, have some new hobbies." *What new hobbies?*

"What new hobbies?" Erik asked. He looked amused, as though he could sense I was lying and wanted to watch me weasel out from under his mother's thumb.

"I'm learning the guitar," I said, realizing I should ask Joe for some lessons. It would be fun to play the guitar. Maybe. "And I've decided to take an entrepreneurship class."

Cat looked up. Since I'd made both of these things up on the spot, no one had heard anything about any of these plans. Myself included. Couldn't I have chosen something more appealing and exciting as my fake hobbies, like, say, "Also pole dancing."

Erik coughed into his napkin, and Laurel's face turned red. "Pardon?" she asked primly.

"Pole dancing." Nothing about water aerobics compared to pole dancing, but I had to fake my way through it now that I'd said it. It sounded fun, and surely would be unexpected. "It's a great workout."

"What's pole dancing?" Pippa asked. Cat shushed her.

"How's your back?" Erik asked, giving me a look that suggested I stop talking.

"My back's better. The pole dancing helps."

"Are you in any kind of therapy?" Erik adjusted his expression so it was more of a command to stop talking than simply a suggestion. Laurel was squirming in her seat, and he probably assumed I cared that she was uncomfortable. She'd have to get used to the new me.

"I've been on some really bad dates, which is, I suppose, a kind of therapy." Now Cat's expression mirrored Erik's. I was being provocative, and I knew it. I could take the high road, and pretend I was the same old Stella, plodding along in a plain old life. Or I could make up a fabulous new existence, and then rise up to meet my lies head-on. I could live the life I was creating right now. Okay, it made me a liar, but there were much worse things I could do. Such as, *sleep with my ex.* "I feel really good these days, actually. Things are going well, thanks for asking."

Erik simmered quietly in his seat. I could feel the frustration rolling off of him, and everyone around the table was silent. I was irritated that I was being subjected to this family dinner full of judgment and expectation. I guess it was my fault for not asking more questions before accepting the invitation, and I really shouldn't have fooled around with Erik again. That, ultimately, was the problem. It was kind of hard to move on when I kept stepping backward.

Suddenly, I could feel the pressure of the bathroom sex, Laurel's expression, the taste of the olives, and Cat's disappointment all crushing down on me.

"I'm sorry," I said, pushing my chair back from the table. "But I feel like I'm going to be sick. I hate to eat and run, but… well, I think I better go." I threw out a quick "thank you" into the ether and fled Cat's house.

CHAPTER THIRTEEN

"Why don't you date?" I blurted this out the next morning while Anders and I sat together on the couch, munching on apricot scones from the bakery. I hadn't told him anything about the dinner at Cat's the night before, afraid I'd inadvertently let some information about my little rendezvous with Erik slip. I knew Anders would make me feel worse about it than I already did.

Anders looked up from his tea, some sort of earthy mint blend that made the house smell like Christmas. He cleared his throat and blinked. "I date."

"You never date anyone worth dating. It's like you don't *want* to find love." I tucked my legs under the blanket we were sharing on the couch. I'd come to realize Anders really was just like a gay best friend—always there, always honest, always comfortable, always a little bit tempting. Also, he was hot. But there was something so inherently wrong about wanting Anders like *that*, since he also felt like my brother, so I'd never considered him as a possible boyfriend. "You always flirt and act like some sort of Cassanova. Before we lived together, I thought you were kind of a man slut, but you're actually quite celibate. So, nice guy, why don't you ever date nice girls?"

"You thought I was a Cassanova, huh? Is that the vibe I'm giving off?"

"Actually, you sometimes give a bit of a gay vibe, but I'm sure you know that."

Anders laughed heartily. "There's nothing wrong with flirting with both sides."

"No, there isn't. But you're leaving a pile of disappointed men in your wake. It's not fair, you know."

"There's nothing fair in love. I'm not gay, in case you're still curious—I'm just sensitive and snarky and intimidatingly handsome, which makes you think I'm that gay best friend every woman feels sure she needs. Is that how you all see me?" He curled his hands around his big mug.

"Maybe." I giggled, thinking about all the times Cat and Lily and I had wondered, guiltily, if Anders was hiding some big, secret love life from us. A love life with hot, strapping male models—the kind of guys who grace the covers of romance novels and bachelorette party stripper ads. (We didn't give him a lot of credit for good taste.)

"Well, I'll have to do more to keep you guessing. It's fun to think I have a reputation. I like intrigue." He chewed at his thumbnail. "So... now that we live together, you must have noticed the girls I date are all very nice," he said, grinning. "It's just that they're also all a little stupid. The kind of girls I don't actually want to bring home."

"Don't you want to find your one true love? Haven't you ever thought about settling down, marrying, having kids? Is it just me who has that fantasy?"

"Don't you watch TV, Stella? According to CBS, Lifetime, and that channel that only plays bad romantic comedies, that's everyone's fantasy."

"Not yours."

"How do you know it's not mine?" Anders sipped at his tea. When he saw me looking at his mug, he offered to make me a cup. I wondered again how he wasn't taken. "Just because I'm not married to my college sweetheart doesn't mean I don't wish that had been my destiny."

"You wish you could have married your college sweetheart?" I asked. "Who was your college sweetheart?" I don't remember Anders ever talking about a college sweetheart.

"Lily, of course." I stared, and Anders laughed. "I'm kidding. I didn't have a college sweetheart. I'm just saying, if there had been one, I would have probably been pretty satisfied had I married her and fertilized her with two adoring children."

"Why aren't you doing more to get that?"

"I'm keeping you company," he said, avoiding the question.

"But I've only been single for a few months. You've been single for as long as I've known you." I considered this fact, and realized Anders had never introduced anyone as his girlfriend—date, maybe. But never girlfriend.

"I'm holding out hope that things will work out according to my master plan," he said, rubbing his fingers together. "Honestly, I just haven't really found the right person."

"That's impossible." I shook my head. "You flirt enough that surely there's been someone who meets enough of your criteria to warrant an extended amount of time in your charming presence. Do you have commitment issues or something?"

Anders laughed. "I told you, I'm just picky. And I'm hoping things will work out, someday. Where is this going, anyway? You're not thinking about Erik again, are you?"

"No," I lied, and a flush crept up my cheeks. "Why? Would that be so terrible?"

Anders threw a pillow at my head. "Oh, Stella, we've been through this. He's never going to change. You're like a different person since you guys broke up—I don't want to see you fall back into old habits and regress."

"What if he has changed?" I asked desperately. "What if we can find that fire again?"

"Like suddenly your sex life would be sublime, he'd treat you like a princess capable of making her own choices, and he'd tell his mom to fuck off?"

"Something like that," I said, and the flush snaked across my entire torso, thinking about the sex and almost-sex I'd had with Erik since we'd broken up. That had to be indicative of something. And the flowers. Clearly, he was changing. He'd admitted he'd taken me for granted. He'd admitted he hadn't seen me at my full potential. And I couldn't help but wonder if guys like Joe were just looking for a fling and a fuck. Is that what was waiting for me out in the wild? If so, I wasn't so eager to be out guy-shopping. I didn't say it out loud, but I really wanted to ask, "What if what Erik and I had all these years wasn't all that bad after all?"

Instead, I said, "Maybe Erik and I could make it work again. Like you said, I'm different now, so maybe I could convince him to reestablish our relationship on my terms?"

"Nuh-uh. Did you hear yourself? *Maybe you could convince him?* That's not right, Stella. You shouldn't have to convince your boyfriend of anything."

"I just keep thinking, maybe I'm being really selfish to insist on marriage. Isn't a solid relationship about compromise? I'm not even looking at things from Erik's perspective."

"And vice-versa, he's not looking at things from yours. You believe in marriage, you believe in having fun, and you deserve to believe in you. I don't want to get all Oprah on you, but I really, truly believe you'd be giving up on yourself if you stayed with Erik. He has this weird power over you, something that's kept you from wishing for anything beyond the most elementary things for yourself. Figure out what you want as an adult, and then figure out if Erik fits into that."

"You're smart for a straight guy."

"Exceedingly good looking, too." He winked.

"Nice. You're a winker, huh? That's a thing that really gets a girl."

"Did you give Erik this kind of snark? Because I find it hard to believe you talked to him like this and still he treated you like such a dimwit."

"I'm evolving."

"Well, evolve further on your date with Joe this afternoon. You need to get laid by someone other than Erik. It's the only thing that's going to get you to move on."

I stood up quickly to throw a handful of crumbs in the garbage, hoping Anders wouldn't see my flushed face. If only he knew what I'd done. Was he right? Had I slept with the wrong guy? The fact that I hadn't told anyone about Erik made me thing the answer to that was a big, fat, resounding yes. But then why had it felt so good?

There were about fifteen people milling around in a small parking lot next to the grocery store where the hash was slated to start that afternoon. I'd spent most of the morning fretting over what to wear, and had forgotten to dwell on the more daunting aspect of this date: the run itself. The people in the parking lot all looked fit, healthy, and spry—and I was feeling old, fat, and guilty.

Old since there were six or seven people in the group who were clearly in their mid- to late-twenties.

Fat because the people who were over the age of thirty appeared to be slim and muscled, that rugged Minnesota urban athlete look (I'd always wondered where all of these people were come State Fair season).

Guilty because I was on a date with an adorable new man, and I could still feel Erik's hands on me from the night before. Clearly, I wasn't wired for the casual dating life, since the idea of two different sets of lips on me within the same weekend made me squirm. Anyway, I suspected I'd be so sweaty and stinky by the end of the run that Joe wouldn't exactly be trying to get in my pants. And he hadn't made any kind of move yet, anyway, so I hadn't quite figured out where things were going with us. I was interested, sure, but I was still a little curious about why he wanted to go out with me again when he had his pick of the mom squad.

"You ready?" Joe adjusted his stocking cap, and looked over at me from the driver's seat.

I glanced at him and murmured, "Maybe we should just get brunch instead?"

He laughed, and reached over to touch my knee. He gave it three swift pats, nothing sexy or flirty, and opened his door to the cold, unwelcoming air. The temperature was hovering around freezing, and I wasn't sure why anyone would choose to exercise outdoors in this kind of weather. "Come on," he said, leaning back into the car. "You're gonna love it."

"I should've picked pole dancing," I grumbled as I climbed out of the car.

Joe lifted his eyebrows. "You really should have. *That* I would love to see."

The other people who had come for the hash gathered around someone's car, jiggling their legs and jumping up and down. Up close, I realized I'd underestimated most peoples' ages, and greatly underestimated weights and fitness levels. It was a pretty normal looking crew, if a little edgier-looking than the average floor full of people at Centrex would be. The guy wearing a pair of Spiderman briefs over shiny blue leggings ratcheted up the quirk factor. Joe introduced me to a few people, then jogged back to his car for beer. He was the Beer Whore that week, he'd explained. I'd lifted my eyebrows at the terminology.

"How do you know Dog Balls?" one of the women he'd left me with asked. When she saw the look on my face, she explained, "His hash name. Is this your first time?"

I nodded, and a sudden chant of "virgin" erupted from the group standing next to us. I blushed just as Joe sauntered back.

"Heel!" he shouted, and Spidey-pants and two guys wearing chunky knit caps lifted their hands in surrender and laughed.

"I'm Slippery Nipple," a ruddy-faced woman in all purple said. "This is Kotex Moments—" she gestured to a small girlish woman who was probably in her mid-fifties. "That's Pooper Scoop." A short guy with glasses (and was that a leash around his neck?) waved. "Just stick with us and we'll keep you safe. What's your name gonna be?" Slippery Nipple and Joe were both staring at me expectantly.

"Stella?" I asked, knowing as soon as I said it that this wouldn't cut it. Joe grinned, obviously aware of my discomfort. He didn't offer any suggestions and stared as I groped for something clever. "Um…?" I racked my brain for something funny. When I tried to channel Lily, the first thing that popped into my head was, "Pole Dancing Ho?"

A slow smile spread across Slippery Nipple's face, and Joe beamed at me. I guess I'd figured out the formula.

"I like it," Joe said, his mouth close to my ear. "Something tells me you just created a whole new you."

I shrugged. "I guess you'll have to figure that out on your own. Maybe I am who I say I am." I grinned back at him. "So when does the running start?" I noticed that the littlest toe on each of my feet had disappeared or frozen.

"Hold your horses, Ho," Kotex Moments said. "We'll run in a bit. Get your panties out of a bunch and socialize for a bit.

Have fun, have a beer. The hare will get things going in a few."
She wandered off, and Joe and I were left alone together.

"What are you laughing about?" I asked. He was chuckling
again. It seemed like he was always laughing. It was actually a
nice change from Erik, who didn't even laugh at old episodes
of *Arrested Development*.

"You," he answered, and put his arm around my shoulders. I
could smell that faint cinnamon scent I'd come to associate
with him. Deep inside, somewhere, something was stirring.
Something much different from what I'd felt with Erik, ever. I
wanted so badly to tuck in closer, nuzzle deeper under his arm.
I wanted him to take me inside somewhere and wrap his arms
around me to heat me up. When I thought about that, it made
me think about other things I wanted him to do to warm me up.
I wondered if he kissed like Erik? Would sex with Joe feel the
same, or would it be something altogether different?

"I need to move around or something," I said, breaking out
of my thoughts. I couldn't think about this. I had to distract
myself. I still had to figure out what I wanted for myself, and
fantasizing about sleeping with Joe was not the right way to get
my head back on track. "I'm freezing."

In response, Joe tightened his arm around my shoulder, and
pulled me in closer, into a half-hug. I heard a sharp intake of
breath, and realized a moment later that it had come from me. I
could feel the heat pouring off of his chest, and his hands
rubbed against my back to try to keep my blood pumping. He
didn't really need to rub to get my blood pumping—just being
close to him was doing the trick. It was the uncertainty of what
would happen now, later, the next day that heated me up.

I kept my eyes down, but I could feel his eyes watching me
from under his knit cap. It was like a million tiny heaters had
been activated under my skin when he looked at me, and when
he took one of his hands away I felt the cold settle in again. I
wanted him to keep touching me. But then I let myself wonder
how many other women were thinking the same things about
him at this very moment. Did I care that I was just one woman
in a long line of women, waiting for their turn with Banjo Boy?

Suddenly, a tall, broad-shouldered woman wearing jeans
announced that we were ready to go. She talked a little bit

about the course, and I followed along, hoping Joe would stick with me to keep me on track. I realized, though, that he was here to get a workout, and staying back with me was just going to force him to go slower than he usually would.

Erik and I had done a charity bike ride together, once, and he'd shot ahead within moments of the start, telling me he'd see me at the finish line. I'd biked along at my slow and steady pace alone, and was grateful when a random guy stopped and helped me get my chain back on when it fell off on a long uphill. I'd cursed Erik through the rest of the race.

As we started to run along the hash trail, I realized there were at least a few other people who would probably be going about my pace… that is, walking with a little jogging thrown in to get the blood pumping. Joe stayed by my side, trotting along sideways to watch me as I made my way through the parking lot and into an alley that was the start of our course.

"You can go ahead, you know," I said. "It looks like there are some other people going at my pace—we can meet up at the beer stops, okay?" I'd learned that we stopped every couple miles along the course to rest, drink a beer, and socialize. Hashing was my kind of exercise.

"I'm not ditching you," he said, pulling his eyebrows together. He grinned at me and I melted a little again. "We're here together. This isn't a competition or anything, so I don't feel any pressure to bolt out front. Besides, Pooper Scoop makes this weird puffing noise when he runs and I often get stuck next to him through the whole hash. It drives me nuts. I'll hang back with you, if you don't mind."

"I don't want you to hang back just for me," I said, but I was happy to hear him offer. "I mean, if you don't want to hear Poopy puffing, I understand, but don't stay with me just because you feel guilty or anything."

"It's not guilt. It's what I want. I invited you to come along because I want to spend time with you. Not sweat separately, then drive home together. Do I seem like that kind of guy?"

I could feel my breath quickening, and was having a harder time chatting now that we were really moving along the trail. I wondered if Joe was going to keep me talking through the whole run. I wasn't sure I'd be able to. I wasn't sure I was going to make it, period. "No, you don't seem like that kind of guy. It's just that most people are pretty serious about their exercise."

"Serious exercise doesn't sound like much fun," he said, and started to run backward. "I'm not particularly serious about anything, actually."

"You must have been serious enough to make it through law school."

"Yeah, I was plenty serious when I was still in my twenties. Isn't everyone?"

"Most people I know still are. It seems like seriousness is enhanced with age."

"Maybe you're hanging out with the wrong people then." Joe turned around to run forward again. He was right beside me, and I could hear him breathing softly. I glanced over at him, and watched his arm muscles tensing as he swung his arms forward and back with each step. They looked strong, and I suddenly had an urge to have them around me again. Then I thought about Erik's arms around me the night before, and that familiar guilty creep crawled across my body. "Was your ex serious?"

It was as if Joe had plucked the thoughts of Erik straight out of my head and introduced him into the conversation. I hoped talking about him would make me think about something other than the previous night's shower scene. "Yeah," I said, slowing to a walk. "Very serious."

"I bet he supported that list of yours," Joe teased, keeping pace with me. "Because lists are serious business."

I shot him a look. "He did, except for the whole getting married thing."

"Do you ever think about what your life might be like if you hadn't achieved anything on your list?"

"I'd be a high school dropout, living in an ugly apartment," I said, only partly joking. I felt like my list had kept life on track after mom died. It was the only thing guiding me along when she was no longer around. My dad had been no help at all, and without my own vision, I would have been a complete wreck.

"What if life had taken a turn and suddenly you just rebelled and did something so unlike you that everything you thought you wanted for yourself went puff? Original goals gone, replaced with new surprises."

"That wouldn't have happened. I'm a planner. I don't do surprises."

Joe stopped suddenly, and I didn't realize he was no longer beside me until I was a few steps ahead of him. I turned back, staring at him as he just stood there on the trail. His face was flushed, and his hat had come up on one side so his ear was poking out into the chilly air. He smiled, and the goofy look on his face made me giddy. The moment lasted only seconds before he strode forward in two big steps, and leaned over to kiss me. I was caught off guard, and by the time I realized his lips were on mine, they were gone again, leaving my skin cold where his mouth had been only seconds before.

"Did you plan that?" he asked. "Or did it surprise you?"

I started laughing. He looked so self-satisfied, ogling me with an amused grin. Joe was so charming, so adorable—I felt like a teenager, being kissed by someone who had never kissed anyone before. He reached out and held my hand, the warmth of his skin seeping through his glove and mine.

"I'm serious," he said. "I bet you wouldn't have picked this as the perfect spot for our first kiss. In fact, I don't even know if kissing me is on your list of things to accomplish this month. But I don't care. I decided that kissing you would be fun, right now, and so I did it. Surprise! Now we have to deal with it, and figure out where to go from here. It's a tangent… what happens when things veer off plan? What will happen next?" He was talking fast, as though he needed to convince me.

That's when I tipped my body forward and brought my lips close to his again. "This," I said, watching our hot breath mingle in the cold air around us. I touched my lips to his, letting them linger before I pressed into him. I felt his arms wrap around me as our lips intertwined. "This is what will happen next," I murmured.

Suddenly I heard hooting behind us, and realized Kotex Moments and a group of walkers had caught up to us along the hash trail. They were clapping and hollering and stomping their feet, and I felt exactly like a kid who'd been caught kissing her brand new boyfriend at a school dance.

My face reddened, and then Joe grabbed me again and tipped me backward and kissed me even more passionately, right there in front of all of them.

"We get it, we get it," Kotex said, shielding her eyes and moving along. "We'll see you at the watering hole." Then the group of walkers moved on by, and we were left alone again.

Joe was still holding one of my hands, and he ran the other up my back. I could scarcely feel his touch through the layers of jackets and shirts I was wearing to stay warm, but the sudden idea of his fingers on my bare skin made me shudder. His hand had crawled to my upper back, and reached around to circle around my neck, pulling me in closer. This time, he moved slowly and put his lips full on mine. I could taste sugar and cinnamon and his smell made me think of Christmas morning. I wanted to curl up with him in a huge armchair and snuggle into his flannel and be wanted.

"You're beautiful," he said into my hair.

"Do you say that to all your women?" I asked, and regretted it instantly.

But he smiled and answered, "Only when it's true." He took his hand off my neck and pulled back the tiniest bit to say, "Why do you think I'm a womanizer? That is what you think, right?"

"Am I wrong?" I asked, realizing that experience with a lot of women probably made Joe really good in bed. "You are a musician after all."

"I play for children, Stella," he said, quirking his eyebrow up like I was a creep. "Not twenty-year-old groupies."

"Children and their moms," I argued. "Moms who look at you like a glazed doughnut. I've been to one of your shows, remember? I see the way they look at you. You're a doughnut to these women."

"I had a doughnut for breakfast this morning," he said, shifting topic. "From Mel-O-Glaze. You've had Mel-O-Glaze before, right?"

"That kiss tasted like doughnuts," I said, feeling dizzy from thinking about the kiss again. Then I blurted out, "But don't change the subject. You can't pretend you haven't slept with half the women who come see your shows with their kids."

He tilted his head at me. "You don't have a lot of faith in faithfulness, girl. Most of those women are married."

"Does that always matter?" I asked, and started to walk with him along the trail again. I was freezing, just standing there in the middle of the running trail, with no movement or kissing to warm me. "Marriage doesn't make for happiness, right? I mean, a ton of people who are married would give anything to get a little escape to fantasy with a sexy musician. Someone who takes them out of their life and into another, more exciting existence." I thought of Cat, and of the man Lily was sleeping with. Neither of them were in healthy, happy relationships. Did I really want a marriage if I was only going to feel ho-hum about life?

"Is that what I am for you? A distraction?" He looked a little hurt, and the smirk had been wiped clean. "An escape?"

"No, that's not what I meant." I groaned. "I don't know what this is. Actually, I'm having a hard time understanding what you see in me, anyway. I don't think it's unusual for me to wonder if I'm just the next in a long line of flings. Not that that's bad, necessarily, it's just that I'm not sure I'm the type of person who's exactly *good* at flings, given that I've been in a relationship for a while now." I kept babbling as we walked along the path, and I barely noticed when Joe wrapped his fingers through mine. I just carried on. "I mean, Anders and Lily both think I should probably have a few flings, some meaningless sex to try to get over Erik, but I'm not sure I can *do* that, you know?"

Joe began to laugh, and I realized what I'd just said. "Not that I'm thinking about sex," I said, horrified. I couldn't stop thinking about sex with Joe, but that didn't mean I ought to have *announced* it to him.

"I'm thinking about sex," he said simply, as though it were totally normal to just talk about something as private and personal as making love. "But Stella, I'm a little worried you think I'm only interested in you for that. I think you're incredibly sexy, yeah, but I'm not intending for this to be a fling. I don't want a fling. That might sound like a line from reality TV, but the fact is, I'm looking for more than that. You're funny and smart and you make me feel grounded in a way I haven't in a long time, if that makes sense. I want to be a better person when I'm with you."

I snorted. "That is incredibly cheesy."

He grinned back at me. "I'll take a fling, if that's what you want to give, but I'm not really big on meaningless sex. If I wanted to have meaningless sex, I would have stayed a lawyer and stayed married to my ex-wife." He laughed humorlessly. "That sounds bad, doesn't it?"

"Kinda," I admitted, and realized we'd started jogging again. It felt good to be out, doing something other than huffing chlorinated air with judgmental women. And I realized I was messing it up. Somehow, a perfectly pleasant afternoon with an impulsive, hot, and yummy kiss was getting side-tracked by my judging and prudishness. I thought about what Joe had said—he wasn't interested in a fling. But he hadn't denied he was a total womanizer. I wasn't sure I could handle the uncertainty of where he'd been before me, and who else he might be doing on the side. I couldn't assume he'd changed, just because I was in the picture and he'd recited a few choice lines from a cheesy dating show.

I picked up the pace, and Joe was suddenly a few steps behind me. I narrowed my eyes, making an effort to refocus my attitude. Starting over was never going to work if I was going to drag all my old insecurities and judgment into things. And who was I to judge when I was actively fantasizing about a hot musician while carrying on with an ex who wanted me back?

I glanced over and saw Joe's face was set and stony.

"I'm sorry," I said. He hadn't asked for or deserved my judgment—I'd just given it to him, mere moments after he'd kissed me and made me feel like the sexiest woman on the planet. I stopped running again.

"Can we decide if we're running or walking and maybe keep to a pace?" Joe had his hands on his hips a few steps ahead of me on the path, his hat askew on his head again. "The stopping and starting is kind of killing me."

"I think we should stop," I said, moving toward him.

"Stop what?" he asked, squinting at me through the crooked sunlight pressing through the sparse evergreen branches hanging heavy with snow above us. "Stop dating?"

I moved closer to him, standing inches away from his body again. I could feel the heat pouring off him, and I wanted him to touch me. I needed to feel him. When I was with Joe, it felt like the days ahead of me had hope and laughter, instead of animosity and forgotten dreams. Maybe I was abandoning comfort and family and security with Erik, but I could make that again. I had to have me in order to have anything, and Joe was the kind of man who would let me figure out who I was.

"I don't want to stop dating," I said, my mouth close to his. "I want to stop running."

His eyes were bright, and I could sense the silly grin on his face even though I was too close to really see it.

"You need to rest?" he asked quietly. I could tell he was going to make me make the next move. My hands were freezing, so I took my gloves off and slipped my hands under the bottom of his jacket, feeling through layers of cotton for the skin beneath. I'd felt his warmth rolling over me all afternoon, and now I needed to touch it.

Joe flinched when my fingers slipped over his stomach, my cold skin pressing against his hot, sticky body. He drew a breath in, and I could feel his breathing coming quick and shallow as I moved my hands from his stomach to his sides, warming my hands against his surprisingly hard body. As I watched his face, Joe's eyes fluttered closed and he leaned his head back just slightly, letting me touch him. It felt so strange and scary to be touching a new man. There was a little trail of fuzzy hair that ran up the middle of his stomach, something I'd never felt before, and I traced it up until I could go no further without lifting his shirt and exposing his tender skin to the frozen air.

My hands crawled around the sides of his body again, stretching to fan out against his back. They'd warmed up, and now my hands were as hot as his body. I pulled him against me and leaned my face in toward his. His eyes were still closed, but he'd bent toward me, his mouth relaxed and open. I kissed his chin first, feeling the scratchiness of several days without shaving. He tasted salty, and I reached my tongue out to lick the little space under his lower lip. Joe groaned, and I moved my mouth to his jawline. His hands were on me now, pulling me against him tighter as I kissed his ears, his neck, the little dip that brought me from his ear to his neck. Finally, I brought my mouth close to his and breathed in his cinnamon scent. I could still smell doughnuts and sweetness, but there was something under all of that I knew was just Joe.

When our lips touched, I could feel the same heat reaching deep inside me. I kissed him eagerly, and my body was overtaken by a spinning buzz that brought me up on my toes. I couldn't even feel the cold air around us. Our bodies were pressed together, shielding us from everything, helping me forget we were in the middle of who-knows-where. All I knew—and I could feel it in every last corner of my body—is I wanted him. I hadn't felt this kind of longing in years, and I knew I needed him.

Joe and I both pulled away from the kiss at the same time, and my hands slipped out from under his shirt. "I think we missed the beer stop," he said, chuckling.

"I think that's okay," I said, still dizzy from the kiss.

"This is the best run I've ever been on," he said happily. "I'm bringing you on every hash from now on."

"Would this really count as an official hash? We only made it about a mile down the trail. And I haven't had a beer yet."

"You've just rewritten the rules of hashing for me." Joe said happily. "I prefer running and kissing to running and drinking."

"Should we call this run officially over?" I was tired of running, and wanted to curl up with Joe somewhere instead of sweating on a rocky path.

As we ambled back down the path toward the start of the route and Joe's car, we held hands loosely. Our gloves were a level of protection between us, keeping me from feeling the tingle that ran up my arm when he touched me skin to skin. I was grateful for the distance—now that I was out of the heat of the moment, I realized it was lucky we had been outside for what had just happened. Had we been inside somewhere, it could have led to... well, anything, and I wasn't sure I was ready for anything yet. Before I went any further with Joe, I needed to know I was mentally ready to let go of Erik. I'd only slept with three people total in my entire life, so this was a big step for me. I wanted to make sure it felt right. I needed that separation, and getting naked with two men in the same weekend felt a little dirty.

Joe squeezed my hand after a few minutes of comfortable silence and asked, "So why is it you're so big on marriage?" When I looked at him out of the corner of my eye—warning him not to start teasing me about the list again—he spoke. "Not that there's anything wrong with that… it's just, the statistics say half of all marriages end in divorce, so why are you a believer?"

Erik had asked me this, too, but with him the question always came out defensively. I felt like I was on trial. In contrast, when Joe-the-former-lawyer asked, it felt like he was just curious. Like he really wanted to know.

"I'm not really sure," I said honestly. I'd thought about it a million times during my years with Erik, and I could never really come up with a rational, well-thought-out reason for my conviction that marriage was the right thing for me. "My parents were always really happy, and I knew I wanted something like they had."

"Your mom must have died really young," Joe said, and I felt his fingers curl around mine more tightly. I let him hold me close, and felt the sense of security I'd often felt with Erik. I knew it was just a superficial comfort now, but I wondered if maybe Joe and I could grow to have the same thing I'd grown to need from Erik… stability, routine, trust that someone would be there and you'd never be left alone.

"She was forty-four. Ten years older than me now."

"Is your dad still around?"

"He pretty much disappeared after my mom died. I mean, he and I lived together, and he was always a good dad—took pictures of me going to prom and all the other things you're supposed to do as a parent of a teenage girl—but it was obvious that a piece of him broke when Mom left us. He started drinking and eating terribly and basically gave up." I paused, checking to make sure Joe wasn't uncomfortable. Most people got uncomfortable when I started talking about this. Joe nodded, telling me to go on. I did. "He died of a heart attack my junior year of college. Even though the same thing had happened to his dad—my grandpa died of a surprise heart attack when I was really little—I'm still convinced his heart just broke after my mom died. Medically, I know it was genetics, but the romantic in me wanted to think he just couldn't make it without her. Maybe I'm naïve and maybe I didn't see the bad stuff, but it really seemed like they lived for one another. They made marriage and love look like such a partnership. I want what they had." I shrugged. "Without the dying."

"You lost both your parents when you were still just a kid." Joe's eyebrows pulled together, concerned.

"Yeah, and that's part of the reason I tend to hold on to the things I have, even when they're not always exactly what I want. I think it was my therapist who taught me that I'm afraid of losing things that make me feel settled—I'm a serial monogamist with friends and boyfriends, partly out of fear of being left alone again." I believed in family and friends and held them close, since I knew how quickly everything could be taken away. I was scared to lose Laurel and Cat and the girls. They were all I had. I wasn't going to get into *that* with Joe. We didn't need to psychoanalyze my breakup. "I spent a few years in therapy that helped me realize my list somehow signifies life with my mom. One of my therapists pointed out that maybe I was trying to freeze a piece of my life so Mom can be a part of my goals and dreams. I wrote the list the year she died, so by committing myself to it, I'm somehow trying to hold fast to a time in my life when my parents were still around."

"Deep stuff," Joe said lightly. He wasn't making light of the situation, I could tell. He was just playing off my tone. I didn't do a lot of moping, or it would have been a long twenty years. In a way, it felt like I lost both Mom and Dad at once, which had made the grieving a little easier at the time. "Do you think that's true?"

I shrugged. "Probably. I don't know. It seems valid enough. I probably could have figured that much out on my own, though, and saved myself more than a few angsty sessions in college therapy offices. I was a real treat my junior and senior year."

"And then you met Erik?"

I nodded. "Yep. Then I met Erik, got back on my feet, and got back on track with the list. It was the one thing that kept me grounded."

"Grounded, or held back?" Joe asked. His voice was still light, and I appreciated the fact that he wasn't getting drippy and emotional on me. Usually when I told new people about my parents, they got overly apologetic and awkward. Joe seemed to sense I wasn't going to break down on him, and was responding appropriately. It had all happened twenty years ago, so I'd pretty much come to figure out how to talk about it.

"I didn't really feel like I was held back until a few years ago. That's the first time I paid attention to the fact that I hadn't edited the list beyond a fifteen-year-old's imagination of what adult life must be like. I mean, really, I didn't even give myself enough to do to get me into my thirties. There are no notes about whether or not I should dye my hair when the grays start to take over."

"You shouldn't," Joe said. "You don't seem like a bottle blonde candidate to me."

I laughed. "And let's face it... you live life off of a list, and you manage to miss a few things."

"Like what?"

I looked at him and noticed his hat was askew again. His ear was poking out of the bottom of it, and had flipped down on itself. His cheeks were ruddy and red, and I once again pictured him as a lumberjack. I was realizing how much I loved unshaved scruff and a rumpled guy. Joe looked a little like a shirt left in the dryer for several days that had cooled in a wrinkled, relaxed heap. He also didn't look at all breakable—versus Erik, who freaked when his hair was out of order—and that was part of the reason I wanted to see what he was like in bed. I cleared my throat, trying to get my mind off Joe between a set of flannel sheets. Would he have flannel sheets? I suddenly really, really needed to know.

"What did I miss out on, you mean?" I asked, clarifying his question to get myself back into the conversation.

"Yeah. You have any specific examples?" he asked, smirking, and I wondered if he could tell I was thinking about what his body would look like stretched out under messy sheets.

"Not really." I wasn't going to admit I'd started living for Erik's goals. It was embarrassing enough that I knew it to be true.

"You just sort of know you're missing something?" Joe eyed me suspiciously.

"Italy," I admitted, blushing when I looked at him walking along next to me. I couldn't look at him without thinking about him naked. Now that I'd touched his abs, I needed to see them. Soon. "I always wanted to go to Italy, but Erik went in college and so the one time we went anywhere fun, we decided to go somewhere neither of us had been before."

"So why don't you go?" Joe asked, and it sounded so sensible that I almost asked him what he was doing for Thanksgiving.

"To Italy? Like, by myself?"

"Sure," he said, swinging our hands through the air between us. "Or you could bring a friend."

"Yeah. Maybe I'll do that." We'd finally reached the car, and I found myself grinning when he unlocked the car door and opened mine for me. It was such an antiquated expression of chivalry, but something no one had ever done for me before. There had to be something more than a womanizer inside this guy... or he was just very, very good at playing the game. Either way, he was a hot distraction while I struggled to escape the pull of Erik's comfort circle.

"So, I have some stuff I have to do for the band this afternoon. I really, really wish we could hang out the rest of the day, but the pull of responsibility means I should probably drop you off at your place, okay?" Joe said this casually as he backed out of his spot and pulled onto the busy street. I was glad he was driving, because he couldn't see the disappointment that flashed across my face.

"Yeah, of course. That's fine."

"I'm glad you came." He reached his hand across the center console and took my hand in his again. "Even though you didn't truly experience a hash."

"I didn't mind."

"Would you like to, uh—try it again sometime?"

"Hashing?" I asked. "Or all that other stuff we did out on the trail? In either case, asolutely."

Joe snuck a quick peek at me and smiled. Then we sat in comfortable silence, holding hands and listening to something that definitely wasn't the Dog Hounds, all the way home. I couldn't wait for next time.

CHAPTER FOURTEEN

"My feet smell like cabbage. Or maybe sprouts," Lily announced as we stood in the twelfth floor pantry at work later that week. She was digging through the cupboards, and sniffed a package of crackers clearly marked "Corinne."

"It's weird. When I wake up in the morning, I swear they smell normal, then I take a shower, pluck my brows, pick an outfit, and that's when I notice they smell like earthy vegetables."

I laughed, picking at the leftover spaghetti I'd heated up in the microwave for lunch. "Your feet don't smell like vegetables."

"They do, I swear. It must be a disease." Lily pulled one foot out of her tall, shiny black pump and held her foot out toward me. "Take a whiff."

"Lil, I'm not sniffing your feet."

"You don't even have to get close. You can probably smell them from there. Put down the noodles and you'll notice."

"You're just being self-conscious."

"If it's not my feet, it must be my breath that smells like rotting earth," she muttered. "There's *something* wrong with me."

"There is actually nothing wrong with you," I assured her quietly, studying my always-perfect friend in the flickering fluorescent light of the pantry. How could someone be so perfect, yet so self-conscious about every little thing? "The only thing wrong with you is your head."

"What's wrong with my head?" Lily hissed, reaching her slender hand up to touch her soft waves. "Oh my god, does my head smell?"

I laughed again, and Lily groaned. "I know it's too small," she said certainly. "But I can't do anything about that. I try to compensate for my pinhead with big hair. Do I need to change shampoos?"

"Lil, I mean you're mentally deficient. No offense, but the only thing wrong with you is your self-esteem. Maybe you should get rid of your destructive, absent boyfriend and the married man you're messing around with on the side, and see if you can find someone who won't make you doubt yourself."

Lily narrowed her eyes at me. "Oh, I see. Now that you're screwing a hot, sensitive musician, you're allowed to get on me about my messed up relationship? I seem to recall you yourself were stuck in—what did you call it?—an unsatisfying relationship for, oh, about fifteen years?"

"Twelve," I corrected, trying to bring the volume of the conversation back down to office-pantry-acceptable levels. "And I'm not sleeping with Joe."

"Ha! There's no way you're not fucking him—"

"Lil, pipe down," I begged, shushing her as a pair of interns walked past the pantry at eavesdropping speed. "And I'm really not having sex with him. We did kiss this weekend, but that's it. Just because you're all full of sex doesn't mean I am."

I thought back to the weekend, and how much I'd enjoyed my date with Joe. Since Sunday, he'd sent me a few emails and had called on Monday night, just to talk. On Tuesday, last night, I'd come home from work to find him sitting on my front stoop with a box of fresh pasta and a jar of yummy sauce from the Italian take-out place near my house. He also had a bottle of wine tucked into his jacket pocket. The impromptu date was quick, since he had to meet up with the band for rehearsal, but the fact that I knew he was thinking of me made me fall even harder. He'd given me a quick kiss at the door when he left, and said, "You taste like Italy." Then he grinned and promised he'd be back for more later in the week.

I'd peeked out the frosted glass in the front door, watching as his hot little ass sashayed down my front steps and back to his car. If only it were appropriate to chase him down and jump him. If I didn't get him naked soon, I'd be forced to do just that.

"Then who are you sleeping with?" Lily whispered, hands perched on her hips. "You're obviously getting some. You're smirking."

"I'm not." I twisted violently at a piece of my hair and dug into the pile of lukewarm spaghetti that was left in the plastic container. Lying to friends had never been my strong suit. I hadn't exactly forgotten about the shower thing with Erik, but I was trying really hard to pretend it hadn't happened. He'd called a few times, but once again, I was letting it go to voicemail. I think I just needed some distance from Erik while things got off the ground with Joe, or I was going to keep messing up.

"Fine," she said, obviously unconvinced. "Lie to your best friend who smells like head and cabbage. I get it." She was sulking. I knew she wasn't really that upset, since she was still trying so hard to make me laugh. "It's because I smell weird, isn't it? You're picking Anders over me for confiding, since he smells like boy soap and fancy cologne?"

"I wouldn't lie to you about sleeping with Joe, Lil. If I sleep with him, I'll tell you." *Maybe.*

"Okay, fine." She started to walk back to her office, obviously expecting me to follow. I did. "So this is going to sound weird, but I need you to do me a favor."

I swallowed the last of my pasta and threw the disposable container in the trash. I groaned. Lily's favors scared me. "Okay…"

She didn't say anything more until we got to her office and she was perched in her desk chair, feet up. "I'm going out with Brad tonight—"

"Oh, Lily, I thought you were going to break that off," I said, settling into my seat across from her. "You need to step away from the married man."

Lily violently thrust her hand into a bag of goldfish crackers that she'd taken from someone's stash in the pantry earlier that week. An intern's name was written in purple glitter pen on the top of the bag.

"I'm trying," she whispered. "I really am."

"So what do you need from me?"

"I want you to come to Plant & Bean with us tonight."

"Like a double date?" Ick. Plant & Bean was the gastro-vegetarian-raw food place. I'd been there twice—once with Erik, once with Laurel—and both times I'd left hungry.

Lily chewed at her lip. "Sure. A double date. Except it needs to be more of a 'work thing.'" She air-quoted me, which reminded me of Hardcore Lil who everyone else at Centrex got to see. I had a feeling she was trying to trick me into something.

"What's the catch?"

"I want you to meet him."

I narrowed my eyes and watched as Lily pulled her Blackberry out of her suit coat and aimlessly scrolled through the emails that had amassed during our short lunch break. I knew she was just trying to avoid my suspicious gaze.

"I don't want to meet him," I said honestly.

"Please, Stella," she pleaded. "We want to go out on a normal date, but we can't really go out, just the two of us. He thinks it looks too fishy."

I snorted. "He put his hand up your skirt at a restaurant after a work meeting. And now he's suddenly worried about what people might think? Can't he write this off as a business dinner? I would think you two have an easy excuse to go out together."

"I totally agree," Lily said in her talking-to-underlings voice. "But he's been a little weird since I freaked out at him about telling his wife."

"As he should be." I met her gaze head-on, and her eyes shot back down to her Blackberry.

"I just want to do something other than take-out in my apartment with him. You're the only person I trust to tell. I'm begging you to suspend judgment, and just give me this one night where we all pretend to be talking about the Centrex-brand toilet paper campaign so I can go out with him somewhere other than this office or my condo."

"He's from the agency you're working with on the toilet paper campaign? This relationship is destined for the shitter."

"Ha-ha." She wasn't laughing.

I was not deterred. "We need to wipe this guy out and flush him."

"Aren't you cute." Lily glowered at me.

"I hope he doesn't *cling on* after you tell him it's over."

"So mature, Stella."

I beamed proudly. "Seriously, if I have to enable an adulterous relationship, I'm not pretending to talk about toilet paper all night. It's going to be toilet paper and bathroom comments flying at you *all* night long." I'd always lucked out of the less glamorous assignments at Centrex, like toilet paper campaigns. My worst project had been the time I'd had to work under Erik, when he was still at Centrex, on a new hand-soap strategy. But it wasn't the product lines that had made those months of work unpleasant. It was the fact that Erik wanted to talk about our plans and campaigns all freaking night long. That month, we didn't have sex at all.

I needed a new line of business, or I was going to have to start to get excited about shit. Literally.

"Fine, whatever. We can talk about the Easter campaign if you want. His agency is bidding on that, too." Lily looked irritated, which had been the whole point of my goading her. I wasn't going to make it easy for her to sleep with a married man, but I was a little curious what the deal was with this guy. If I joined them, I could see what his damage was, and hopefully I'd have a better strategy for getting Lily the hell away from him. "It's not like we're actually going to talk about work. It's all for show. And you can bring Joe."

I got excited for a minute, thinking about seeing Joe again. But then I remembered something. "Isn't Joe an old frat brother of Chad's? I'm not lying to Joe, so if he comes we really will have to talk about shit or the Easter campaign or whatever. It will be a true agency-client dinner."

"No, no, you're right." Lily ran her hands nervously through her hair. "Fuck."

"I'm not coming alone. I do not want to be a third wheel in an already-awkward situation."

"What about Anders? He'd come with you. I'll pay."

"I'll ask him. But I will not make any guarantees about how either of us will behave. You have to take your chances. We might talk about whether we load the TP roll over- or under-handed all night."

She studied me for a minute, then said, "You're not a bad person. I'll risk it."

Later that day, as I sat in my cube dragging images around on my half-assed, in-store soft drink strategy presentation, I saw an email pop up. Every time that little envelope appeared in the lower corner of my screen, I dropped whatever I was doing and clicked to open it. Didn't matter who it was from—it had to be more interesting than what I was doing.

A few years ago, James hired someone to come in and teach us personal efficiency (thanks to an intern, who'd graciously suggested Centrex people needed the course, and then left for a job analyzing men's underwear at Wal-mart). The efficiency coach had told us to block fifteen minutes off on our calendar every three hours to respond to emails. She'd said opening them as they came in would ultimately lead to a less effective workday. Well, I'd tried that, and found I would just stare at the little unopened envelope icon for two of those three hours, and I began missing important coffee outings and illicit in-office happy hours coordinated by email. Now I opened and responded to every email immediately. It could be someone announcing free cupcakes in the pantry, and if I didn't see the email right away, they'd be long gone before I could scurry over there.

There were two new emails. I opened the one from James first. Our boss often sent out motivational emails to his staff, little quotes or excerpts meant to rally the troops. Once, he'd scanned and emailed the first four chapters from a management book—a long series of anecdotes about great battles in military history, and the reason they were won or lost and the leadership strategy that had been employed. Today, the email was an announcement about a new training program, "Hope to Dream." Sounded cheesy.

The second email was from Joe. The subject line said, "Turkey Day." I opened it up, thinking, *is it too soon for holidays together?*

Joe: "What are you doing for Thanksgiving?"

I took a deep breath in. This wasn't the first time I'd thought about Thanksgiving. What was I going to do for Thanksgiving? Did I need to stress out about the significance of Thanksgiving? Couldn't I just order Chinese in, alone?

Me: "Are you going to invite me to your grandma's house for homemade potato latkes? (I'm still considering all of my offers for next Thursday.)"

I hit send, laughing a little. Within seconds, I had an email back.

Joe: "My grandma makes lefse, not latkes. Does that matter?"

Oh. Did he actually have a grandma who made lefse? I had been joking about the grandma thing, but now I was a little worried. I wasn't actually sure I was prepared for a new family Thanksgiving. Did he already think after just a few dates, we were serious enough for a family holiday gathering? I liked him more than I thought was possible (considering he wore overalls in his job—not that I'm judging), but were we there yet? We hadn't even had sex.

Me: "Do you make the turkey? Or are you one of those eat-too-much-and-pass-out-in-front-of-football guys?"

While I waited for a response back, I re-read the email from James so I could delete it. But when I clicked the link attached to his email, I found that Centrex had set up a career development program. It looked like I could enroll in classes in just about anything—not pole dancing, sadly—and Centrex would pay for it.

I thought back to dinner at Cat's. I'd told Laurel and Erik I was taking a class on entrepreneurship, which had been a lie. But it didn't need to be a lie. I'd hated and been uninspired by my job at Centrex for years, but I'd never done anything about it. I had always found it easy to criticize Erik for never pursuing his dream of starting his own business, but now I was stuck in a dead-end job, working eighty-percent, and hating one hundred percent of it. I'd always thought middle-management marketing was enough for me, but that was back when I thought Erik was enough for me.

It couldn't hurt to take a class to learn something new. It's not like I was short on time. Maybe I could even get Joe to start teaching me the guitar after Thanksgiving dinner. I could picture it: him sitting behind me on his grandmother's sofa, legs on either side of me, his hands over mine to show me what to do. Maybe Thanksgiving with Joe wasn't such a terrible idea.

The email icon popped up, and I opened Joe's response.

Joe: "Actually, I usually just get sushi. What *are* you doing next week? If you don't have any big traditions, want to come to Iowa with me?"

Oh, god. A holiday *and* a trip? I needed to talk to Lily. This seemed crazy.

As I stood up to find her, another email popped up.

Joe: "We have a gig on Friday. Another parade. It just *happens* to be Thanksgiving weekend. Am I freaking you out by asking you to come on a holiday trip with me? Too impulsive? Maybe I should have talked to you about this in person..." Then there was a little emoticon, one I'd never seen before, with squinty little eyes and a lolling tongue. What was I thinking, trying to date a guy who uses emoticons?

A few minutes later, I had Lily cornered in a conference room. "Who uses emoticons?" I asked, giving her a quick run-down of the email chain. "I knew there was something seriously wrong with him."

"I don't think you should be judging him on a few emails, Stella. It's kinda early for you to go away with him for Thanksgiving, but I guess if he's worried that maybe you don't have anywhere to be..." She shrugged. "I don't know, I think it's kind of sweet. Iowa, though?"

"I know."

"You should do it."

I stared at her. What did I have to lose? It would be fun to get away, and it would give me a perfect excuse for missing Laurel's Thanksgiving. "It's not too soon?" I asked Lily warily.

"You're thirty-four years old, woman! You're allowed to go away with your boyfriend."

"But I wouldn't necessarily call him my boyfriend yet. I still have some issues with him."

She heaved a huge sigh. "Of course you have issues with him. You're scared, and freaked out by the fact that you're seeing a new man who is totally unlike Erik. It's all really strange, I know. But this is normal, Stella. You have to move on—you *want* to move on. You've got to let yourself do things if you want to start fresh."

"But he sleeps around," I said pitifully. "Do I really want to stay overnight in a hotel with a guy who I *know*—for a fact—sleeps around?"

"That's what you're worried about?" Lily laughed. I blinked, wondering what was so funny. "Everyone sleeps around."

I held up a hand. "I don't."

"No, you don't. But that's because you've been stuck in a relationship for a thousand years. If you'd been single all this time, you, too, would have slept around a little bit." She curled her upper lip into a frightening-looking smile. "At least, I hope you would have."

"He was married."

"Exactly. He was married, now he's divorced. The guy had to make up for lost time."

"He's a womanizer." I was trying hard to poke holes in Joe, but failing miserably to convince myself or Lily that there were valid reasons for me not to sleep with him.

"At least he'll be good in bed. You would hope."

"What if he has diseases?"

Lily actually snorted at that. "Is this a nineties made-for-TV movie? That's unlikely. He's an intelligent adult… I'm going to assume he's been safe, and smart, *especially* if he likes, uh, *entertaining* women." She wrapped her slender arm around my shoulder, and guided me back out into the maze of cloth cubicles. "You're making this harder than it needs to be. Just have some fun."

I nodded. "You're right. I like him. A lot. I'll go."

"That's my new Stella." As she led me back to my cube to write back to Joe and settle my Thanksgiving week plans, she said, "You're going to need a wax, you know. I can practically see the little puff of pubes through your skirt."

That night, Anders and I were running late, which made me extra tense as I prepared to meet The Brad. I'd promised Lily we'd meet them in the sparse front entrance of Plant & Bean at seven. But Anders, who had been less-than-enthusiastic about the date, had dragged his feet and taken the world's longest shower, before announcing he had to stop for a quick haircut on the way to the restaurant. I rolled my eyes, but went with it, since it had taken a lot of begging to get him to come at all. He only agreed to come after I told him Lily was paying and I had every intention of ordering double-appetizers. Even then, he didn't look happy about it, but I guilted him into coming.

Lily confessed that Anders had known about Brad for a while, but she'd also asked him to keep it quiet. I wasn't surprised she'd told him—Lily and Anders had been friends forever, and I knew she relied on him when things got bad.

"I just really wish I'd known you knew about this, too," I told Anders as we parked at a meter half a block from the restaurant. "I hated not talking to anyone about it! It's stupid that we were both keeping her secret, when we could have at least vented to each other."

Anders' head was dipped low, searching for quarters in the car's center console, but I heard him mutter, "I didn't really want to talk about it."

I stepped out of the car and watched him stewing while he jammed quarters into the meter. "I only have to plug this until eight, right?" He scanned the street for parking signs. The scarf he'd wrapped around his neck made him look dapper, as always, and his cheeks were flushed from the bitter November wind. He looked sad and angry, even through his handsome shell, and I could tell he was pissed about something.

"How much more do you know about this whole thing than I do? Have you known for a while?" I narrowed my eyes at him, linking my arm through his as we hustled down the street.

"I found out a few weeks ago," he said. "Right after the Halloween party, I think."

"Why do you look so grouchy? Aren't you worried about frown lines?"

"She always does this sort of thing," he grumbled, and then he wrapped his arm around my shoulders to keep me shielded from the wind.

"Thanks," I said, tucking into his arm. "What do you mean? Has she cheated before?"

"No, not *this* exactly. But she just always fucks up her relationships. I wish she'd just figure it out."

"Figure what out?" I asked, surprised at his bitterness. I'd never heard him actually criticize Lily—they often teased one another for fun, but this level of frustration was new. "You know Lily."

He sighed so loudly I could hear it over the wind. "Yeah, I know Lily. And she's genius at picking men."

We'd reached the front of the restaurant, and I stopped short of the door. "Are you going to be like this all night?"

"I'll try to be nice."

"That's the best either of us can do, right?" I smiled at him, and he gave me his best fake smile back. Then he opened the door to the restaurant.

As I walked through the door, Lily was the first thing I saw. She was dressed in a bright red, skin-tight dress, black suede heels, and her hair was bigger than ever. If she weren't my friend, I would seriously wonder if she'd been hired as someone's date for the night. God, I felt like a jerk for thinking that, but it was true. I could sense Anders' reaction next to me, and the way his body stiffened at the sight of her made me think we were on the same page. Not that she didn't look amazing, but she looked... desperate. Like she was trying so very hard, and had something to prove.

Brad, on the other hand, was understated in a pair of gray dress slacks and a sport coat. The sport coat didn't have leather elbow pads, but it could have—that's how much he resembled someone's father. He was obviously good looking, but his style was so tight and rigid, it was a wonder someone like Lily would ever set eyes on him.

"You must be Brad," I said, extending a hand. Anders, who was hiding behind me, didn't bother shaking his hand.

"Thanks so much for coming, guys," Lily said, and I could see she'd been crying.

She accepted a hug from Anders, and her shoulders released as he held her in his arms. "You okay?" he asked quietly. Brad wasn't listening.

"I'm fine," she said, smiling. "Great. But you guys are late!"

Neither Anders nor I said anything, following as Lily trailed behind the hostess and Brad to our table, which was conveniently set in the back of the restaurant, surrounded by palm fronds and a small pond. I noticed there was a dead fish hidden behind a leaf in one shadowy corner of the pond. God, I hated raw food, and this was making it worse.

There were ample pleasantries, but no one really asked anyone else any questions, since none of us really had any interest in getting to know anyone else. Anders and I chatted on one side of the table about nothing in particular, while Lily and Brad looked awkward on their side of the table. After we ordered, Lily tried desperately to find a connection between all of us, but it was obvious she was making an effort where she needn't have wasted her time. Before our first course—sushi, which was so wrong, considering the floater a few feet from my chair—it was clear to everyone that this had been a mistake.

By the time the main course came, Brad had started to sweat and the sport coat came off. Lily put her hand on his arm, and we all noticed when Brad shook it off under the table.

Before dessert, Brad got a phone call and made excuses about why he had to leave. Frankly, I wasn't surprised. I'd been waiting for him to take off all night, and even before he'd retrieved his coat from the coat check, Anders was visibly more relaxed.

"Well, that was fun," he said, watching as Brad strode down the street toward the car. "I'm so glad we could meet him."

Lily heaved a sigh, and she shook her head. "I'm so stupid," she said. Both Anders and I nodded, not at all interested in disagreeing. "Why did I think that would work?"

We all looked at each other uncomfortably. I didn't really want to be the first one to talk—both Anders and Lily were more honest and abrupt than I tended to be—but someone had to say something.

"You guys, there's a dead fish in the pond." I pointed to the bloated orange fish. "That seems oddly symbolic."

Lily started to laugh before Anders, but then we were all in hysterics. When our dessert arrived a few minutes later, Lily took the one Brad had left behind.

"I get it," she said though mouthfuls of foamed caramel. "He's probably not coming to my mom's for Christmas, is he?"

"No," Anders and I said at the same time.

"Stella's boyfriend invited her to Iowa for Thanksgiving, and mine won't even stick around through dessert." Lily glowered over her bowl of sweet foam. "This is revolting, by the way. Completely unsatisfying. Is there even butter in a foamed dessert?"

I took a bite of my own fruit and "flash-frozen-fresh" sheep's milk cream. It tasted sort of gamey. I almost felt like I could taste the little sheep fur, infused in the icy milk. I pushed it aside, and dealt with Lily.

"No, he's not going to be there for holidays, and he won't be there on Sunday morning when you want someone to get you a latte—" I glanced at Anders appreciatively. "Not to be harsh, but he's not even the kind of guy who'll be there when you're having a bad day. If your bad day coincides with his daughter's piano recital or his son's soccer game, your bad day isn't going to matter." I knew it was harsh, but with Lily, it wasn't worth beating around the bush. She wanted people to give it to her straight, and I'd wasted enough time fooling myself that I didn't need to fool my best friend, too.

She began to cry—probably for the second time that night. "I want someone to buy me lattes," she said pitifully.

"I'm a latte guy," Anders said quietly. "I can buy you lattes." There was something in his tone that made me look up from my dessert, which I'd started to pick at again. He was looking at Lily with this… something. I'd never picked up on it before, but now I realized I'd seen him looking at her like this before. There was hope, and respect, and something that went beyond anything the rest of us had with Lily.

Oh, I thought, watching Lily be completely oblivious to Anders' offer. *He loves her. Lily is what he's waiting for.*

It was devastating, now that I saw it there. I wondered how long Anders had loved Lily like this, and how many times he'd had to watch her make stupid choices about men. How many times he'd had to watch her pick men who were a thousand times worse than himself. How many times he'd wished she would notice him like that.

And I'd told him we all thought he was gay! Ack. I was officially the shittiest roommate ever.

"Do you want to stay at our place tonight?" I offered, before I realized it was a good idea. But it was a good idea. She didn't need to be alone, and the only way for me to show her that Anders was the perfect guy was for her to experience it herself.

And then, even though Lily fought hard for the check when it came, Anders insisted he would cover it. That was just the kind of guy he was. Lily would notice that someday. I was looking forward to that day coming.

CHAPTER FIFTEEN

"Have you slept with the singer yet?" Heather tugged at her swimsuit, and one of her breasts got stuck in the fabric. She'd had a mastectomy on her left side, so that half of the bathing suit always slipped on easily, leaving the right breast behind. She told me once she forgot there was still a boob there. How could you forget about a boob? I guess if there was only one to think about, it might be easier to lose just the one, but I think she just got distracted.

"I messed up," I admitted, for the first time since it had happened. "I slept with my ex again."

"Well, was it worth it?" Heather asked, tugging at the fabric of her suit. I watched out of my peripheral vision as her skin stretched and finally gave in. Halleluiah, she was clothed. "I hope you knew what you were doing."

"I did," I said. Then, "At least I thought I did. But then I went out with the band guy again."

"Ah," Heather winked. "Slept with him, too?"

"No." I'd thought about it plenty, but that didn't quite fulfill the same need. "But I really like him. I think he's a good guy."

"So what's the problem?"

"I don't know," I admitted. "No problem. He invited me to Iowa for the weekend."

"This weekend?" Heather started her slow walk toward the showers. "It's Thanksgiving."

"I know."

"That's significant."

"I know." I turned on the shower and rinsed off. "I can't figure out what's wrong with him."

Heather glanced at me before taking my arm to shuffle out to the pool deck. "Why are you looking?"

"For flaws?"

"What's the point? You're going to find some. So why bother?"

"I'm not going to be stupid about this. I need to know how serious his issues are before I get in too deep."

"If you'd known your ex was a selfish piece of shit, would you have hung around for twelve years?"

I thought about that while we made our way down the ramp into the pool. The truth was, if I'd looked hard enough, I probably would have realized how Erik and I would have ended up. Or would I? Maybe that's why I was being so careful about Joe. I didn't want to waste my time. Was it really worth leaving everything behind for an uncertain future?

"I didn't know as much then as I know now," I answered. "I'm not leaving one mistake for another."

"So you're already expecting him to be a mistake?" Heather scoffed. "Sounds promising. Invite me to the wedding."

"That's not what I meant." Ugh. Smart old people pissed me off. "I mean, I'm not going into this with my eyes closed. When I met Erik, I was still looking for something. My parents were both gone, I needed a family, and he gave me the consistency and stability I'd been looking for. He held me together when things were really bad, and eventually I grew out of it. If I'd been in a better place, I might not have clung so hard to Erik when I first met him. I might not have lost sight of myself after a few months together."

"What you're telling me is, you're *not* looking for anything now? This situation is somehow different?"

The cool pool water tickled my ankles, then rose up to my knees and hips, before I sunk down to my shoulders, letting myself float away from Heather. "I like to think I know myself now."

Heather lifted her hands in the air, keeping as much of her body out of the water as possible. Or maybe she was cheering about what I'd said? It was unclear.

"If that's true, then you must know yourself enough to know if this guy gets you going. Does he make you feel something?

If he does, then maybe you shouldn't be so quick to search for the flaws. Why don't you just enjoy it?"

I looked around and saw the other nosy women in the pool were all nodding at me. Why did Heather have to be so irritatingly wise?

I had a boyfriend. A real, honest-to-goodness, banjo-playing boyfriend.

Joe and I had seen each other almost every night for the past week, and I was falling hard. I felt like one of the giddy little girls at the Dog Hounds concert I'd gone to with Pippa and Heidi—I was really, truly smitten, and I'd finally managed to shake the mental image of Joe in overalls. Now, when I daydreamed about him, I thought about how warm I felt when his flannel-clad arms were wrapped around me, or how his butt looked inside his loose jeans when he'd dance around my living room (which he did fairly often).

Even Anders had stopped making fun of him, and we'd had a couple of nights where we all sat around watching TV or making dinner or just talking. Lily was won over when he brought us both coffees one day, just because he was downtown and wanted to see my inspiring cube. The next day, he'd brought me a piece of red flannel fabric to pin up on one wall so it wouldn't be so drab. He'd even helped me find a "Start Your Own Business" class I was going to take right after Christmas. I felt like Joe was becoming a part of my life—it finally felt like I had my friends and I had my boyfriend and I had my life, and they all fit together in a way that fit me.

The only thing missing? We still hadn't slept together. I had come to grips with the idea of making love to someone new—and had told Erik I couldn't see him, even in casual situations, for a while—but it just hadn't happened yet. I was a little surprised, given Joe's reputation, and I wondered why someone with a reputation as a player was so slow to start with me. I didn't want to ask, since I was trying hard to stop poking around for flaws, but I really hoped we'd finally get there in Iowa. Every time I thought of the feel of his skin and the way his hands moved on me so softly and gently, like he was playing his guitar and making love to me with his hands, I wanted to beg him to spend the night. But I could wait, and when it finally happened, it would be right.

Joe and I drove to Iowa in his car on Thanksgiving morning, just the two of us, with all the band's gear piled into the back of his station wagon with the seats down. The other guys from the band were leaving early Friday morning, and driving back the same night, after the gig. They had families, and Joe had agreed to go down early and get things set up and ready so they could hustle in and out, and be back in time for the long weekend with their families.

While we drove, Joe told me his parents lived in Florida and both his sisters were still in Detroit. His grandmother lived in Minneapolis, and that was part of what had drawn him to Minnesota in the first place. It sounded like he was closer to her than to anyone else in the family.

"Don't you spend Thanksgiving together?" I asked, watching Joe tap a rhythm on his knee with his fingers under the steering wheel. I reached over and took his hand in mine, and he looked over at me briefly, just to smile.

"Sometimes," he said. "She's busy. And she understands the band thing. She gets it's a business, and that it makes me happy. My sisters still take every opportunity to give me grief about my ex—they feel like I really screwed up when I left my practice and my wife and 'regressed.'"

"They're not big on the band, huh?"

"Not many people are," he said. "I'm a thirty-four-year-old, overall-wearing, small-time children's musician. Some might say I threw away a perfectly good life for nothing much at all."

"But your face is on billboards," I teased. "That's worth something."

"I actually hate those billboards," he said. "Frank had a friend who sold outdoor advertising, and he had all these leftover units at the end of last year, so he gave them to us free. We just had to produce the boards, and they gave us the space. So Theo's wife designed them, we printed them at Kinko's, and that's how my face came to be on billboards. Am I more attractive to you because my face is a face of fame?"

I laughed. He had a phony, billboard-quality smile on his face. "You should go for bus stop benches next. Somehow, the realtors have really cornered that market." He squeezed my hand, then I pulled it away and ran my fingers up his leg. I heard him suck in a breath and he glanced at me sideways.

"Driving," he reminded me, his voice a warning.

"I know," I said, and my fingers trailed lazily back down his leg.

"How much longer is this drive?" he asked with just a hint of whine. His voice had grown low and husky, and I felt his body stiffen under my hand. "Maybe we've gone far enough for today?"

I laughed, and kept tickling my fingers across his leg, up his stomach. I moved up to his face and touched his jawline, rubbing my thumb against the tiny bit of stubble that always seemed to be there. My hand found its way to his hair, and I teased at the curls, twisting into them, feeling their silkiness against my fingers. I watched his profile as he watched the road, and I knew it was going to be a long hour before we would be at our hotel.

"Can you stop at this rest stop?" I asked suddenly, spotting a green sign and the off-ramp. "Just for a sec?"

He bit his lip and jerked the car toward the off-ramp, ignoring the signs pointing cars to the left and trucks to the right. He followed signs for the truck parking, and pulled into the empty lot. He put the car in park, and took a deep breath before looking at me. I could see the fire in his eyes, and I literally dove over the center console to kiss him and wrap my hands around his neck. There was nothing comfortable about my position, but I wanted to touch him so badly and I couldn't wait until we were there. It had to be now, or I'd explode.

The car was still on and the heat vents were blowing warm air against my back while Joe's breath warmed my neck. *Such Great Heights* by The Postal Service was on the radio, and my boyfriend's hands were on me and I was happier than I'd been in years. I closed my eyes and my butt began to go numb so I couldn't feel the rough edges of the center console digging into my jeans under me. All I could feel was Joe's mouth on mine, and his hand reaching behind me to pull me closer. His hand was inside my shirt, pressing into my back. I leaned into him, and readjusted so I was sort of sitting on his lap, sideways, and he held me close so my elbow wouldn't press against the steering wheel. His hand had moved, and suddenly it was against my stomach, climbing upward. Somehow, my bra had come undone and his hand was on my breast, while his mouth pressed into mine.

He reached down and pulled at the lever that released his seat back, and we both thudded back against it. I brought one leg over him, and sat straddling him while we kissed in the rest stop parking lot. I could feel him hard under me, and I wanted him right then and there. I reached down and started to unbutton his pants, but he took my hands in his and brought them back up.

"I love the spontaneity, Stella," he murmured. "But let's not do this here."

"Yes," I whispered. "Here." Even in my hazy, sex-obsessed stupor, I knew this would *not* have been the place I would have planned to make love to Joe for the first time, but there was something about him that made me throw my rules out and rethink everything. I wanted him, and I wanted him now, and I wasn't going to wait. I couldn't wait. I'd waited long enough, and this felt right. Somewhat uncomfortable, and my leg was half asleep, but still it felt good.

"Not here," he said again, chuckling, his voice a whisper. "I've been waiting to do it right, and I don't want to screw it up by making love to you in the car. You deserve better." He pulled me against him and kissed my ear, sending shivers across the top of my neck. "Let me wait. Please."

I looked at him, and saw that he meant it. His eyes were pleading, and I could tell it had taken insane amounts of self-control for him to stop things when he had.

"Okay," I said, biting my lip. He reached his finger up and pushed a curl out of my eyes with his thumb. "What if I told you I put sex-at-a-rest-stop on my list?" I asked, leaning down to kiss him quickly, one more time. "Would you really make me stop?"

"You have sex-at-a-rest-stop on your list?" Joe asked, his eyes sparkling. "Really?"

"I'm not telling," I shrugged.

"I don't buy it. You wrote that list when you were fifteen. I highly doubt that's going to make your list of life goals as a fifteen-year-old… sex in rest stops wasn't a big feature of John Hughes or Hugh Grant movies."

I lay against his chest and listened as his heartbeat slowed. He was so soft and warm under me, and I wished we could just teleport to Iowa so I could lay right where I was for the rest of the drive. We stayed like that for a while, with his arms wrapped around me and mine twisting into his hair, until I started to fall asleep and I realized I could very easily crush him if I stayed where I was for an entire nap. I could see the headlines—maybe it would even be on one of those big, electronic billboards—telling everyone that the much-beloved lead singer of the Dog Hounds was crushed to death by his girlfriend in a rest stop parking lot. That would not be good press. Pippa and Heidi would hate me. So I climbed off and settled back into my own seat. Joe brought his seat back up and looked over at me.

"Ready?"

"Can we drive a little faster?" I asked hopefully. "I'm ready to be out of the car. Let's get there already."

For much of the rest of the drive, we talked about stupid stuff—anything to distract us from the sex waiting at the end of our drive. Movies (we were both big chickens when it came to horror films), music (he was a proud Britney Spears fan… I promised to have another listen, with an open mind—though I knew he couldn't change my mind even if it made him dance adorably around the room), and family. He told me about his sisters, who sounded a lot like me, and his parents, who lived in a retirement community in Florida.

"I've always kind of wanted to live in a retirement community," I admitted.

"You really are a planner," he teased. "You're already thinking about retirement?"

"No," I said. "I mean now. Like, I'd kind of like to live in a retirement community now. I think I'd enjoy the feeling of being surrounded by friends and people who would be there for you if anything were to go wrong. I'm sure there would always be someone up for a game of cards, and it just seems like the kind of place where you would never be lonely."

"You want to live in a retirement community as a thirty-four-year-old unmarried woman?"

"Well, not *immediately*. But it's something I wish wasn't frowned upon."

"Who frowns upon it?"

"People," I said, though I'd never actually discussed this idea with anyone. I was just certain people would think it was weird if I were to move in with a bunch of seventy-year-olds. "But I think it would be great. I like playing cards. I'd like having someone shovel and rake for me. It would be really relaxing. I don't have any grandparents of my own, and with my parents gone, I've just always craved that feeling of being looked after." I thought about Laurel, and how her "caring" had always been more judging, but at least it had felt like I had someone thinking about me.

"Don't the ladies at your water aerobics class sort of do that for you?"

Of course—Heather and Barbara and the other women at the Y. I had recovered from my back injury well enough that I could surely be doing some other form of exercise by now, but I'd continued to go because the women there had grown on me. I liked the way they seemed to have their eye on what I was doing, and were going to make sure I didn't screw anything up too badly.

"Yeah, you're right. I guess I could really use a grandma."

"You can borrow mine," Joe said, finally pulling into the lot at the little hotel we'd booked for the night. "She's going to like you."

It made me happy to think about meeting Joe's grandma. I was oddly touched that he *wanted* me to meet his grandma. I suppose we were on a trip over a holiday together, but talking about meeting family made it all feel that much more real.

I watched as Joe covered all the gear in the back of the car with a few big blankets, and then we grabbed our bags and headed into the hotel. As we walked toward the door, he took my hand and looked over at me and I felt that heat boiling up again. Now that I knew we were this close, I was suddenly, inexplicably nervous. We had been *this* close just an hour earlier in the front seat of the car and I hadn't had even an ounce of nerves... but now that I had time to plan for it and think about it and stress over how it might go, I was letting myself get jittery.

Joe squeezed my hand and leaned in to kiss me. When he did, I felt that now-familiar tension building in me and smelled his cinnamon scent and felt the rub of his flannel shirt against my neck and the fear all washed away. I didn't know if I could stand waiting while we checked in and found our room. But I had to, and I did, and in the space of no time at all, we were in our room and our bags were left in the entryway and he had me pressed up against the wall with a passion so intense, I could hardly even breathe.

His hands were everywhere, touching and holding and pressing me in ways I'd never felt before. While we kissed, I held my breath and teased at the buttons on his shirt. Then I had it open, and finally I exhaled when my hands were free to touch the skin I'd felt for the first time the weekend before, when I'd warmed my hands on him on the running trail. I held him away from me for just a moment, so I could look at his chest, and run my hands down to that little patch of hair I'd felt at the bottom of his stomach. As I let my fingers trail across his body, he closed his eyes and breathed in, and I felt my bra snap open.

"You're good at that," I said. He laughed, then shut me up with another kiss.

The way he touched me was unfamiliar, but it was as if he knew how to turn me on in a way I'd never imagined possible. He guided me in the direction of the bed and slipped my shirt up and over my head. I felt his eyes on me, looking at me in a way that made me feel like my body was special and prized and maybe a little off-limits. My bra dropped to the floor, and I stood half-naked in front of a new man. His eyes took me in and a slow smile crept onto his face, before he moved his mouth to my neck and then down to each of my breasts. Time moved so slowly, and everything went still as we savored every step. I stretched out on the milky-white duvet and let him touch me, resolved to make this last as long as possible. I wanted to revel in his touch, feel the way his hands explored my contours and made my skin hot.

Joe obviously had the same idea, since he was taking his time moving his mouth from my breasts to my stomach, and then back up to my mouth. When our lips touched, our bare chests pressed together and I could feel his hot skin searing into me, and I wanted more. Moments later, we were both in just underwear, him in boxer briefs that hugged his delicious ass in the most perfect way and me in one of the two pairs of sexy underwear I owned.

It was at the moment when I decided I couldn't possibly wait one more second to feel him inside me that my phone rang.

Fuck.

I ignored it, but both Joe and I tensed a little every time it jangled in the background. He was on top of me, and I could feel him pressing against me, and I arched up to meet him just as my phone started to ring again. I growled a little, pissed at whoever was bothering me. My friends all knew I was here, they knew I was with Joe, and someone was being irritatingly persistent. I rocked against him, and moved on top of him, pinning him against the bed with my hips. I pressed into him harder every time the phone trilled at the end of the bed, willing both of us to forget it and move on.

He bit his lower lip, and I leaned down to take his mouth in mine, biting his lip for him. He groaned, and I kissed him harder.

My breasts pressed against his body, and his hands were wrapped around my butt when my phone rang again. I sat up, pissed.

"Someone really wants to talk to you," he said.

"My friends aren't usually this persistent," I murmured apologetically, still sitting astride his hips. "I'm getting seriously frustrated."

"Maybe you should check and see who it is?" he said, just as it started ringing again. I kissed him one more time before moving to the end of the bed to grab my phone out of my pants pocket.

Erik.

He hadn't called since I'd told him definitively that we needed to stop talking. He'd told me he respected my decision, and promised not to call. He had promised. And now he was being annoying at the very worst possible moment. Count on Erik to figure out how to insert himself into a part of my life that was most definitely not his.

I stared at the phone as it rang, unwilling to answer. But when it began to ring again, mere moments after Erik's call was logged in the Missed Call directory, and Laurel's number popped up on my caller ID, I decided I might as well just answer. Joe and I would have no trouble getting back to what we'd been this close to doing just moments before, and if I didn't answer, they would obviously just keep calling. I seriously hoped this wasn't about Brussels sprouts.

I pressed answer. "Hello?"

"Stella," Laurel's voice was so unwelcome at that moment I almost hung up. But I didn't, and then she said, "Stella, it's Cat and Travis." Her voice choked. "And the girls. They've been in an accident. We need you."

CHAPTER SIXTEEN

I felt the walls in the hotel room close in around me as I listened while Laurel told me Cat and Travis and the girls had been on their way to Peter and Laurel's for Thanksgiving dinner when their minivan had gone off the road. It rolled, and rolled again, and they were all in the hospital. Cat was banged up and had a broken rib and was in stable condition, but Travis was unconscious and they were saying it was critical. And the girls. My beautiful little girls were both in surgery. I could see Pippa's tiny face, and Heidi's little smile, and I wanted to hold them and comfort Cat and—I had to be there. I needed to be there now. They were my family.

"I need to go back," I told Joe when I'd hung up with Laurel and had the details on which hospital they'd been taken to. I couldn't shake the image of my beautiful little girls in the back of an ambulance, and I began to sob. "I have to go home."

He didn't ask any questions as we got dressed and grabbed our bags and loaded back into the car and got on the road. I sat in stony silence and cried in the seat next to him, hating the uncertainty and wondering what I'd find when I got there. No one knew what was going on, and no one knew what was going to happen to the girls… and Cat was there, helpless, and I knew exactly how she must be feeling.

Through tears, I told Joe what I knew and he didn't ask any stupid questions or press for more information. After we'd driven for an hour in silence, I began to talk. I needed to distract myself, and I couldn't figure out how to do that other than to talk about something. I told Joe more about my mom, and how I'd felt completely abandoned after she died.

"When I was pulled out of class, and told there'd been a car accident, I didn't really think about anything until my dad came and told me she was gone. I didn't realize how much I'd counted on my parents, and I'd never thought about how much would be lost if they ever just weren't there." I stopped talking, drawn back to those feelings of loneliness and abandonment and fear. There were no sisters or brothers for me to lean on, and it seemed like everyone else—aunts, uncles, cousins— were so busy comforting one another that they forgot I had no one. It was in the space of one morning that I was left alone. They all had each other, and my partner was my dad. But no one noticed my dad was essentially gone, and so it was just me. I knew I would never be able to watch anyone suffer alone like that, knowing what I'd gone through that year and the years that followed.

I stared out the window, thinking again about how afraid I was to go to the hospital, but I knew Cat and the girls and the rest of my family—they were still my family—needed me. My mind flashed to Erik, and I wondered how he was coping. He was alone. He didn't have a partner, and I knew how scared he would be. Laurel would be useless, and Peter would be silent, and Erik would be absolutely lost. He'd been there for me when I had finally come to terms with losing my parents, and now I needed to be there for him. After our years together, I knew I owed him that. I wanted to give him that.

When we got to the hospital, Joe dropped me at the front door and asked if I wanted him to stay. I shook my head and told him I'd call, then pressed inside the hospital's front doors. They directed me to trauma, where I found Laurel and Erik and Peter all huddled together in a cold, windowless waiting room. The TV was tuned to *SpongeBob*, which reminded me of the girls and weekend mornings, and I immediately asked, "How are they?" I sat next to Erik and took his hand when he offered.

"They're both out of surgery, but Pippa's in a medically-induced coma," Peter said. Laurel just sat there shaking her head. "She has a lot of swelling, and they want to take extra precautions." He didn't want to say the word brain damage, but we'd all watched enough TV to know what that probably meant. "When the car rolled, they think she may have been hit with something that was on the floor of the van. Travis is still unconscious, and he's in the critical care unit."

"What about Cat? Where is she?"

"She's in a room resting."

"Does she know about Travis and the girls?"

"Not yet," Erik said. They all looked at each other nervously and Laurel hid her face behind a perfectly-manicured hand. "We couldn't. None of us could. They gave her something to help with the pain. It knocked her out, and she's been asleep since."

I stood and made my way to the room Cat was in. They all watched me go, and I saw Erik's eyes flick toward SpongeBob for some distraction. There was an empty bed near the door, and Cat was hidden behind a curtain by the window. She looked so peaceful, so beautiful, and so small. It was always a shock when I realized just how tiny she was without heels and make-up and her big voice and naughty words. Machines beeped, and things whirred, but all I could hear was her breath, soft and tiny and fragile, pressing out and pulling in as her body lay resting. I'd always given her grief for being a terrible driver, and now I felt guilty that I'd never actually pushed harder. What if something terrible were to come of all of this? What if Pippa never woke up? Or Travis?

My fingers trailed along the top of a nubby, fabric-covered chair by her bedside, and eventually I sat on the edge of it, watching as she breathed and machines whirred and stirred around her. Who would tell her? Was it my job?

No.

Surely someone other than me had to be more equipped to tell a mother her daughter may be dying or brain damaged and her husband was very possibly lost? But when her eyes fluttered and she stirred, I felt her hand reach for mine, and I knew it was up to me. Erik couldn't handle this, and Laurel was surely thinking of her own worst nightmares—they needed me to do this. She'd want to hear it from me. She had to hear it from someone.

"The girls…" she said, trying to sit up. Cat cringed, and I gently pressed her shoulder back against the bed.

"You broke ribs," I said, keeping my voice as calm as possible. "You need to lie still."

"But the girls," she said, and I saw panic flash across her face. "Travis."

"The girls are both out of surgery," I said soothingly. "They're taking good care of them." I looked at her dazed expression, and knew I couldn't tell her about Pippa yet. We didn't know enough for me to tell her anything. It would just freak her out, and there was nothing she could do. She might not even hear what I was saying, and for all I knew, the doctors might take her out of the coma that very day—I didn't know, and I didn't want to alarm her.

"Travis?"

"He's in critical condition. We don't know much yet. But I'm here, and I'll stay with you. Your parents are waiting outside the trauma unit with Erik—they're waiting for the girls and Travis. But I'll stay with you. I'm not going to leave you."

Her eyes fluttered, and I saw she was sinking again, fighting to keep her eyes open while the pull of the pain medication dragged her under. Her eyes were huge with fear, but the lids dropped and slipped and pulled her back into unconsciousness, where I hoped she could forget for just a little while, before it would be impossible not to remember.

We all waited. We waited minutes and hours and eventually days, and we just sat, thinking and wondering and holding each other. Cat was recovering, and Heidi was in a room with her, where they were both being nurtured and cared for and fed. Travis had woken up, but he couldn't remember anything, and there was a lot that was broken. He'd been in the passenger seat, and it had taken the brunt of the force when the van rolled. He'd been squashed, they told us, but in more medical terms. He'd been battered. He was definitely broken, but we didn't know yet just how bad it would be.

Pippa was still asleep. The doctors were concerned, and they didn't want to wake her prematurely for fear of permanent damage. So she just lay there, still and sleeping, where she looked bruised and cut up, like a little doll that had been thrown around in the backyard too many times. I wanted to pick her up and hold her and wrap her in her blankie, but they wouldn't let us do that and so we had to settle for just sitting and watching and waiting and telling her stories.

Most of the time, Erik and I sat together, each of us on either side of the bed, making up adventures that took her far away from where she was—first I would begin, telling her tales of princesses who liked macaroni and cheese, and then when I would get stuck at some point where Pippa would usually prompt me about what should come next, Erik would take over and introduce a dragon or a family of nice bats that liked to eat salami. Through the hours that passed at the hospital, Erik and I found comfort in each other, and I knew Laurel was relying on me as the one person who could keep things under control.

I would go home late at night and wake up early in the morning, with everything in my life revolving around those sweet girls and my tiny friend and the family that needed me. I didn't see Joe, and we didn't talk, and I didn't think of him very much at all. Things had changed, and I began to feel myself slip into old habits and settle into a routine that felt like my life. There wasn't enough space in my brain to think about anything beyond the superficial needs that faced me every day, and I focused everything I had on filling those needs and just keeping myself and the Wesleys afloat.

I watched the way Laurel and Peter supported each other, and I saw a love there that I'd never noticed before. To me, they'd always seemed like separate planets, orbiting around the same life, but never touching or interacting, their atmospheres as different as could be. But now, in the face of this, while we all had to be strong and hope and want with all our hearts for this to pass, I saw them come together for each other. They had one another, and for the first time they were relying on each other to keep moving.

In much the same way, I watched as Erik clung to me, holding tight to our years together and knowing I was something he could count on. I accepted the role, and started to feel myself floating back to him as we spent those hours together at the hospital. First, it was our hands. They'd cling to each other as we sat beside Pippa, or we'd link them together behind our backs as we stood before Cat, telling her the latest news from the doctors. Sometimes, he'd rest his hand softly on my back as I cried in the waiting room, wishing I could just tell Cat that Travis was fine and her little girl would be fine, and we could all go home. Eventually, it was our bodies, pressed up against one another in the waiting room while we watched TV, or leaning together as we sat side by side on the edge of Heidi's bed.

Joe called, of course, and he sent me emails, and several nights when I'd get home late from the hospital, there would be daisies left for me on the dining room table or a box with a piece of cake from my favorite bakery waiting on the counter. One morning, he'd left a hot coffee on the stoop. But I didn't see him, and he must have understood I didn't have room inside for anything more, that I couldn't fit any more people in and I had to focus on the family. Because he didn't try to see me, and he didn't press, and eventually, I started to think of him as something distant and past, a memory of something that had happened so long ago, in such a different life, that it was a wonder so little real time had passed.

After a few days, they released Cat and Heidi and they were sent home to recover. They went to Laurel's house, where they would be taken care of and watched and where we could all be together. I moved in to the guest room, helping with Cat and Heidi while Laurel and Peter were at the hospital. Because Heidi was home, Cat went, too, but she spent large parts of her day at the hospital with Travis and Pippa. We all chipped in and did our part, and we began to work as a unit, taking care of the people who were home and hoping for the ones who weren't.

Finally, the day came when Travis could remember and he could speak through the swelling. The doctors were confident he was going to get better. Though he would never be perfect again, and his leg would be pinned, he'd come home in one piece someday soon, and I watched as Cat cried in relief and exhaustion.

"I love him so much, Stella. He's always been good to me," she said as I drove her to the hospital to see him. "If I'd lost him, I don't know what I would have done. If I'd been left alone…"

I thought about that, and I let it sink in, and I wondered, not for the first time, why I'd set myself up for a life alone. There were no guarantees with Joe, or anyone else, and though Erik had never agreed to give me exactly what I wanted, I knew he'd never leave me and I'd always have someone. Someone who'd be there through the hard times, and the challenges, and the nights when I was scared. Maybe that mattered more to me than perfect passion or total happiness or fulfilling the needs of a list that was really all about family, anyway. If holding tight to family, holding tight to my mom, had led me to the list in the first place, then why was I letting the list drag me away from the only family I'd ever known after I lost my parents? Surely, some things could be sacrificed for stability and the knowledge that I was surrounded by good people who would never do anything to hurt me.

I was living at Laurel's, and even though nothing beyond a few gentle touches had passed between Erik and I, we sometimes slept in the same bed, holding each other late at night when everyone else was asleep. I wouldn't say either of us was happy, but we both felt comfortable and cared for.

In early December, I had to go back to work, and it was then that I saw Joe for the first time since Thanksgiving Day. He came to the front desk, so I went to the lobby to see him, even though I didn't really want to. I was emotionally exhausted, and I didn't know how I'd respond when we were face to face. I'd convinced myself to forget him, and let myself believe I had been a fool for falling for him. But when I saw him, I felt the same desire and lust and want I'd felt when we'd been together the last time. I pressed it deep down into the depths, and focused on Pippa and Cat and how they still needed me.

"I missed you," he said, coming forward to wrap me in a hug. But I bristled, and he sensed it, and stepped back to look at me. "I'm so sorry, Stella."

"Thanks," I said, shuffling as we walked toward the coffee shop in the skyway. I felt his hand reach for mine as it hung by my side, but I stuffed it in my pocket, unwilling to take it and feel that heat knock against me and trick me into falling for him again. I was empty, and I didn't have anything to give. "How have you been?"

"I'm lonely," he said, laughing, obviously oblivious to my signals. "I've been dying to see you." I tensed, and he said, quickly, "I can wait, though. I know you still have a lot going on. Anders has kept me up to speed. If there's anything I can do..."

"I appreciate it," I said honestly.

After a few minutes of walking in silence, he said, "Stella, listen, I just want you to know I'm here for you. I've been trying to stay out of the way, but I don't want you to think I'm not here to talk whenever you want to. I can help at the hospital—I was thinking, the guys and I could come, or just me, and play some songs for Pippa if you think that would help?"

I felt tears creeping to the surface as I thought about how much that would mean to her, and I nodded. But I couldn't let him do this, and lead him on, if he thought it meant there was still any hope for us. I didn't know him enough to trust him, and there were still doubts, and listening to Cat talk about how Travis had always been there for her and how she trusted him had made me think about how well I really knew Joe and whether I could trust him.

Suddenly, I just had to get away. Without thinking, I blurted, "I know you've been with a million women, but one of the things I need to know is, have you slept with any of the women who have come to your shows?"

He waited before answering, looking at me with a mix of hurt and confusion. "Yeah, but that was before."

"Were they still married at the time?"

"Some of them," he said quietly. He didn't look proud, but he also didn't look as ashamed as he ought to have.

"Right," I said. *Wrong*, I thought. It was reckless passion that had drawn me to Joe, and I had to step back and let reason and sensibility guide me again.

"It's not something I'm proud of—" he started, but I cut him off.

"I actually don't really want the specifics," I said tightly. "You know I'm a big believer in marriage and commitment and believing in someone, and I have a hard time feeling great about someone who makes a habit of screwing married women." He looked more appropriately ashamed.

"I get that," he said, scratching at his head. "I can't change the things I've done," he said. "But I can make different choices in the future, and that's what I've been working on. With you, I—I'm not—"

"Joe, it doesn't matter anymore." I cut him off. If I'd learned anything from Erik, it was that guys don't change, even if you wish on every falling star. "I hardly even know you, and I don't feel any pressing need to have you justify yourself to me." I thrust out my chin, hoping it would give me the confidence to say what I needed to say. "We were just having a good time, and it's not like I'm interviewing you for marriage."

As I said it, I realized it was true. I knew what I was getting with Erik, and that had to be the safer choice. I was giving up too much by letting him go. I looked at Joe without any emotion at all. I was spent. "I'm sorry."

"It's fine," he said, but I could tell he didn't mean it. I could tell I'd hurt him, and he had more he wanted to say, but I didn't want to hear it. I didn't need to hear it, because it wasn't going to change the kind of person he was, or the kind of person I was.

I stood in front of him outside the skyway coffee shop, ready to turn back and go to my cube and the predictability of a safe life surrounded by things that I knew wouldn't change. "I'm sorry," I said again, and I really did mean it.

"It was different with you, Stella," he said, and I ached with guilt and anger and frustration. "I want things with you I didn't think I'd ever want again. For what it's worth, I was falling in love with you, if you'd have only given me a chance."

I looked at him one last time, and then I walked away, leaving him there in the skyway to watch me abandon what could have been, if only things were different.

If only I wasn't me.

CHAPTER SEVENTEEN

Life carried on, and all of us settled into a routine of waiting and wishing. I continued to live at Laurel's, helping with Cat when I wasn't at work, spending my nights keeping an eye on Heidi while everyone else was at the hospital. Erik and I had become a team, usually going back and forth from the hospital together, and staying at Laurel's together. Sometimes, we would sleep together in the spare room, but it was just for the company. We didn't make love, and we didn't talk about how we were falling back together, slipping into the old patterns and conveniences and customs we'd both grown comfortable with over the years.

We also didn't kiss, and it was one day while I was reading an escapist novel filled with sex and passion that I realized, sadly, I didn't even miss it. I didn't want to kiss Erik. I told myself it was only because Erik and I weren't there yet. There were still things we had to build, and trust and passion that needed to come back before I would be comfortable going there with him again. I knew there was no rush, since what we'd had had built up over years, and it would take more than a few months to break it down again. We had time, and I was taking that time to just be with him.

"Are you happy?" Cat asked me one day, as we sat together in front of a movie. Erik had gone home for the night, and I'd picked *Notting Hill*, a movie Erik hated and never wanted to watch.

"No," I told her honestly. "I've been better."

"I mean, are you happy with Erik?" she asked. When I didn't answer, she asked, "What happened to Joe?"

"It wasn't meant to be. I was never going to get what I wanted. And he could never be the kind of guy who would want the things I want."

"What do you want?" she asked. "Marriage?" She lifted her brows, as though it would be criminal of me to lust after that.

"I thought that's all I wanted, but it's more than that," I said, hearing myself repeat out loud what I'd told myself for the past few weeks. "Marriage stands for something, I guess. Stability. Trust. Love. What you have with Travis, what my parents had. It's nothing I could ever get from Joe. He's not the kind of guy who could commit like that."

"But it's what you have with Erik?"

"Yeah, I guess," I lied, but I couldn't look at her.

Her feet were resting on my lap, and she wiggled her toes in my face to get my attention. I looked at her, and she said, "That's not what you have with Erik."

I shrugged. "Maybe not. But at least Erik is a sure thing. The last few weeks have reminded me how much I need to know I have someone."

She sighed, and that was as far as it went that night.

It was in those days while I was living with Laurel that she and I began to change the way we interacted, too. I felt, somehow, I was becoming more of a friend and—if it was possible—like a daughter, rather than simply Erik's life partner. I felt the judgment passing, and I could feel her relief at my being there. She hadn't brought up my hair in weeks, and there were no longer comments about shoving Erik and I back together. Perhaps that was partly because he and I were spending so much time together, and it gave her hope we'd stay together. But I felt it was more than that.

I actually kind of liked her, and began to enjoy spending time with her, rather than looking at her as a necessary evil that came with Erik. Of course, I'd relied on her heavily over the past twelve years, but it was always on an uneven playing field, and I'd never really let myself understand her as a woman and an individual. Now that I was watching her lead her family—

okay, so she wasn't leading, but she was at least organizing things effectively—through a difficult time, I felt like I started to know her as *Laurel*.

Laurel had been comforting herself and everyone else with her cooking through the hospital ordeal. In fact, she'd decided to revise her Foodie Channel segment to focus on what she was calling "Soothing Food from the Heartland," which she believed was a cross between comfort food and southern cooking—made by a Minnesotan. In fact, her recipes were all hot dishes, the staple of Minnesota church potlucks.

"They're comforting, and they freeze well," she'd told me when she finalized her change-in-strategy. "The rest of the country has a lot to learn from people who understand a deep-freeze and can plan ahead in the face of tragedy."

I wasn't sure how well food connected to tragedy would go over on the Foodie Channel, but it was an interesting change-of-pace from their usual programming. It wasn't like Laurel was suddenly going to be the new face of America's kitchens, so whatever made her feel good about herself was what she should cook.

"You're a good girl, Stella," she announced at random one afternoon while she and I made a homemade tater-tot-topped casserole for the family. It was a little condescending, but there was no malice or sneer in her words. "You know you're part of my family, no matter what." She'd focused her intense gaze on me, and I could see the dabs of stray mascara that dotted her upper eyelid. She'd really let herself slip during this ordeal.

"I know. Thank you for that," I answered, and wondered what she thought was going on with me and Erik. "I love you guys."

"Some of us more than others," she muttered.

"No, I love you all the same," I said, absentmindedly chopping already-chopped carrots into miniscule bits.

"That's not dicing," she snipped and pulled the cutting board away from me. "That's mincing. Those are irregular pieces. I needed perfect squares."

"Sorry," I grumbled. Her scolding momentarily distracted me enough that I forgot what we'd been talking about, but late that night as I lay in bed alone, I thought about what she'd said.

Some of us more than others. Was she right? I felt infinitely more comfortable with Cat than I ever would with Erik, and even Laurel had begun to grow on me. Did I love them just a little bit more than I could ever love Erik?

That weekend, I sat in Pippa's room with Erik, reading stories aloud from a Brothers Grimm collection, when a familiar voice in the hallway startled me out of the world of *Hansel & Gretel.* The velvety richness of Joe's tenor carried through the plastic curtain that hung beside Pippa's hospital bed, and I fought against the nerves that rumbled in my stomach at the thought of seeing him again. I couldn't believe he'd come, even after everything I'd said to him.

I heard the door swing open, and the sounds from the hall came barreling in, along with the sound of Joe's leather boots tapping against the linoleum floor tiles. He peeked around the curtain, and his smile was unrestrained and warm, as though our last conversation had never happened.

"Hey," he said, smiling at me with the easy, warm smile I recognized from his stage persona. "I'm Joe," he said to Erik, reaching across me to shake hands.

I wasn't sure how much Erik knew about Joe, or whether he realized this was the guy I'd been dating. I decided it wasn't the best time to tell him, and chose instead to say, "Erik, this is Joe, from the Dog Hounds—Pippa's favorite band."

"Oh, hey, man," Erik said, pulling out his cool-guy voice. "Thanks for coming—did Cat call you?"

Joe glanced at me, then said, "Yeah. I wanted to play for Pippa, and see if I could help. Sometimes music therapy can do something. It's worth a shot."

"Cool, man," Erik said, and I rolled my eyes. "Give it a crack." He nodded in that slow, lower-lip-out sort of way he did every time we listened to songs he was supposed to like. "Rock on."

I found it impossible to be squeezed between Joe and Erik, when Joe was so naturally, perfectly cool and relaxed and Erik… well, I couldn't help but wonder if Erik had a little metal ball tucked up between his ass cheeks, and someone had told him he'd go bald if it fell out.

I felt bad for Pippa, who had to listen to him posing and posturing. *I* had put myself in this position, but she was trapped in a coma listening to her uncle pretend to be Mr. Cool Guy while her musical hero stood three feet from the foot of her bed, charming us all with his beautiful curls and sensual voice.

Joe had brought a guitar—more versatile than the banjo when he was playing solo, he'd told me—and settled in at the foot of Pippa's bed. His hand patted her ankle, covered under a sheet, and then he began to play. It was soft and gentle, a song about kangaroos and koala bears and dancing in the rain. His voice had life and humor, and I just hoped somewhere in there, under the IVs and medicine, Pippa could hear the song he was playing only for her. Joe didn't seem deterred by his lack of audience, but played and sang for almost an hour, while I sat still and listened, wondering why I'd never asked him to sing for me.

After Joe had played a few songs, Erik left to get some lunch, but I stayed and watched. Joe's eyes locked on mine while he sang about koi and carp and wishes that sprinkled down like fish food in a tank. I tried to think of anything other than the way a curl fell across his eye, and how he probably smelled like doughnuts or cinnamon or the winter wind from his run that morning. But instead of distracting myself, I found I was drawn in, pulled into the swirling of his voice and the way it comforted me and wrapped around me, even when he was singing about pickles and focusing his everything on Pippa.

Cat and Travis came into the room after he'd been playing for a while, Travis in his hospital gown with a walker, his body still wrapped and broken but finally functioning. We all sat together at the foot of the bed, and I could feel Cat watching me while I restrained myself from staring at Joe. I kept my eyes down, and uttered a simple "thanks for coming" when he was done, hoping no one noticed how much it hurt for me to see him here, to watch him with Pippa, and to recognize just how much his presence relaxed me.

He left, and Cat fixed her gaze on me. "WTF are you doing, Stella?"

"Is it okay that he came?" I asked casually. "I didn't think it would upset her, and he offered, and it just seemed like she would love it." I glanced up, and saw that Travis was leaning on Cat and she held him up, all five feet of her supporting the weight of his body somehow. "If it comes up, can you tell Erik you invited Joe to come?"

She shook her head. But when she saw the pleading look on my face, she agreed. "Sure, hon. I'll do that if it comes up." She paused. "Stell? You know what happened to us doesn't change the fact that you chose to leave Erik the first time." When I didn't respond, she sighed. "Thank you, Stella, for having Joe sing for her. Pippa is lucky to have you in her life."

Perhaps it was something about the kangaroos and koalas, or maybe it was sheer coincidence, but the doctors told us later that afternoon they felt confident Pippa was ready to come out of her coma. They'd recognized positive signs, and felt there was a level of consistency in her brain functioning that made it safe for them to release her from her medical hold.

We all gathered at her bedside the next morning as they began the process to pull her out. The doctors had told us it would take days, if not weeks, for her to recover fully from the heavy dose of medication she'd been relying on, and they warned us that she probably wouldn't talk for a while and would have trouble remembering things we told her later. But it didn't matter, since she was finally going to wake up. She was finally coming back to us, and from the tests the doctors had run, it looked like she'd recover fully.

I stepped back when I saw her lids flutter, watched from the shadows outside the circle of family that pressed in around her. I was fairly certain waking up with a small army of people hovering over you would be shocking and scary, and I didn't need to be *right there*. I knew I didn't need to be physically present to be a part of this. I didn't need to hover in order for her to know I was there for her.

Cat cried when Pippa's eyes finally opened and she stared up at her. Travis held Heidi tight as Pippa focused on the people who loved her. Pippa's eyes opened to her future—and strangely, when I imagined what that future would be and where her next steps would take her, I knew I would be a part of it.

At that moment I was sure, without a doubt, that I'd always be in her life. Even if Erik wasn't beside me, pulling me into the folds of the family, the bonds I'd formed with Pippa and Heidi and Cat—even Laurel—would carry on. No matter what happened between Erik and I, no one could take away the connection I'd built with the other people I'd come to love as a family of my own. They were a sure thing.

True friendships and the kind of bond I'd formed with Pippa and Heidi couldn't fall apart if you held tight, not if you clung to them and cherished them and *wanted* them to carry on. A bond like the one I had with the girls only broke when you gave up on it, or *let* the person drift away into a thing of the past—when you said goodbye because it was time. I would never be ready to let go of those dear girls, and I knew I only had to if that's what I chose to do.

I could hold on to them, and still find a way to hold fast to me.

Erik reached for me, pulling me forward into the circle of family surrounding Pippa, and I began to cry. I cried for her, and I cried for Cat, and I cried for me.

I cried because I knew by continuing to fit into this circle as Erik's partner, holding fast to his crisp shirttails and clinging to him simply because I needed to feel like I belonged and because I needed someone to need me, I really had given up on me. Completely. At that moment, watching Pippa creep back from the scary shadows of a temporary world, I could see how my life would slowly creep back to the way it was, if I let it. And that's the thing that scared me.

I'd been foolish to think things could be different between Erik and me, now that we'd had this experience together. To think that the accident had happened because somehow, the universe wanted us to slip and slide back into the familiar coexistence that had left me empty and unhappy in the first place.

I felt sick, realizing a future with Erik would never give me the same rush I'd felt in his office that day, or in Cat's upstairs shower—it would just be more of the same. More coping and existing, simply because that's the way our life was. Because that's the life we'd found together. Because it was the best life I could wish for myself when I was with him.

The life I had with Erik was the very one I'd designed and plotted and planned for as a fifteen-year-old girl, imagining it in my mind before working toward some specific and intangible endpoint. But then, like a sand castle left forgotten on the beach at the end of a summer's day, I'd stepped away and let someone else shape it and mess with it and eventually create something entirely different from my original design. Hell, that someone—maybe it was my own insecurity, or Erik, or a wicked combination of the two of us together—had stomped on my castle and left it in pieces. But I guess a piece of me could still see the outlines of my creation sitting there in the sand—and the ghost of what I'd once wished my life could be kept making me want to try to build it up into something again. At some point, I'd let myself believe it was too late to make something different, to build a new life.

I was cheating myself out of a fair chance at happiness.

Erik's hand reached for mine, and habit and hope and a little bit of fear propelled me to let him take it, but there was a distance in our touch unlike anything I'd ever felt before. It was as though a great crevice had split the floor between us, miles deep, that would never allow either of us to cross the divide from him to me and back again.

We stepped out of the room after a few minutes, giving the immediate family some time to reconnect.

"I'm so glad you were here for us all this time, Stella." He paused. "It meant more than you'll ever know. To me, especially. I—" He cleared his throat, picking at his top button, pushing it open, closed, open, closed. "I know we have a lot to figure out, and now that things are going to go back to normal, I hope you'll consider coming home?"

Home. To his house. To the way things were.

"Stella?" he asked, pressing on before I had a chance to say anything. "I was thinking, if you really want to get married…" He laughed. "I know you do want to get married, but—well, if you still want to get married, we can do that, you know."

"Get married?" I asked, stunned. "Are you proposing, Erik?"

He shrugged. "Yeah. Of course, I'll ask you properly, too, but I just wanted to let you know I'm willing to do that for you. I don't want that to be the only thing keeping us apart. It's stupid, and there's no reason for us to break up over a formality."

"Erik, there was so much more that was wrong with us than just a 'formality.' It wasn't just the marriage thing."

"I know there were other little things, and I get that you needed some time to find yourself or whatever, but a wedding was the biggie, right?" He smiled. "Because we can fix that."

"I'm sorry, Erik, but we're beyond repair." I knew then that it was true.

"But you've seemed so happy the last few weeks. We've been so good! I thought you'd figured it out, and that you were getting back to normal."

That's normal for him? I wondered. *No feeling or connection, just sort of generally* being *in the same place?* "You're right. I *have* figured it out," I said.

As I strode out of the hospital, walking away from Erik for the last time, I was absolutely certain if I wanted to have any hope of living a life less lonely, I needed to leave a sure thing. I may have been walking out alone, but I knew I'd never let myself feel so lonely and forgotten again.

CHAPTER EIGHTEEN

"I'm starting to realize it's actually sort of easy to leave someone, but it's not quite as easy to find yourself again." I looked up from the ever-growing pile of apple slices on the counter in front of me. "How many do you think we need? Is this enough?"

"Are you kidding me right now?" Lily shook her head and ignored my apples. "That's the stupidest thing I've ever heard." She snagged an apple slice and popped it in her mouth.

"I'm reading self-help," I said with a shrug. "It's soothing. They write poignantly in quotes—it's actually really clever."

Lily groaned. "It's stupid. Stop reading self-help. You don't need soothing. You need to get laid and just move on already. We went over this the first time you left Erik. Do we really need to have the same conversation again?"

"I do need soothing. I'm busy liberating myself, and someone has to tell me how to do that." I pushed the pile of apples to the middle of Lily's kitchen island and set my knife aside. I was supposedly teaching her how to bake apple crisp, but so far the tutorial had involved me chopping up all the apples and mixing the ingredients for the topping, while Lily took tiny bites and helped with nothing. "I know I made the right choice—"

Lily cut me off to say, "Took you long enough. Here's what bothers me: How could you possibly have had sex with that guy again? Was he really good enough in bed that you were desperate to go back for more? Erik doesn't strike me as a stallion. He's less Patrick Swayze in *Dirty Dancing*, more Lloyd Dobbler from *Say Anything*."

"What's wrong with Lloyd Dobbler? He was a nice guy! See, this is what's wrong with your taste in men... Lloyd Dobbler is classic romance, the perfect guy. Patrick Swayze was a man-whore in *Dirty Dancing*. Also, he had a mullet."

"Lloyd Dobbler is *fine*," Lily sighed. "But the point is, no one fantasizes about sex with Lloyd Dobbler. The guy's name is Lloyd. Lloyd is like Erik and his pleated khaki pants... seriously, who fantasizes about one last quickie with a guy who wears pleated pants?"

"Okay, so I *eventually* made the right choice, but now that Erik is out of my life for good, it's hard to figure out what to do with myself. The Internet dating and the stuff with Joe..." I took a breath and pushed around the pile of apples, hoping Lily wouldn't ask about Joe again. I was trying not to think about him. Trying not to wonder what might have happened if things had gone differently. Trying not to remember that afternoon in Iowa. Trying not to remember how I'd told him off, and how he'd come to sing for Pippa anyway. "I guess it just feels like I was practicing being an adult for the past few months. But now the game has started—the whistle blew, so to speak, and I'm not sure what position I'm supposed to be playing."

Lily stared at me, open-mouthed. "If you're going to keep talking like this, with those stupid metaphors and self-help language, I'm cracking a bottle of wine."

"It's eleven in the morning."

"Some people are driven to drink at eleven in the morning. Specifically, people who are friends with self-help authors."

"You'd like self-help. It's a big industry, you know. There's money in it."

Lily rolled her eyes. "Are you ever going to bake that crisp? I'm hungry."

As I piled the apples into a baking dish and sprinkled the crumbles of butter and sugar over the top, I thought about the past week. After I'd walked away from Erik in the hospital, I'd felt at peace almost immediately. In many ways, life was better than it was the first time I'd left him, since I knew now that I could truly move on. As much as I had absolutely believed I was ready to move on when I first left Erik, the finality of that last goodbye felt completely different.

The first time I'd left, it had been—in large part—a response to Erik's actions. This time, I'd walked away because I firmly believed I would be happier without him. I wasn't leaving because he wouldn't commit, but because I didn't want him to anymore. It was liberating to be free, but also somewhat lonely. I knew there was something better out there for me, but I still had to figure out how to get to it.

"Have you talked to him at all?" Lily asked, settling into the couch.

"No, not to Erik directly. Laurel has called every day, though. Aren't I lucky?"

"I think you've actually started to like her," Lily said, putting her feet up on the coffee table. "I bet you'd be a little disappointed if she didn't pester you from time to time."

"Yeah, she's not bad. But she's been calling because she still insists I join her for this Foodie Network segment. I sort of feel like I have to—it's almost impossible to tell her no, even though she has no hold over me. She's very convincing."

"Erik obviously got it from someone," Lily said, closing her eyes. "You're your own woman now. Don't do anything she tells you to do if you don't want to do it."

"I won't," I said, but knew that was easier said than done. "Obviously."

"Yeah, there are a lot of things that are obvious, but you have trouble seeing them sometimes." She peeked at me from one half-opened eye.

"You're not really one to talk," I said, and glared back at her. "Anyway, it's easier to deal with Laurel now that I'm not constantly worried about how much insight she has into my sex life. I always vaguely suspected Erik confided just a little too much in his mother. She would look at me, like—" I made a puckered face, and Lily laughed.

As I was sliding the crisp in the oven, I heard a key in the lock and jumped.

Anders peeked his head in the front door, and looked as surprised to see me as I was to see him. "Oh, hey, Stella." He grinned at me, then at Lily. "I forgot I stole your key that, um, that day you, ah... Well, anyway, here it is—back to you! I was just bringing it back to you."

I looked from Anders to Lily and back again. I had a hunch Anders and Lily had been spending a lot more time together while I'd been out of the house. They'd always been close friends, of course, but there was something about the way I'd noticed them acting around one another since I'd moved back home that felt different. There was a new level of respect, and a little less snarkiness. But neither one of them had said anything about it, so I wasn't going to bring it up yet. I loved the idea of them finding each other, and I had a feeling if I pushed too soon, it would crumble.

"Want some crisp?" Lily offered, scooting over on the couch so Anders could sit next to her. I admired the way Lily was always so comfortable around Anders, so sure of herself. I hoped she would have the opportunity to love someone who would cherish her and help her see herself as beautiful and amazing. She needed a sexy Lloyd Dobbler. Someone who wouldn't make her fret over bra lines or uneven breasts. "Stay and hang out. Stella's baking."

"Actually, I'm supposed to be *teaching*, but Lily is a horrible student. This is worse than cooking with Laurel. She's bossy, but at least she participates."

"I'm a great director, but a terrible doer. I don't like to get all wrapped up in the details. Details bore me. I have different talents—marketing bath tissue and toothbrushes to the masses, for one. Want some coffee?" She grinned at Anders, then turned to me with a firm expression and a cold voice. "Stella would be happy to get it for you. Thank you, dear."

"Oh, I see how it is," I grumbled, filling a cup of coffee for Anders. "I'm only pouring this cup of coffee because it's for Anders. *Not* because you ordered me to. I don't do your bidding, Lily Sparrow. Hardcore Lily may scare some people, but she doesn't scare me."

"Hardcore Lily is hot," Anders said, settling back against the couch to watch the drama unfold. "I'd like to see you boss Stella around some more. You're sort of sexy when you go all executive, Lil."

I'd heard Anders say things like this to Lily before, but not with the same earnest tone of voice he'd just used. It didn't sound like banter, it sounded real. Slightly creepy, but very real.

She beamed. "Sexy, huh?"

"Very." They stared at each other, and I suddenly felt like I was watching something I wasn't supposed to see.

"Well, then," I began to gather my things. "I guess I should go. I was going to go for a run, or do some laundry, or something."

"Your crisp..." Lily said, vaguely pointing to the oven. "Don't you want some crisp?"

"You guys can eat it. You made it, after all."

A week or so later, just before Christmas, Cat, Anders, Lily, and I sat in the living room at Cat's house, drinking wine after the girls had gone to bed. We had moved our drinks night to Cat's house so she wouldn't have to leave Pippa, who had finally come home from the hospital.

Pip was feeling better, but still had momentary flashes of bad memories and dreams after the accident, so Cat was understandably reluctant to leave her. She also wanted to be near Heidi and Travis—they all sort of marched around the house in a pack, cuddling each other in the most adorable way. The accident had obviously pulled them all even closer together. Cat had gigglingly confessed that she and Trav had finally started to sleep together again, even. A few good things had come of the accident.

"Let's all discuss the elephant in the room," Lily said, dumping the rest of the contents of the wine bottle into her glass. She was drinking "Italian-style," as she called it, using a big water glass to drink her adult beverage, rather than a proper wine glass. "We're all together, and I think enough time has passed that we can finally discuss it."

"And that is?" Anders said, touching his fingers to Lily's knee. I averted my eyes. Every time Anders touched Lily, I cracked up. I'm not sure why—it wasn't really funny, exactly—but I could not wrap my brain around the fact that they were dating (or whatever you would call it) now. They still hadn't *exactly* confessed to anything happening between them, but I'd seen the change in the way they related to each other—the touching was a fairly overt sign—and I knew it was just a matter of time before they'd come out with it. Lily had broken things off with Chad, and hadn't seen Brad since our disastrous date with the dead fish. "Which elephant?"

"Stella's sex life, moving forward." She lifted her eyebrows at me. "So? Let's talk."

"I'd say the larger elephant is sitting on Anders' fingers, right there on your knee." Cat pointed and giggled, which made me feel a little better about my own reaction. "Is there a little sumpin-sumpin happening here?" Cat hadn't witnessed the shift in how Lily and Anders been acting around one another—for her, seeing them touch was obviously somewhat shocking. "Give me the deets!"

Anders started to pull his fingers away from Lily's leg, but Lily dragged them back.

"Perhaps something *is* happening here," she said grinning. "However, I have a tendency to screw up every relationship, so I'd rather not talk about it." She looked at us haughtily, but it was hard to take her seriously with a water glass full of wine squeezed between her knees.

Cat and I *oohed* in unison.

"Lily keeping quiet?" I asked, realizing Anders was squirming on the couch beside her. "You know the less you say, the more we'll press."

"How about you give us a few weeks to see how badly we're going to fuck this up, and then you can 'press' all you want?" Anders pleaded. Lily smirked, aware that because Anders had been the one to ask, we'd probably comply. He had a way of making things sound so reasonable that only a real asshole would pester him after he asked us to lay off.

"Sounds fair," I said.

Cat agreed. "Just please don't fuck it up," she pleaded. "With you guys, it's a little harder for Stella and I to pick sides if you get twitchy around each other."

"They're already twitchy around each other," I told her. "Look how Anders' hand keeps jumping on and off her knee." Cat and I leaned against each other and laughed. "He's nervous. Aw." I guess I was the asshole who felt compelled to push.

"This means you're the only one of us not getting any now, Stella." Lily beamed, clearly proud of her ability to turn the tables on me. "Unless you are…?"

"Things have been pretty quiet at our house," Anders announced. "No scarves or bras—or overalls—on the door. Where is our friend Joe?"

I took a big swig of wine. "I told you. We broke up. Over."

"That was temporary," Cat said. "Right?"

"No, it was real," I said pitifully. "It's a problem that he makes a habit of sleeping with married women." I'd spent the last few weeks convincing myself I'd done the right thing when I'd walked away from Joe. After all, he was a player who had no interest in committing. He had probably broken up families… families just like Cat's. "Besides, I don't really want to be the idiot who falls for a stupid musician who's doing groupies in the back of the band van."

"Is that what he does?" Cat looked abashed.

"I don't know," I muttered. "Probably."

"Probably?" Lily laughed. "Maybe so, but I doubt it. They don't even *have* a band van. And anyway, Joe's a really nice guy. I thought you were having fun with him."

"He's a nice guy because he's busy trying to get in women's pants." My friends didn't look convinced, so I continued. I spoke aloud all of the excuses I'd given myself for why I couldn't call him again. "For one thing, he's in a children's band. If that weren't bad enough, he also makes a habit of sleeping with the adoring mothers who come to his shows. I actually do have hopes of maybe, someday, finding someone who makes me happy and wants to spend his life with me, and I know Banjo Boy Joe just isn't going to be that guy."

I heard myself saying aloud all the things I'd told myself over and over again, every time I began to fantasize about Joe or thought about that day in the car on our way to Iowa.

"He's already been divorced once, and now he's just trying to have a good time. He's hot, and funny, and incredibly charming… and that's why he's trouble. I know you all think I need to have a fling or two, but Joe's not going to be it. I need to be more responsible with my time."

My friends stared at me with matching smiles on their faces. "Stop looking at me like that."

"Did you at least sleep with him before you said bye-bye?" Cat asked.

"Or did you *love* him too much to fuck him?" Lily teased.

"You guys are getting all junior high on me. We went out on, like, seven dates. You could hardly call it love. Lust, maybe. But yeah, I really liked him. A lot." I felt myself starting to flush, and wished I could trick my friends into talking about something else. Every time I thought about Joe, I missed him. I regretted being so rude to him when he'd been nothing but gracious with me, and I wished it had ended differently. Not that it would have ended with us riding off into the sunset together, but maybe it could have ended with a little sex? Just a tiny bit, so I could have seen what it was like to feel those thighs on mine. "And no, we never did sleep together, to answer that classy question."

"You can't stop thinking about him," Anders announced. "Let's not kid ourselves that you're not thinking about him right now."

"I'm thinking about him right now because we're talking about him." I polished off my wine in three huge gulps, and felt myself opening up as the buzz crept in. "But yeah, I still think about him a lot. I wish I hadn't told him off so definitively, but I did, and I need to stick by it." My resolve was crumbling, but I went on. "It's over. I have principles."

"Why the hell do you need to stick by your word? Obviously, your incredible resolve to trap yourself by your own stupid decisions has left you completely unsatisfied for the last ten years or so." As Lily got worked up, she edged closer to Anders. Was his hand under her butt? "Maybe you should stop sticking by your stubborn guns and let yourself change your mind and change course?"

"Stubborn guns?" Anders asked. "Is that a real thing?"

"Mixed metaphor, maybe? But the point is made." Lily grinned at him.

"For reals, Stella," Cat chimed in. "You could just call him and see if maybe, possibly, you were a little harsh? Tell him you want to see him one more time?"

"It's too late. I was really rude." I knew that probably wasn't true. Joe was the kind of guy who would forgive. He wasn't the sort to bear grudges or linger forever on stupid mistakes. But carrying on with Joe wasn't going to get me anywhere—it was time to grow up and figure out what I really wanted.

"Wah-wah." Lily rolled her eyes. "You're depressing me. It's never too late for anything." She glanced at Anders, and the significance wasn't lost on any of us.

"Call him," Anders agreed. "It can't hurt."

"Don't you want to cuddle up in his flannel-y scruff again?" Lily asked, giggling. "Nuzzle up to the sounds of his crooning Banjo Boy voice?"

I shrugged and poured myself more wine. The thought of Joe, his warm chest wrapped in soft flannel and his adorable curls poking out from under that silly winter cap, was not something I wanted to think about. Because when I thought about him, I knew there was unfinished business between us. But what would another night, or another few months, or any amount of time with Joe, do for me? It wasn't going to help me figure out where I wanted to be in life, or what I wanted to do, or get me any closer to the settled, secure life I wanted.

What was more important: A little more time with a hot guy who might turn into another mistake, or the confidence that I was making smart choices for myself? The answer was clear.

I knew I had to pick smart choices, but part of me wished it was possible to have both.

CHAPTER NINETEEN

The next morning, I went back to water aerobics for a final pre-holiday gossip session. Before and after the last few classes, I'd given the Y ladies a run-down of the month, and had filled everyone in on my final-for-real-this-time break up with Erik.

I'd also shared the details of my last conversation with Joe, which had not gone over as well as I might have hoped, but did go about as well as I would have expected. Rae and Fran and even Barbara hissed and booed, but I knew they would. They sometimes forgot my life wasn't a movie and that a girl didn't always end up with the sexy guy. Sometimes, the girl made more practical choices, which—they'd informed me—didn't make for quite as good a plotline.

Even though they were all pissy with me about the Joe decision, I was looking forward to seeing them all one last time before Christmas. I suspected it would probably be the last time I'd see the Y crew for a while. I had no idea what my schedule would be like once I started my entrepreneurship class after the new year. But I did know it was time to settle back into a routine, and now that my back was feeling better, maybe it was time to do some real exercise.

Even though the ladies-of-the-pool deserved better, I'd brought a guest with me for my final class—someone who needed a few friends closer to her own age, so she'd stop bugging me.

"This is an old person class!" Laurel hissed as she stood, fully clothed and very pissed, in the locker room at the Y that morning. "They're all minutes away from death!"

"We may be old, but we *can* hear you," Heather muttered from a few feet away. Loudly, she asked, "Who's the angry bitch, Stella?"

"Heather, this is Laurel... Erik's mother." I gave her a pointed glance that said, *Let's not share my secrets, shall we?*

Heather smirked. "Let me guess—this is the stiff's mom?"

Laurel stomped on the floor, making me think of a toddler or an angry bull. "My son is not a stiff," she said stiffly.

"Ignore Heather," I said. "She's senile."

I smiled at Heather, warning her to keep her mouth shut. At least until I was no longer coming to water aerobics. Then they could say whatever they wanted to Laurel. I was actually hoping they'd torment her a little—it was part of the reason I'd suggested she come. She could use a good dose of what these ladies had to dish out. I had a feeling Laurel would fit in well with the water aerobics crew.

"Where, pray tell, do I change?" Laurel looked at me archly, her body stiff and rigid as she noticed all the naked figures around her. "Certainly not here."

"You can get your fat ass into a swimsuit here, or you can hunker down over a toilet back there. But Barb squats when she pees, so there's usually a bit of piss on the seat." Heather smiled back at me. She was really laying it on thick for Laurel.

I pulled my own swimsuit on quickly, while Laurel huffed and puffed at my side.

"You're going to have to change eventually. Here, try this." I showed her the trick of wrapping a towel around herself while pulling her swimsuit up discreetly. But she lacked some coordination, and the towel fluttered to the floor mid-pull, leaving Laurel naked and screeching while Barb, Heather, and Fran crowded together at the end of the aisle laughing. Laurel shrieked and pulled her suit up, but not before everyone had a good laugh at her dramatics.

Laurel obviously wasn't seeing the humor in the situation. She glared at all of us. "It's impolite to laugh at another woman's misfortunes," she pouted. This made the others laugh harder, until finally they got distracted.

"Those women are terrible, Stella," she told me. "I'm a Foodie Channel celebrity… they should have more respect. You should know better."

"You're not a Foodie Channel celebrity yet," I warned her. "They haven't even come to film you."

"Well, the cameras will be on me soon, and then these women will have to treat me with more respect." She grumbled and patted at her hair, making sure she was pulled together for class. "That's the only reason I'm here, really. The camera adds five pounds, you know."

"Isn't it ten?" Heather asked with a smile. She always waited for me to walk her out to the pool deck, but today I sort of wished she'd leave us. I felt like a traitor, but I had a feeling coaxing Laurel out to the pool would be a little like coaxing Pippa into the doctor's office for a shot.

The only reason Laurel had agreed to water aerobics in the first place is she wanted to slim down a bit for her Foodie Channel filming, which was finally scheduled for the week between Christmas and New Year's. Laurel had started herself on a cabbage soup diet and vowed to exercise, hoping she could shed at least ten pounds in less than two weeks.

"Who's farting?" Fran asked suddenly, her voice cutting through the din in the locker room. She sniffed around in Barb's aisle, then poked her head around to peer at us. "It stinks to high heaven in here."

"It's Stella's friend," Heather announced helpfully. "She's gassy. Let's get her under the water and the bubbles will give her away."

"These women are crass," Laurel hissed to me, her face turning crimson with embarrassment. I had to agree. The fact that they'd devolved to a discussion of bodily functions didn't help, but it wasn't like the ladies at the Y ever held back on much. "I don't want to be here anymore. Polite company doesn't discuss flatulence." I fought hard to hold back my laughter, but it was impossible. I giggled and Laurel got even redder. "Seriously, Stella, you're better than this. Do I need to worry about how you're going to present yourself during my Foodie Channel filming? Need I worry about how you're going to represent the family?"

I'd told Laurel many times it made me uncomfortable to be a part of her Foodie Channel segment, but she never seemed to hear me. We saw each other infrequently enough that I hoped she'd just sort of give up after a while. Unfortunately, she called too often, and every time we spoke, she acted like it made total sense for me to be right there by her side when she filmed her bit about comfort food from the Heartland. I just couldn't come up with a decent excuse for why I couldn't do it, so Laurel refused to hear me. I know she understood Erik and I were over, but I wondered if maybe this was her way of holding on to me a little longer. Maybe she thought I'd slip away if she didn't continue to cling and act needy.

"For your information," Laurel announced haughtily. "I'm on a diet of cabbage soup and grapefruit. It's glorious for weight-loss, but the side effects are challenging."

The other women in the locker room stared. Rae spoke first. "So I take it this means we should keep you away from the bag of cookies after class?"

"Why diet?" Barbara asked. "You're chubby, not fat. You need the spare tire for when you get old and wither up, like Heather." She lifted her eyebrows and surveyed Laurel with the keen eye of an observant retiree. "It's a good thing you're at aerobics, though, since it looks like you'd benefit from a little strength, but all in all I wouldn't mind having your figure."

Laurel wasn't sure whether to take this as a compliment. She frowned, then tried to hide behind an open locker door to finish getting dressed.

"I've been selected for a segment on the Foodie Channel," Laurel informed the others as we walked out toward the pool deck. She lifted her chin and told the other women about her segment, and about her magnificent kitchen, and carried right on to explain how Cat and I would be a part of the show with her. About how it was everything both of us had ever dreamed of, which was obviously incorrect.

I caught Heather watching me, noting my discomfort.

"When are they coming to film this?" Heather asked, glancing at me quickly before easing into the pool.

"Right after Christmas—they fit me in on the Friday before New Year's, which will be ideal, since my ceramic Christmas village will still be up on display on the buffet." She breathed out as the water reached her midsection. "I always take it down on New Year's Day—I feel it's inappropriate to stretch a holiday past its limit."

"Obviously," Heather muttered. "That would be a sin." She glanced at me again, and I shrugged. "It's just bad timing," Heather said, more loudly this time.

"Why's that?" Laurel asked. "My house never looks as good as it does during the holidays, and my hair will be in the perfect place between cuts. I think the timing of their visit is ideal." She lifted her chin and dared Heather to challenge her.

Heather shrugged. "It's just that I was going to see if Stella wanted to join me on a little holiday jaunt..." She trailed off.

"What kind of jaunt? You mean, a trip?" I asked, curious. I liked Heather. A lot. And I liked jaunts—or, at least I liked the idea of trips. It wasn't as if I'd been on a multitude of adventures, but still. On the other hand, Christmas was just days away, and I had things to do. Gifts to buy for the girls, pre-reading to do for my class, cookies to bake for the office (I *always* baked cookies for the office). How could I possibly consider a *vacation*. "Where are you going?"

"I'm headed to Venice," she uttered casually, letting the tiniest hint of a smile tug at her mouth. "A last-minute thing. "

"California?" I asked, narrowing my eyes.

"Stella..." Laurel began, her gaze darting between Heather and I. Rae, Barbara, and Fran were all watching the conversation with great interest from their perch on the side of the pool. "You wouldn't let me down, would you?" Tears pooled in her eyes and a Laurel-pout crushed her lips into a squishy line that looked like a row of raisins lined up end to end. "I need you."

"Not California. Italy," Heather said, wiggling her dumbbells through the water. Little chlorinated ripples lapped at the sides of my body. "I've got a nephew in Italy, and he's invited me to visit for the holidays." She grinned. "I might stay for a while, actually. See if I can snag a man. Got nothing better to do."

Barbara snorted and Rae huffed.

"You're going to Italy for Christmas? Since when?" Fran demanded.

"Since I decided it would be fun," Heather chirped back. "And I'm inviting Stella to join me because she's young and *single*—" She cast a meaningful look at Laurel, who stared right back at her. "And besides, she'll help me pee on the plane. Spending Christmas on the Venice canals should be decent." She shrugged. "It's just an invite, no pressure. You can run your own life, Stella. I'm certainly not going to tell you what you should or shouldn't do." She turned away, but I could hear her say, "Nobody wants to be alone at Christmas."

"I appreciate it," I said, finding myself getting a little emotional at the kindness and surprise of the offer. Here I'd been sniping and griping about these ladies and making fun of my water aerobics course, and Heather was offering to save me from a Christmas alone. It was almost as though she was stepping up, offering to be my Nana—or, at the very least, a crabby and reliable friend. I was happy with either—and overwhelmed by the idea of a Christmas in Italy. "I'll think about it. But with work, and my class starting, and…" I broke off, realizing how sad and thin all of those excuses sounded in comparison to an on-a-whim trip to Italy. *Italy!*

I could practically taste the tiramisu in my mouth when Laurel spoke. "But you're all booked up with the Foodie Channel segment. Don't forget about our segment. I'm counting on you, Stella."

"I don't think there's much risk of her forgetting," Rae muttered, rolling her eyes.

"You know you don't *need* me," I said to Laurel. "But I appreciate that you *want* me there with you." I smiled warmly. "That alone means a lot to me, but what I would really appreciate is the chance to make a choice for myself for once, without anyone giving me a hard time."

Laurel wiped at her eyes and mascara trailed from the corner of one eye to her temple. She smiled wanly, unwilling to let it go without the extra dash of drama.

Jean started class then, and as we lifted and stretched and wiggled our bodies through the water on noodles, I thought about Heather's offer. I had the money, I had no other plans

that thrilled me, no Christmas traditions of my own, and I
certainly wanted to go… so what was keeping me from going
for it?

When James Davis peeked over the edge of my cubicle wall
later that morning, just moments after I'd returned from a
coffee break with Lily, I was distractedly scrolling through
Google results for Venice. I'd slipped off my cowboy boots—
the ones I'd impulsively bought for that first date with Joe—
and I was sitting at my desk in socks. I'd been asked to come in
on a Friday, my day off, even though I wasn't actually being
paid to work. This irked me, but I was a good corporate soldier
and didn't want to ruffle feathers, so I'd come. But so far, I'd
spent the day wasting time and getting as comfortable as I
could in my bland cube.

Around elevent, James' slippery voice cooed, "Working
hard, Stella bell?" and I jumped out of my rolling chair so fast
it shot back and rammed into the cloth wall behind me.

"Please don't call me Stella bell," I said coldly, minimizing
my browser before turning to face James. Because he had my
career in his little hands, I feared him. James was shorter than
me, and younger than me, and ickier than anyone, but he was
Important. I didn't like the way he could sneak up on us, or the
way he seemed to lurk around corners waiting to bust someone
for having a life outside Centrex. Even still, I wasn't sure how
a guy who reminded me of Vanity Smurf could intimidate me.
His coif was pomaded and pressed into a shape that roughly
resembled the secret underbelly of a Smurf's hat, which should
have made him simply comical. But he was sort of scary, and I
didn't like that he'd bullied me into coming into the office on a
Friday, my company-mandated "free day."

"Up a little early for cheer today, eh, little Bear?" He
grinned, flashing the fronts of his teeth all the way back to his
molars. He gestured to my boots and said, "Cowboy boots. Not
really Centrex-appropriate, are they? Have you checked the
dress code intranet site to see if they're on the approved list?"

I lifted my eyebrows and said nothing.

After pushing one of my boots toward me with his toe, James cleared his throat and moved on. "Anyhoo, sorry to make you come in on a Friday—I'm sure you've gotten used to sleeping in and watching movies all day on Fridays, now that you're a lady of luxury." He chuckled, though I didn't think him making light of my corporate downsizing was particularly funny. "I'm going to make it up to you, but you know, we're all team players and sometimes, Stella, we have to work on our own time to get the results we're looking for in our lives."

"No problem," I said, gritting my teeth. "I'm happy to help out."

"The reason I had you come in today," James said, getting comfortable in my guest chair. "Hey, cute flannel," he said, suddenly distracted by the piece of red flannel Joe had brought me weeks ago to spice up the bland walls of my cube. James looked at me and laughed, as though we were sharing a joke or enjoying a funny together. I stared back at him and he turned to rub his finger across the surface of the fabric. Then he studied it carefully, pinned as it was to the wall of my cube like some kind of masterpiece. "Is this art?"

"Please don't touch it," I snapped, trying hard not to laugh. "It's from a gallery in New York, and it was very expensive. You know you're not supposed to touch art with bare, greasy fingers, right?"

James pulled his hand away and jammed it in his pocket. "Sorry about that. It's a great piece." He nodded appreciatively. "As I was saying, the reason I had you come in today is we're kicking off a new project that I want you to be a part of. I see opportunities for you here at Centrex, Stella, and I want to make sure you're engaged in every aspect of this organization." He paused, taking a moment to adjust his hair.

"You've worked on a number of fantastic projects in your years here, and I know you must feel lucky to be a part of such a team." I didn't bother telling him how wrong he was. I hated my job, and it just seemed to be getting worse. At least it was a job, I reminded myself... if only eighty percent. There was that.

James rolled along, without pausing for comments. "See, a few interns have recommended a new strategy I'm excited to run with. We're going to be launching a new campaign in support of high-frequency items—toilet paper, paper towels, things of that nature. The sexy stuff we sell at Centrex." Again, he laughed. I did not. "I'd love for you to be a part of the team leading our toilet paper—er, bath tissue—program. We need to fill the ranks with people from every level, to ensure we get a variety of ideas and experience supporting the project. One of our summer interns is being brought on full time to lead the task-force and bring the plan to fruition." James grinned. "Isn't this exciting?" He reached over and patted my knee. "Let's see a little of that Care Bear cheer, huh?"

I tried. Really, I did. But the thought of sitting on a task force to figure out a fun way to market toilet paper, of being responsible for people knowing Centrex was the place to turn when you had to use the restroom, was so deeply depressing that all I could do was sigh. Loudly.

"Isn't this exciting?" James repeated. "You can thank me for getting you a slot on the team. I stood up for you, insisting you be a part of group. I know your morale has probably been a little squishy since the whole cutback business, but this should help. You'll need to come in some Fridays, obviously, until we've got the plan nailed down." He smiled thinly. "Since it's a special project, it's going to require a little special time." He air-quoted around special time, which made it all feel so much worse than it needed to.

"So does this mean I go back to a full-time position?" I asked quietly. "Or am I still reduced?"

"Still reduced," James said, pushing his lower lip out into a pout and running his hand across his forehead. "Sorry I can't do anything about that. But you'll be part of the team that's going to change the way people look at Centrex. You, along with the rest of this team, have the opportunity to make something *big* happen here. This is a marketing dream job. Finding our way into customers' pockets through creatively marketed *frequency* items. What could be more fun?"

What could be more fun? Oh, I don't know... teaching water aerobics? Playing the banjo in a children's band? Maybe even marketing hand soap, like Erik? Just about *anything* sounded more fun than trying to sell toilet paper, and I knew that meant my run was over at Centrex.

I didn't quit then, but that was the moment I knew I would. I wasn't going to storm out that day, or even that week or month or maybe even that year, but I was going to get out of my job— soon. I wouldn't let what happened with Erik happen in all the other parts of my life. I would escape Smurfy-James, and on-site-off-sites, and corporate yoga. I promised myself I would not let my career dreams top out at marketing toilet paper to suburban families. There had to be something better out there, and I promised myself I would find it.

Instead of storming out in a blaze of glory, I rebelled just a little bit that day, just enough to make me feel somewhat in control of my career and my choices. When my cell phone began to ring in the middle of our conversation, I pointedly turned away from James and answered.

"Yoo-hoo," James said, tapping me on the shoulder in a way that let me know we weren't finished with our conversation.

On the other end of the phone, Cat's tiny little voice rasped, "Hello? Stell? Where are you? "

"I had to come in to work. What's up?" James cleared his throat behind me, but I ignored him. I was thirty-four-years-old, for God's sake. I could take a call from a friend on *my day off* and not fear the wrath of my boss like I had feared every one of my grade school teachers and college professors… and Laurel.

"Work? That blows. You're not supposed to work on Fridays."

"No shit, Shirley."

"Who's Shirley?" Cat asked, distracted.

"Shirley's made up. '*No shit, Shirley*' is just a saying."

"A stupid saying you must have learned from farmhands in Iowa—or Erik. He says stupid stuff like that. Don't say it anymore. I need to mentally separate the two of you, okay?" I sighed and Cat continued. "So, can you take off early today? Like, two-ish?" she asked. "I'm going on a little field trip you might enjoy. The girls are coming, too."

"Sure," I said, then covered the mouthpiece with my hand. "What time is the TP meeting?" James glared at me and held up two fingers. "Shoot," I told him, snapping my fingers. "I have plans—they'll just have to fill me in later on what I missed."

I was at liberty to leave whenever I damn well felt like it. A few frozen yogurt coupons and free lunchtime yoga weren't going to motivate me work for free when I'd been twenty-percent laid off. Fridays were my time, and if they were keeping twenty percent of my cash and filtering it into intern-led-toilet-paper-taskforces, I'd do what I chose with my Fridays. I was going to hang out with Pippa and Heidi and Cat.

"You know what? I'm ready anytime—I'm not supposed to be here today anyway, right?" I grinned at my boss, who shook his head and passive-aggressively slunk out of my cube without comment. What was the worst thing he could do? Fire me? That was probably better than sitting on a toilet paper committee, anyway. If marketing toilet paper was supposedly the pinnacle of my career, it was definitely time to find a better one. And if I got fired, at least then I wouldn't have to quit or look at James' inappropriately hard hair anymore. A mini rebellion was well deserved.

"Where are we going?"

"It's a surprise. I swear it will be fabu."

CHAPTER TWENTY

I should have figured out what Cat had planned when I saw the short, high-pitched crowd gathered in front of the glass-encased suburban library. But it wasn't until Pippa, Heidi, Cat, and I walked into the paisley-carpeted, lower-level performance space and I saw Joe strumming his banjo across the room that I realized she'd taken me to a Dog Hounds concert.

"There he is, Auntie Stella!" Pippa cried happily, hugging my arm. She was still moving slowly, and didn't have the verve she'd had before the accident. But her sweet little smile was as pretty and perfect as ever, and her voice was filled with joy and life. "It's Joe!" Both Pippa and Cat grinned at me, but for different reasons, I was sure.

"It sure is," I murmured, wiggling my toes in my boots. I took a moment to watch him before he realized I was there. He was wearing the usual uniform, including those awful overalls and the fluffy hair. But beneath the ridiculous get-up (which was practically see-through as far as I was concerned, since my mind just kept thinking about the stomach and chest he had hiding under it all), his eyes shone in that way I had come to adore and his goofy grin made me want to run over and wrap my arms around him. He was talking to a pair of little boys wearing cowboy hats, but paused when he noticed me and Cat and the girls.

The sweet smile that had been on his face while he was talking to his tiny fans widened as he made his way toward us a few seconds later, and the dimples at the tops of his cheeks crept into place. My cheeks flushed and my insides squirmed. I guess I'd been fooling myself that I was over him, since my body was telling me I was absolutely *not* over Banjo Boy.

"Pippa!" When he reached us, Joe immediately crouched down and held his hand out to give Pip a low-five. "Let me see that smile."

Pip grinned, clutching my hand tightly in one of hers while she placed the other timidly inside Joe's.

"And hello, Miss Heidi," Joe said, bowing his head and winking. "Ladies." He nodded at Cat and I, letting his eyes linger on mine. My stomach flipped as I waited for him to say my name or touch me, even in the most innocent of ways. "Joining the mom circuit, eh, Stella?"

"I guess so," I said nervously, trying to find a way to flirt. Did I *want* to flirt? Yeah, I really did. "A *single* mom. Or maybe just the really fun aunt?"

He leaned in to speak close to my ear. I breathed in deeply when I smelled his familiar sugary smell and felt one of his curls tickle my cheek. "Well, that's even better then." The rustle of his breath on my hair made my neck tingle, and I had to stop myself from turning to bring my mouth to his.

But he wasn't my boyfriend, and I'd been rude, and whatever had been building between us had been cut down when I'd—rightly—criticized him for sleeping with married women. Joe leaned in even closer and my breath caught in my throat as his hair brushed against my cheek again.

"Not that something like a wedding ring is going to stop a guy like me from hitting on you. Isn't that right?" He stepped back and plucked at the strings of his banjo. When he quirked up one corner of his mouth, I knew he didn't hate me for judging him. And I also knew I really didn't care that he'd been a player.

All that really mattered to me was that we had some seriously unfinished business. Screw sensible. With Joe in the picture, sensible was out. I'd been robbed of good sex with a hot musician and I was going to get it, no matter how bad an idea it was. Joe leaned into me again and whispered, "Nice boots."

I clicked the heels of my cowboy boots together and blushed. After that, the concert was painfully slow. The girls squeezed into the front row and got comfortable right in front of the stage, singing along and waving their arms with the Dog Hounds as they sang about clouds and cupcakes and going with the flow. I sat with Cat at the back of the room, both of us uncomfortable in metal folding chairs. Cat spent most of the show shopping on her phone. I kept my eyes on the band, but found it hard to focus on anything other than Joe's lips and the way I knew my body would feel if his arms were wrapped around me again.

"Oh, eff," Cat murmured as the show was wrapping up. "The girls and I have to get home ASAP. Amelie put regular dish soap in the dishwasher again, and she's freaking out. Last time she did this, she was curled up in a fetal position on the couch, eating Doritos and watching a *Top Model* marathon, while the dishwasher spewed soap all over the kitchen floor. So dramatic. I swear, au pairs are a real pain in the *bleep*," Cat rolled her eyes. "Do you think…" she looked at me and smiled, "…you could get a ride home with Joe?"

"Well, aren't you subtle?" I whispered back.

"Do you hate me?" Cat asked kindly. "As far as I can tell, it doesn't seem like he's holding a grudge. And in case you've put a lot of stock in the mommy-circuit gossip, I checked in with Jenell Matthews and she asked around and found out Joe has actively dismissed a wagonload of hot moms who have flashed their tatas at him over the past three years. Apparently he has more class now, but unfortunately, his man-whore reputation stuck." She grinned. "It seems a shame to waste something so pretty."

I bit my lip and nodded. "Sure, I'll ask him for a ride."

Joe did not mind giving me a ride home, so Cat, Pippa, and Heidi fled to rescue their nanny from a chip binge while I waited for the band to gather their things. I chatted idly with Theo while Joe loaded instruments into the back of his car, wondering all the while how much the other guys in the band knew about what had happened between me and their banjo player.

Once everything was in place and he'd changed into jeans, Joe and I walked together out to his car. He ambled along slowly and I matched his pace. He'd left his cowboy hat with the rest of the band gear, and was now wearing a knit cap over his mess of fluffy curls. "It's good to see you," he said quietly as we made our way through the cold, silent parking lot. Our boots made matching clicking sounds against the pavement.

"You too," I answered. My fingers knocked into his as I swung my arms loosely by my sides. It was an accidental touch, but then Joe reached for my hand and I let him squeeze it. Just as quickly, he dropped it, and I wondered what it meant. I wished he would hold on. "I'm sorry I was a judgmental bitch when you came to see me at work that day."

"S'okay," he said, smiling at me like he really meant it. "I get where you're coming from—pieces of my past are not all that pretty. Since the divorce, especially, I've done some stuff *I'm* not proud of, but I like to think I'm evolving. It's all part of growing up, right? I'm happy to talk about it further, if you want, but would really like to just move on. I have." He nodded resolutely.

"So does that mean you're definitely not sleeping with your little groupies' moms anymore?" I smiled sweetly.

"Just put your questions out there. Please… don't be shy," he said, laughing. "And no. I'm not. What's done is done, can't take that back. But past regrets lead to better futures."

I nodded. "I hope so." The wind whipped at my exposed skin as I walked away from Joe to go toward the passenger side of the car. Joe followed me and unlocked my door first, touching my shoulder as I slipped into the chilly, still silence of his car. I wanted his touch to go further, but that was all he gave me.

"Do you need to get home right away?" he asked, settling into the driver's seat. "Want to grab some food?"

"Sure." Food was fine, but what I really wanted was to kiss him. Or, better yet, to trail my fingers along his stomach and have his hands crawl up my back, to melt against him as our bodies pressed together. I shivered, practically jumping out of my skin to climb into his seat with him.

"Are you okay with Matt's Bar? A couple guys I know are playing a set there, and I told them I'd swing by so I can give them some pointers. I guarantee the music will be terrible, but the burgers should make up for it."

"Adult music? Like, a rock band?" I asked. I couldn't remember the last time I'd gone out to listen to a band—something other than the Dog Hounds or the symphony or a string quartet at a charity event. "Yeah, it would be fun to see a real band."

"A real band? Lady, what do you think the Dog Hounds are?" He shot me a hurt look. I started to protest, but he cut me off. "I should probably manage your expectations anyway. These guys are far from a real band. They're never going to make it, but I figure we've gotta support peoples' dreams. It's not really my place to tell someone to give it up..." He grinned. "Even if listening to them play is a form of torture. It won't be as bad if you're with me."

Joe put the car in drive and headed back toward the city, while I tried hard not to stare at him. There was something about the curve of his jaw, and the way his smile crept all the way up his cheeks, that made me want to touch him. But that would be weird, I reasoned—it's not like you could just start grabbing at someone, like no time had passed. We'd broken up—if you could even *break* up when you weren't even officially *anything* to begin with. I couldn't assume he was interested in me like that anymore.

Just as I was thinking that, Joe reached over and touched my cheek.

"I've missed you," he said in a low, rumbly voice. "Is this okay?" He pushed my hair behind my ear and his hand reached for the back of my neck.

I nodded. I reached up and touched his hand, pulling it in closer to brush his fingers against my lips.

Joe said, "I'm glad everything is okay with Pippa... it was hard to see her—and you—at the hospital. I stopped by your place and checked in with Anders the next day. He told me she'd been taken out of the coma. Are they all home now?"

"Yeah," I said. "Finally. And I'm back at my place again. I was living with Cat's mom, trying to help. Trying to figure some stuff out and just keep myself distracted. But it's good to be home."

"That guy at the hospital—the ex-boyfriend?"

"Yup. Erik."

"Figures. He seems fun." I looked at Joe, and noticed he'd thrust his lower lip out and was nodding slowly, the way Erik had in the hospital. "Rock on." The impression made me laugh. I guess I wasn't the only one who had noticed. "Has he seen your list? I bet a guy like that would love a list."

"Lay off the list, buster."

He grinned. "I can't. It fascinates me."

"Much like your smarminess and inability to wink fascinates *me*."

"You still think I'm smarmy?" He pulled the car over to park across the street from Matt's Bar. "I prefer the term 'silky.' Aren't I sort of a smooth and silky guy?"

"That sounds very wrong." I laughed as we walked into the bar. We sat down in a booth near the back, our faces lit by the neon beer signs dangling from the wall. The band hadn't started yet, but a few guys were hurriedly stuffing instruments into a small piece of empty floor in a corner of the restaurant. A television playing women's hockey was propped up on a rickety-looking board hanging from the wall above them.

"You were great that day with Pippa, you know." I played with a menu and peeked up at him shyly. "Do you know you never sang for me when we were together?"

"Whenever you're in the audience, I'm singing right to you, baby." I snorted, and he shrugged. "It may sound silky—"

"Smooth," I interrupted, laughing.

"...But it's true." He reached over to touch my hand. "Maybe I'll get to sing to you in private sometime, too." He smiled at me and I practically melted.

As we waited for our food, we talked about everything and nothing at all. I was eager to steer us toward topics of conversation that would keep me from thinking about how much I wanted to be somewhere private with him *now*. So I filled Joe in on the beauty of my new toilet tissue campaign, and he told me stories from some of their pre-holiday gigs. It was meaningless conversation, but it felt good to laugh with someone again.

Just as our hamburgers were delivered to our table, the guy who'd been hauling most of the gear into the corner strolled over to fist-pump Joe. Joe stood up and gave him one of those guy-half-hug things. When Joe turned to introduce us, I finally got a good look at his friend.

Even without the tux, I recognized him immediately. "Hi, Jonathan."

"You know each other?" Joe asked.

Jonathan grinned. "Yeah, Stella's my Gran's friend. We went out. You two on a date?" He held his hand up for a high-five with both of us. "I guess Stella here likes the smoldering musician type, eh, brother?"

Joe looked about as disgusted as I felt. "I guess that must be true, ah, *brother*. Stella does have exceptional taste."

Jonathan winked at me. "You two lovebirds enjoy the show, all right? We're working on some new stuff. Joe, you mind if I check in with you tomorrow to see what you think?"

"Sure, give me a call." Joe nodded and sat back down. "So you and Jonathan?" he asked, once Jonathan was out of hearing range. "Just a fling, I assume?"

"Yep," I said, smiling sweetly. "Just a fling. Nice guy, that Jonathan. He's got a great place. He lives down in his grandmother's basement, you know. Very practical."

"That is practical. Sounds perfect for you," Joe said, laughing. "I can see the two of you together. Jonathan. Now there's a guy who has his shit together." Jonathan's band started to play—a loud, screeching horror show of sound.

I cringed. "Yep. He really understands where he's going in life."

"Yep." Joe studied me carefully. His eyes focused in on mine when he asked, "Did you really hook up with Jonathan?" He spoke loudly enough for me to hear him over the band. "I don't know him that well, but I think I know both of you well enough that this is something of a surprise…"

"No one ever said I hooked up with Jonathan." I took a bite of my hamburger, then folded my arms across my chest. "You just jumped to conclusions."

"Huh," he said, leaning back in his booth seat. I strained to hear him over the shouting and angry guitar noises. "I guess that reminds me of someone else I know—a lady who assumes just because I have a history of being something of a player, I'm still sleeping with half the moms from every preschool around town. Someone who doesn't seem to realize I'm not the least bit interested in all the moms around town when there's a hot girl with a flair for spontaneity and whimsy sitting right in front of me." He grinned.

"I'd assume you were talking about me," I said. "But I don't really have a flair for spontaneity *or* whimsy."

Joe shook his head. "Oh, but you do. Right now, I'm specifically remembering one afternoon in particular. An afternoon at a rest stop."

"You're thinking about that?" I asked, wishing we could recreate the scene from the rest stop in the back of Matt's Bar.

"I might be," he said, lifting his eyebrows. "It's a good memory. One that's haunted me for the past few weeks." He flagged the waitress over and asked for the check. We split the bill and headed out into the frozen night. When we got back to the car, Joe looked over at me.

"You know," he said slowly. "You've never been to my place."

"You're right," I said, suddenly feeling a lot warmer. "I haven't."

"So? Can you come over for a while?" He lifted his eyebrows, then blinked exaggeratedly.

"Are you trying to *wink* at me right now?" I asked, laughing. "That's so sad."

"Not smarmy? I'm going for smarmy." He flashed a huge, toothy smile. "Silky."

"Whatever it is that you're doing, it's actually a little creepy. It's like you're leering at me. That grin is disconcerting."

"I *am* leering at you," he said, converting the toothy grin to his signature smirk. "And inviting you over."

"I'd love to," I said, my heart beating and fluttering as I thought about tucking inside Joe's sheets to warm up. "Maybe we can work on your winking for a while."

"There are other things I'd rather do," he said with a growl, and put the car in drive. Then he blinked hugely again, laughed, and drove on.

By the time we got to his house, I was practically floating with anticipation. I'd spent the past month reasoning through why I should or shouldn't be with Joe, but it had taken only one afternoon with him again to realize the only thing I wanted to do was linger in the moment and enjoy myself. I didn't care what my list said, or where this night would or wouldn't get me—all I cared about was having some fun and doing something I *wanted* to do. Something I *really* wanted to do.

I stepped out of the car and followed Joe up the front walk. He lived in a tiny bungalow with dead plants crammed into pots on the front stoop that looked like they were waiting hopefully for more summer days. The front door was painted a cheerful yellow, and when he opened it, I immediately recognized the smell I'd come to associate with Joe. I breathed in and stepped into the front hall, wondering who might make the first move and if it would be awkward or uncomfortable given our time apart.

I didn't have to wonder long. The moment I walked over the threshold, Joe reached one arm past me and shoved the door closed. I stepped back and he stepped forward and before I knew what was happening, he had my body pressed up against the front door. Without a moment of hesitation, his mouth was on mine and it felt like no time had passed since we'd last been together. His strong arms were on either side of me, and his body held me so tightly in place against the door, I could feel his heart pounding through the layers of our clothes. Layers I wanted *off*.

Suddenly, we were all over each other and all I could think about was how badly I wanted to wrap my legs around him and let him take me anywhere. He tasted like cinnamon doughnuts, and his lips were soft but his kisses urgent. I was uber-aware of what had been building up in me, and I knew suddenly and without a doubt that I was very much not alone. We were acting desperate, eagerly tasting and touching each other.

My body relaxed into Joe's and he reached his hand around the back of my head to pull me even closer. His hands twisted into my hair, then trailed down my body, and suddenly I felt myself lifted off the ground. I wrapped my arms and legs around him and held on so tight, I could feel the buttons on his shirt pressing against my chest.

Slowly, we stumbled from the front door to the couch, until eventually we were in a room at the back of the house that I assumed was Joe's bedroom. I reached down and unbuttoned his jeans, and watched as they fell to the floor. He kicked off his boots. There was something so adorable about the way Joe stood there in red boxers and a flannel shirt and his silly knit cap all askew, that I couldn't keep myself from giggling. This made him do a little dance, and then he grabbed me up in his arms and swung me around, kissing me full on the lips before finally pulling me to him again.

My jeans were already unbuttoned and I'd lost my shirt somewhere in the hallway. When Joe unclasped my bra and held my breasts in his hands, I shivered, despite the heat we'd built up between us. When I was totally naked, Joe took off his shirt and wrapped it around me, then pulled back his covers to reveal a set of cozy plaid flannel sheets. He took my hand and led me into bed. I curled in happily, giggling and tucking my body into the heat from his chest. My whole body tingled when he touched me, and all I wanted was more.

I let my hands linger across his chest, then I pressed myself against him and felt our bodies melt together. Something like a growl sounded from somewhere deep inside him as he kneeled over me and touched every inch of my naked body that was wrapped inside his shirt.

"You look so sexy when you're in my clothes, but that shirt has *got* to come off…"

He unwrapped me and lowered me into a pile of soft pillows as his mouth worked its way down my body. His tongue left me both cold and hot—skin steaming the moment his lips touched me, frozen and desperate when he moved to another space to light a different piece of me on fire—and all the while I wished his lips could be everywhere at once.

Joe's hands played with my body the way I'd always known they would—expertly, like he was making music meant only for me. It was as if my body had been out of tune and only knew what to do when Joe was touching me. As first his fingers, then his mouth, reached between my legs, I moaned and rocked under him.

"I want you," I whispered. "Now."

He looked up at me and smiled, then played on. Just when I was sure I couldn't hold out another second, he kissed his way back up to my mouth. He pulled out a condom, keeping his eyes on mine the whole time he put it on.

"Stella…" he murmured, teasing my legs further apart with his own thighs. His eyes fluttered closed for a moment, but he opened them and locked his gaze on mine as he pressed himself into me. I gasped as he slid inside, moving slowly at first, then with increasing intensity. Our bodies moved together perfectly, and it was between those flannel sheets that I finally realized what seriously hot sex was like.

After, we lay curled together for a long time, kissing and holding each other and just relaxing into the soft blankets draped across our bodies. He kept his muscled chest tucked up against my breasts and his strong arms held me against him. Joe moaned every time I moved even the tiniest bit, pulling me in closer. Over the next hour, we talked about everything and nothing, wasting hours laughing and enjoying each other. He brought in a bottle of wine and some crackers and brie long after the sun had gone down.

"I have a proposition," Joe said, late in the night, after he'd sung to me and lulled me nearly to sleep before waking me with more fantastic sex. "It's just an idea, but let me know what you think."

"You want me to become your official bell-ringer at Dog Hound shows? Professional bell shaker?" I teased. "How thoughtful of you. All my dreams are answered."

Joe leaned over to kiss me. "I'm sensing just a wee bit of sarcasm. So let me suggest something similar—without the bells."

I nodded. "Okay."

"Come on tour with us," Joe said, lifting his eyebrows hopefully. "We just booked a winter-spring tour that's going to take us out to the West Coast, through Colorado, then back along the Mississippi later this spring." He rolled over so he was propped up right on top of me, looking straight into my eyes. He spoke apprehensively, as though he was nervous to suggest it—or maybe he was worried about telling me he was going off on tour. "Quit your job. We can drive across the country together. Come with me."

"You want me to quit my job and come on tour with the Dog Hounds?" I said reluctantly. "Like one of those people who used to follow Phish? You want me to be like a Phish Head!?"

The low rumble of his laugh echoed through his ribcage and I could feel the rhythm of it through his chest. "Not exactly the same thing," he said, then leaned down to kiss my forehead. "But it's a very flattering comparison." He rolled onto his back, but pulled me with him so I was laying on top of him now. My legs wrapped around him and my hands tucked under the back of his neck to feel his soft curls between my fingers. "So? Good idea?"

I kissed him, hard, then pulled back and said, "Good idea. But not now."

He nodded. "Okay. Mind if I ask why?"

Quitting my job and touring with Joe—just going where the band went and seeing the country and *enjoying* myself— sounded perfect. But I knew it wasn't *my* plan. It wasn't my tour, it wasn't my life, it wasn't my adventure. If I followed Joe, I would be following someone else and forgetting to force myself to make a decision—again. I wouldn't be figuring out what *I* wanted to do next. I'd been stuck in a rut for as long as I could remember, and I knew I needed to try to shake myself out of it and fly plan-free for a while.

One of my counselors had told me once that it takes six months to unlearn bad habits. Joe certainly wasn't a bad habit, but *I* was. I had to get myself unstuck before I could trust myself to not get stuck to something new. I couldn't settle for folding into Joe's life... I had to learn how to live *my* life before I could fall into someone else's orbit again. I owed it to myself to see where life could take me when I wasn't so busy planning for it.

I didn't get into all of that with Joe—he'd figure it out eventually, if this thing between us went where I hoped—and thought—it would go.

What I did say was, "Because I'm going to Italy. I'm leaving in a few days. One of the ladies from my water aerobics course invited me to join her, and it sounds exactly like what I need right now. I'm not quite sure how long I'll be gone. And then, when I get home, I'm going to take some time to decide where to go next. On my own. But hopefully there will be a lot of *this* happening?" I kissed him again. "You won't mind if I come and visit you on tour, will you?"

Joe smiled. "You'd better come visit me." He pulled me in closer. After a few moments, he whispered, "I'm glad you're finally getting to Italy." He kissed me tenderly, then said, "But before you go, I hope you don't mind spending most of your time between these sheets. Because I've got plans for us."

I kissed him again and curled up inside his arms. "I don't mind at all. You know how much I enjoy a good plan."

CHAPTER TWENTY-ONE

A few days later, I strapped my seatbelt, grinned at Heather, and dug through the seat pocket in front of me. Ten minutes to take-off, and then I was officially on my way to Italy.

I'd organized the seat pocket so my book, gum, and a magazine were close at hand. I didn't like to get up before the pilot gave his permission to do so.

"I bet you're the kind of person who reviews the safety instructions," Heather observed as I shuffled through the papers in the fabric folder in front of me.

She wasn't wrong. But I wasn't going to admit it, so I ignored the draw of that laminated little card (but seriously, what *would* I do in the event of a water landing?) and pulled out the airline magazine, flipping to the back.

"Ooh, look at all the movie choices!" I announced giddily.

"Woop-de-doo," Heather muttered. "Wake me up when we get there." Then she pulled an eye mask out of her purse and strapped it on. In elegant script across the front, it read: *Wake me for coffee. Otherwise, let me rest in peace.*

In less than twelve hours we'd be in Italy. How could she sleep? All I could do is squirm in my seat and think about how much had changed for me in the space of just a few months (and wine. Who wouldn't be thinking about wine?). This was the first time in more than ten years that I'd decided what I wanted to do—all by my adult-self—and *done* it. No list, no checking with Erik, no worrying about who might have another big idea about what I should do instead. Joe and I had left things up in the air, promising to figure out what would happen next *sometime*. Not before I left, not necessarily next week, or before he left on tour, but eventually. We were enjoying each other without forcing a label on it, and that felt perfect to me.

As I listened to the hum of the engines and watched the safety video and tried to ignore the fight happening between a teenage girl and her mother behind me, I thought about my list of life's goals and how something so seemingly well thought-out had led me so far astray. It probably should have taken me less than twenty years to figure out that a fifteen-year-old really shouldn't be making decisions for a grown woman (as evidenced by the argument I was eavesdropping on behind me). The fact that a boy with a mullet and taco breath and a probable case of genital warts was on my life's list at all should have told me something sooner, but alas, you live and learn.

Sure, the list had served me well in some respects. I had plenty to show for what I'd done and seen and learned. I certainly wasn't going to waste time now regretting the uptight tendencies of my twenties, much like I wasn't going to continue plodding along toward a predetermined future.

As a first step to my "list recovery," I'd finally showed Lily and Anders the wedding dress still wrapped in plastic at the back of my closet. Instead of throwing it away, I decided it would be fun to throw myself a kick-ass thirty-fifth birthday bash in a few months. I'd invite everyone to wear the skeletons of old dresses... futzy-prom-fluff (left unzipped to fit), bridesmaids-dresses-from-hell, or a never-used wedding dress. I figured everyone had a few old relics in their closet they'd get a kick out of resurrecting for a night. What could be more fun than laughing at bad decisions from the past over a few drinks? At least those bad decisions would get to step out of the closet for a nice night out on the town.

There was still that one big thing left unfinished on my original list. I still wanted to get married—but it didn't need to be now. I'd realized finishing every single thing on your list of life's goals before you were thirty-five was even more depressing than never finishing at all. So the wedding that had seemed so important when I was with Erik would just have to have to wait.

When I finally gave myself permission to move forward without a plan, I had easily come up with some new stuff I could add to my list of life's goals. But I had decided rather than spell them out and stress over the details of whether or not I finished what I set out to do, I'd finally scratched the list altogether. It was gone, stuffed unceremoniously in the shredder at Centrex.

The airplane's engines roared and I glanced out the window, watching as we rolled onto the tarmac. The only list I was keeping now was in my head, and it had only one thing on it: go with the flow. And that's what I was about to do. The plane raced down the runway and we soared into open air.

ABOUT THE AUTHOR

ERIN DOWNING has written more than a dozen novels for adults and young adults. She loves writing funny, contemporary stories filled with sexy men, hilarious friends, and women who can stick up for themselves. When she's not writing, she enjoys drinking wine with friends, watching cheesy romantic dramas on TV, and walking her adorable dog (and kids) around the lakes near her house.

Before becoming an author, Erin worked as a book editor, spent a few months as a cookie inventor, and also worked for Nickelodeon. She has lived in England, Sweden, and New York City, and now resides in Minneapolis with her amazing husband, three charming children, and one fluffy dog. More information about Erin and her books can be found at: www.erindowning.com.